The Shadow Realm

DISTANT MEMORIES

J.L.KEATHLEY

Published by Merfire Publishing

Merfire Publishing, LLC
209 E. Broad Texarkana Ar, 71854

ISBN: 978-1-949770-00-1 (Paperback)

The Shadow Realm

Book 1

Chapter One

Four guardians broke through the locked door of the old warehouse I was hiding in, telling me, by orders of the Elder's Council, they needed to escort me to Nyidular. Falcon was starting to change from being human into his animal form and Luna was showing her fangs ready to attack. "No, stop, let them take me!" I screamed. I didn't want my friends to get hurt. They had already helped me with so much. I let the guardians take me to a black van with dark tinted windows that looked like a typical secret government agency vehicle. They didn't have to restrain me; they were stronger and had more training than I did. I didn't want to use any magic on them either. I wasn't sure how much they knew about me and I wasn't going to provide them with any new information.

I was surprised they found me so quickly. I thought my invisibility spell was strong, but I was wrong. I should have been more careful. I had a feeling I was being watched, but I thought I was being paranoid. The Elders had spies everywhere. I should have known they were trying to find me; there hasn't been anyone like me for centuries. On the way to Nyidular, all I could think about was how my life had changed so much. I used to be a normal teenage girl who was excited about turning sixteen. I felt so naive. I had no idea what type of world really existed and I was supposed to be someone who noticed things. That saying "ignorance is bliss", was so true. I didn't see anything odd because I didn't want to, even though the signs were right in front of me.

I wanted more time to spend with Luna. Was that too much to ask for? I had searched for her for months. All I got was a couple of hours with her. Why couldn't the Elders wait a few more days to send their soldiers after me? I didn't hurt anyone and I stayed to myself mostly. I was only trying to find out where I came from, who I was, what I was supposed to be. I didn't know why I was different from everyone else or why I had more powers than others of my race. All I wanted was answers and to be left alone to live my life as normal as possible.

The van finally came to a stop hours later. The guardians wouldn't stop for a break. They were probably scared I would run. They had no reason to be worried, I wasn't going to try to escape yet. Everything and everyone I cared about was mostly gone. I'm sure they didn't bring the others with me. I just hoped they were still alive. Guardians weren't supposed to kill people from the Shadow Realm. So of course, they had to be fine, I assured myself. Honestly, I was hoping they let them go. I told them if anything ever happened to me, to just live their lives and forget about me. I was sure they wouldn't listen, but I wanted them to try.

Before letting me out, the guardian who sat beside me put a blindfold on me. I didn't care where we were going. I was sure it would all be over soon for me anyway. I was a hybrid and we were not allowed to exist. I was dragged from the van and told to be still and not scream. The guardians were firm and direct with what they wanted me to do, but they weren't cruel about it. We walked outside a short distance. I could feel the heat from the sun on me and smell the freshness of the earth. We stopped walking about twenty minutes after we left the van. We were at a portal. I could feel the energy pouring from it. I wondered where we were. I should have known we wouldn't be traveling like humans the entire way to Nyidular.

When I was pulled through, I could feel the cold energy touch my skin taking me from the Human Realm to the Shadow Realm. I had imagined what it would be like to go to the place where all the creatures that the humans feared had originally come from. I had hoped I would be visiting this world one day on my own free will, instead, I was a prisoner.

The blindfold was taken off of me as soon as I made it through the portal. The view was more incredible than I could have ever imagined. The green sky had waves of blue and purple blended in with it. The sun was dark blue in the sky instead of yellow like the human world. The air smelled cleaner and felt purer. There wasn't any pollution or chemicals mixed in with it.

In front of me was a large gray stone castle that was more than fifty feet tall, with a tower on each side, and several openings in the walls for windows. The castle was surrounded by clear blue water. There was a wide long wooden bridge with thick chains connected to posts on the castle walls. It took me a minute, but I realized it was a drawbridge. Before I could look around at the rest of my surroundings, I was pushed forward and told to walk, by the large man who was sitting next to me before.

I took some deep breaths and walked towards the metal door that was slowly opening. After entering the castle, I was immediately placed into a room with a modern table and chairs. There was some food and water on the table. I was told I should eat and drink something to keep my energy up, and blood would be provided later. I was going to do my best to hold out as long as I could. I didn't trust anyone who worked for the Elders.

I really thought I was going to be thrown into a dungeon to be chained up. That is what happened to creatures that were feared. They were locked away and tortured. I tried to stay brave. I could handle this. Out of everything that has happened to me, I could survive this. I just needed enough time to come up with a plan to escape.

Six months earlier...

Seven young women were dancing barefoot around a large bright fire while singing a beautiful melody. *The green flames were contained by rough dark brown and gray stones. All the stones had white moons and stars etched into them. The symbols began to light up as the song continued. All the women were beautiful in their own way. They had different skin and hair colors, and each one was a different size in height and shape. The only thing that connected them to one another was their auras. I could see the white mystic energy surrounding all of them but one.*

The shortest woman's aura had a hint of blue around the edges. Each woman was wearing a simple dress made of the same shimmering white material that formed to their bodies perfectly. Each dress had a unique design that suited the woman wearing it.

Out of the seven women who were dancing, the one in the middle caught my attention and held it. She looked familiar to me, even though I had never seen her before. I couldn't forget someone who looked like her if I tried. She was

not the prettiest, but she was the smallest.
However, there was something that made me
want to keep watching her. She had dark
brown hair almost to the point where it could
be considered black, hanging in loose spiral
waves cascading down past the middle of her
back. She had ivory skin shimmering with different shades of blue and green depending on
the way she moved. Her eyes were hazel with
a hint of mint green. She had pointed ears that
made her look like an elf. On her left arm was
an odd light blue mark. It was a crescent
moon with a tiny star above it on the right
side.

The dancing slowed down and came to a
stop as the song dwindled down to silence. I
was sad it ended. The song brought me peace
as if the words were meant to comfort and
guide whoever listened. The song was in a
language I didn't understand. It wasn't English, but it could have been Latin.

They all fell to the ground with exhaustion,
but they were smiling at one another and
laughing. Even their laughs sounded like
beautiful music exploding in the night's sky. As
the laughing died down, they stared quietly at
the sky, gazing up at the moon and the stars

as if they were seeing it for the first time. The night's sky became darker, the gold moon and stars shined brighter, as the flames of the fire dwindled down as it released its energy contently into the atmosphere.

No one had moved in what seemed to be hours. I was starting to get worried. Looking closer, I could see they had fallen asleep. Each one had smiles on their faces, as though they were having pleasant dreams, except the one with the mark. She looked like she was trapped in a nightmare. She was frowning and I could see tears running down her face.

I felt the need to watch over them, to protect them from something, but I was not sure what. I kept staring at the arm with the strange mark. It looked like it could be a birthmark, but birthmarks didn't generally look like that. Maybe it was a tattoo?

Dawn was slowly approaching, the sun was rising in the sky, producing dark shades of red, orange, and purple creating a perfect sunrise. The view was incredible. I had not paid much attention to my surroundings until then. Looking around, I noticed we were in a clearing of short grass with beautiful wildflowers scattered around everywhere. The clearing was surrounded by lots of different species of tall trees. The trees were not like what I was used to. They were more vibrant with different purple, pink, and orange colored leaves, their barks were dark brown, and each tree was full of energy and life.

The women started to wake up when the light from the sun hit their faces. They stood up slowly and stretched before leaving the clearing. I followed them down a narrow dirt path through the large forest for a little while, until we came to a small opening that led into a village.

Little smooth stone houses and huts made out of bamboo sticks with straw roofs were scattered around everywhere. Wooden fences with sheep, cows, goats, and chickens enclosed within them were on the far end of the village. In the middle, there were rows of vegetables. A few I recognized. Along the sides of the houses and huts were lots of fruit trees. I could see apples, oranges, and peaches, and some fruit I had never seen before; it all looked so delicious. Even in the village, the colors were more illuminating than I thought possible.

The elf looking woman had caught my attention again. She went to a tree that had dark red leaves with blue and white roundish fruit on it. She picked one and smiled softly. Then started to walk toward one of the stone houses. I followed her to one with a white crescent moon on the front circular wooden door.

Before she made it all the way to the door, a man and small child came out from inside the house and greeted her affectionately. The man was tall, slightly tanned, with light blonde curly hair, and blue-green eyes that glowed a little when he looked at the pointed ear women. He bent down and kissed her on the lips softly.

"Hello wife, how was your ritual gathering?" he asked with a bright smile on his face.

"Informative, I know what I have to do now", she said, looking troubled.

The man nodded in acknowledgment, but seemed sad at the news. His smile faded for a moment, but returned quickly.

"That is good. What did the great power tell you my love?"

"He explained to me that I have to go help our people. I am the healer of the Cardamines and one of our strongest warriors. I cannot let our warriors fight alone. The humans don't have fairy magic or guardian strength, but they have their own type of weapons that can hurt so many."

The small child then tugged on her mother's white dress trying to get her attention. The elf woman looked down and smiled at the face staring up at her. She then bent down and scooped up the little girl. They looked so much alike. The girl had the same dark hair, but her eyes were bright green and her ears weren't pointed. She looked human. The girl's skin tone was lightly tanned, a lighter shade than her fathers, not pale and shimmery like her mothers.

"Lavender, I missed you, my sweet little fairy girl", her mother said before handing her the round fruit she had picked earlier. Lavender smiled back at her with loving eyes. She then turned her head and looked straight at me.

♋

I was jolted awake by the annoying beeping of the alarm clock on my smartphone. I rolled over to it. It was beside the picture of my parents on the nightstand. The screen was too bright, as usual. I had to remember to turn down the brightness at night. Squinting my eyes at the well-lit screen, I could see it was a little past six in the morning. Looking out my windows, I could see the sun wasn't out yet. I must have been in a deep sleep because my alarm goes off at six and the annoying beeping didn't wake me. Those dreams I was having were intense.

It was time for school again. School wasn't terrible really, but waking up early every day was. I was a sophomore at Twin-City High. I was not the most popular, not that I would want to be. I didn't like to be the center of attention. I had a small group of friends; they were all I needed. Of course, I had a best friend as well, but what teenage girl didn't.

Getting out of bed, I started my usual morning routine: brushed my teeth and hair, and put on a little makeup to look like I was not wearing any. Getting changed into day clothes: my usual style was some old faded jeans, cute t-shirts, and flip-flops. It had been that way since my mom stopped picking out clothes for me. Shoes always bugged me, but I had to wear them, so flip flops was the next option to going barefoot, in my opinion anyway.

Before leaving my room, I always looked in the mirror, but nothing ever changed. I still had the same light brown hair tumbling past my shoulders, hazel eyes that changed to green depending on my mood, and I was still short. At least I still had a little of the tan I got during summer, so I wasn't too pale.

Giving one last look around my room, I could see the aqua blue colored walls, the white old-fashioned canopy bed, the four-drawer dresser, and large desk. The furniture was built for me especially. I requested it to be built in that particular style. The furniture wasn't all that old, but the furniture style was supposed to look like something from the early 1800s. I didn't care for the modern style furniture made in the past several years. My room had the same wall color and style furniture for the past couple of years, ever since I came to live with my grandmother. Change wasn't for me. The past couple of years I had plenty of it.

It had been awhile since I thought about the death of my parents. I was told it was a robbery gone wrong. It happened when my parents came home from their special date night on a Saturday evening. No one knows exactly what happened, except both my parents were found in the living room, bleeding out from multiple gunshot wounds. I didn't want to know where they had been shot. I didn't care for the gory details. It was too much for a young teenager to deal with at the time. My grandmother told me that the police statement said electronics and some jewelry appeared to be missing. That's why a robbery gone badly was suspected. There weren't any fingerprints, strands of hair, or any other type of evidence found. The police never found the person who broke in, so it became a cold case. I wasn't sure if knowing the truth about that night would have helped me anyway.

I felt horrible and still do because I wasn't there that weekend. I wanted to give them some alone time since they hadn't had any in a while. That night, I was staying over at my best friend, Maxine's house. I haven't talked to her in years, not since that horrible night. We were out getting tacos and some movies with Maxine's parents, Mr. and Mrs. Jones, when a call came in from an unknown number on my flip phone. I wasn't going to answer it, but I had a feeling I should.

"Hello?" I asked a little nervously.

"Is this Jade Dixon?" asked a sad rough voice on the other end of the line.

My phone had made the sound for my text message tone, dragging me back to reality. The phone was still on my nightstand. I walked over to pick it up, knowing without a doubt who sent me a message. Yep, it was Alexa, my best friend for the past year and a half. I laughed a little, thinking who else would have sent me a text message this early in the morning.

I met Alexa my freshman year. I was new to the school, after having recently moved from a small town in Texas called Friendship. Alexa told me she heard a new girl around her age was starting school that semester and she wanted to meet her. She was the president of the school's Welcome Committee. Even as a freshman, Alexa had the ability to take control of school events and clubs. She said it would look good on her college applications. Even back then, she was thinking of her future.

Alexandra, Alexa for short, had light cream skin, big dark brown eyes, long dark brown hair, and a strong competitive personality. She was taller than me, but who wasn't honestly. She always wore dressy casual clothes. We were the complete opposite. I think I was more down to earth and go with the flow, whereas Alexa, not so much. She was a little controlling to say the least, but I loved her anyway.

I walked into the main office at the front of the large red bricked school. My first day of freshman year. Alexa was waiting for me impatiently, all starry-eyed and grinning creepily. I was the first newbie, as she called it, to be shown around by her, the president of the Welcoming Committee. She even had a badge, which she was quite proud of.

She handed my class schedule for the year to me and excitedly explained we had a few classes together including homeroom. We also had Algebra 2 and Gym. We bonded instantly over the fact neither of us liked Gym. "I'll figure out a way to get out of gym. I have to be able to use my Freshman Class President status for something", she joked. After that first day of school, the two of us were inseparable. Also, she did get us out of gym. She took up tutoring and I joined the Gymnastics Team. I thought it was better than running laps in a circle or playing some boring sport that involved a ball.

Looking back down at the phone screen, I read the message she sent me. "You're going to be late today, if you don't hurry! We have a huge biology test first period, and you know how the wicked witch is when certain people are late (meaning you)!"

She didn't like to use text jargon. She preferred full sentences, even though no one else did. That was an Alexa thing for sure. She didn't care that she could say the same thing with less syllables. Laughing to myself, I responded back. "Blah, yeah, ikr, omw... skipn brakfst..." my phone said message sent. A second later, a new message came in, asking if I was crazy, and to grab a protein bar at least. That made me smile. She was always looking out for me. Alexa was always the one person I could count on, no matter what.

I'm taking back what I said about school not being all that bad. First class of the day was advanced biology. I used to like science a lot, but I stopped when we got a new teacher. She was seriously awful. Her nickname among us lowly students was "wicked witch," and it suited her well, I promise. The only people who cared for Ms. Silvia were the teachers and other faculty staff. Although she was nice to them of course, she hid her true nature from the other adults. She had been at the school for maybe three or four months, but it seemed so much longer than that.

I made it to my seat right before the final bell rang. Thankfully, my Grams drove me to school that morning before she went to the nursing home. I usually have to ride the school bus, but I missed it that day. Too much day-dreaming that morning. That was something I needed to work on. I sat in the back of the class to avoid Ms. Silvia, not that it really helped. I got called on a lot by the evil teacher even though I didn't raise my hand, ever! It was as if she hated me more than all the other students. I couldn't figure out why. It was not like I started the whole "wicked witch" thing.

I never got into trouble. I hated to break the rules at school or anywhere. I always did my homework and even tried to do extra credit work, when offered. I wanted to get into a well-known college after graduation, well... maybe. I still didn't know what I wanted. My plans had been changing a lot lately. I had been thinking about traveling for a couple of years to find my-self, even if it was a cliché. I felt so confused sometimes about life; honestly, I wanted my parents to be proud of me even if they weren't around anymore.

The school day went by fast after first period was over. Nothing really exciting happened. I was quite sure I passed the test in AP Biology. I had a special talent. I have always been able to read something from a book, pamphlet, or any form of words and look at any photo one time and remember it completely, every word and detail. I was also good at figuring stuff out quickly. I loved mysteries, because the answer was always so obvious. I had always been a fast learner, so it made school easy. That was why I took so many advanced classes. No one knew how smart I really was. Too many people would make a fuss over it, especially Alexa. She would have tried to get me to join some academic teams or some club she was in charge of. I had plenty of school, I didn't need more of it.

For fun lately, I had been reading different versions of encyclopedias. They belonged to my dad. Something he really cared about. The books were in Gram's storage shed for a while. They stayed there after we packed all the stuff up from my old house. I started to use what my friends called "big words" to annoy them. They hated it, but it was funny to me. I needed to stop though, Alexa had been hinting about the debate team or the school newspaper. I didn't want any huge commitments, anything could change at any time. I knew that better than anyone.

I was relieved it was Friday. My friends and I had the weekend to do whatever we wanted. There wasn't much to do in Texarkana. It was a small two state city. Both Texarkana, Arkansas and Texarkana, Texas had the same attractions. There were a couple of bowling alleys, a skating rink, movie-theater, and a mall. I know a mall sounds exciting, but it was not very big, and there was always too many people with the exact same stores, which were mostly clothing. I didn't like to shop for clothing or really anything at all. However, my girlfriends were the opposite. They loved clothes, shoes, and all that girly stuff. Unfortunately for me, I got dragged to the mall a lot even though I protested every single time. Although, that weekend it was my turn to choose what we did, thankfully. I just had to figure out what I wanted to do.

Chapter Two

It was Friday night and I had homework to do, so I made plans to go out with everyone the next afternoon. I thought about going to see the new movie Dracula Goes to Mars. I had heard it was supposed to be really scary and bloody. I thought the title was a little odd, but the weirder the better. Can't judge a movie by its title. I could hear the groans through the messages coming to my phone. "They are going to have to suffer this weekend. It was payback for dragging me to the places I never wanted to go to," I said a little evilly to myself.

I loved everything supernatural and mythical. My friends thought I was weird, except Alexa. All of it fascinated me. In all the movies I had seen and the books I had read, everyone appeared to be human to most of the world, but they were not even close. The creatures changed into bats and drank blood, during the full moon they changed into wolves, witches cast evil spells and flew on brooms, and then of course the zombies crawled out from the grave and ate your brains. I knew it was not real, but maybe that was why I liked it so much, because it was an escape from the real world. It was all a crazy fantasy, so I thought. Of course, you had all your other different creatures as well that were never talked about much.

I did say that I would pay for burgers and fries at our favorite 1950's style diner. That was probably why everyone stopped blowing up my phone with "why are you being so cruel" and "anything else we can do??" I was not rich by any means, but I got a monthly allowance of five hundred dollars. Then, when I turned eighteen, I would get the rest of the money from the life insurance policies my parents had. I first found out about the money, a few months after I started living with my grandmother. I tried to give her money to help with the bills and groceries, but she would not accept it.

She was like that: strong, independent, and did not want help with anything. She retired from her long forty years of service working at a hospital as head nurse in the emergency room. She owned her house, so there was not any rent due and she got retirement checks every month to cover everything else. Anyways I did not spend a lot of the money I received. I put most of it into a checking account that Grams helped me set up a few months after I started getting the money. My parents always told me to be responsible with what I had. They also liked that old saying "money doesn't grow on trees."

Finally, my homework was finished. That took a couple of hours (teachers were cruel). I tried to read for a little while to relax. I was re-reading a vampire series, I know... I know... I liked what I liked. These vampires were not the typical ones who couldn't walk in the sunlight because they would burn up, they sparkled. I mainly liked the story because the rules were different for the supernatural world. It didn't follow the normal myths that vampires slept in coffins and wolves only changed during the full moon. There was also the love story between the girl and two guys who were mortal enemies. The best part was that the girl was so open-minded, even though the world she entered into was scary. She simply didn't care. She didn't fit into the human world and she didn't want to. I knew all this was not real, but it would be neat if it was; to be something special other than human. I read for about an hour, but started to get restless so I quit.

I got Legs out of her tank. My adorable rose hair tarantula. She had eight brown fuzzy legs and her abdomen was more of a purple color than pink. I got her during the summer. I couldn't pass her up. She was a little skittish at first, but she was coming around. I slowly sat on my bed to let her walk around on the blankets and me for a bit. Other than Alexa and Grams, she was my best friend. Maybe it was because she listened to whatever I said and didn't talk back. The only people who were not terrified of her was Alexa and Grams. I got Legs from a cute little pet shop downtown that was closing due to lack of business. It was a few doors down from the burger place we always went to.

I would visit the pet shop often, but I didn't buy anything. Now I wish I had. It was the closest thing to a zoo we had in Texarkana. The closest actual zoo was over two hours away. The owners did let us hold the animals for educational purposes, which was pretty awesome. Anyways, the owners just gave her to me. It was probably because I always went straight to the tarantulas and snakes when I came to visit. She was one of the last animals they had left. They also gave me a used tank with a hide and water dish to keep her in. My boyfriend Nick, named her Legs. I know it was not very original, but it worked for her. He claimed he wasn't scared of her, but he didn't want to handle her either. It could also be that she caused your skin to itch sometimes. I thought it was cute that he didn't want to seem nervous around me. I know not everyone in the world likes the creepy crawlies.

Nick and I had been together for about eight or nine months. We started hanging out in January. Alexa's boyfriend introduced us because Nick was the new kid in school at the end of last year. His parents split up, so he moved here with his dad who had gotten a new position as a detective at the police station. Nick seemed super proud to tell me that a little while after we met. I was proud for his dad too, even though it made me miss my parents even more; not that I would have told him that. He was your typical boy next door, with short bleached blonde hair and brown eyes. He wasn't much taller than me, but he had some muscle for a sixteen year old. He wore fitted jeans or khakis and polo shirts. He wasn't the typical guy I thought I would go for, but he made me laugh and had decent manners, so I figured why not. He was the first boy I had ever dated and he did make a great boyfriend.

I didn't remember falling asleep, but I guess I did after I started reading again. Thankfully, I was reading an e-book so I didn't lose my place. It was early in the morning still, the sun was coming up and my phone said it was a little after seven. I was wide awake and a little annoyed because it was Saturday and I wanted to sleep in for more than an hour. The past few weeks I had not been able to sleep very long, which wasn't fair. That was probably why I drank so much coffee. On the bright side, I was relieved I didn't have any dreams. They seemed to be getting a lot weirder lately. Maybe I had been reading too many supernatural books. I kept dreaming of fairies and elves; if not that then vampires and werewolves. They weren't scary dreams. They just seemed strangely familiar and real, like I had been to those places before. I knew that it sounded crazy; creatures and secret worlds didn't exist. Nope, we were all boring normal humans on planet Earth. To get out of my head, I decided to jump in the shower really quick; to feel fresh before I started my day and to get me in a better mood.

I was not meeting anyone until about three in the afternoon, so I had hours to kill. I didn't want to stay home all day though. The weather was supposed to be amazing. Sunny with cool autumn air and the leaves on the trees had already started changing colors. My favorite season of the year was fall. I liked that it was cool and not too hot. It was perfect weather for bonfires and s'mores. Also the best holiday ever was coming up in just a couple of weeks, which was Halloween by the way. It may also have had something to do with my birthday as well. Yep, I was a Halloween baby and proud of it. Alexa thought that was why I liked all the "weird stuff". Something about Halloween made me feel alive and more like myself than any other day. Unfortunately, that would make me the center of attention, but it was only one time a year, and it was my birthday. I liked birthdays, it was the only day a year that was special to that one person. Yes even though a lot of people shared the same birthday, it was their special day, not like a holiday that was for everyone.

Leaving the house with a caramel iced coffee, I was ready for the day. I thought I would catch a bus and walk around downtown for a while. I was not sixteen yet, so that was my means of transportation, unless Nick took me somewhere. A couple more weeks and I would have my driver's license, and I was also hoping to get a car. I had enough money saved up to get one; a cheap previously owned car. My grandmother had a friend who was selling a Volkswagen Beetle Bug. He said he would hold it for me. He was doing this as a special favor for Grams. Luckily for me, it was an automatic and the interior had decent soft dark gray fabric. It did need a paint job really bad though. The yellow paint on it was peeling off. Nick said he would get some help from his friends and paint it for me. The car was going to be blue of course since it was my favorite color. I just had to figure out what shade of blue it would be. I was leaning more toward sky blue. My grandmother told me I couldn't buy it until I got my driver's license. I had already memorized the drivers' manual; it only took me a couple of hours. Grams and Nick had been teaching me to drive on the back roads outside city limits, so I was a decent driver. The only things I had to really work on was parallel parking and driving in reverse. With height being an issue, it was not easy, since both of them drove large trucks. At least the Bug would be my size.

The bus ride downtown didn't take too long. It didn't usually, if you got up and around before noon. That was when the whole town started to wake up and started doing their weekend stuff. It was still early so there weren't very many people downtown, just a few shops that were starting to open up and the museums. One museum was for kids mostly and the others were for people who liked history a lot. It was mainly about trains and how our city was founded. The train museum was free to get in, but they did take donations. I didn't go to the others much anymore; they didn't change and I had been to them so many times that it had gotten old. Tourists loved them though, so that helped get people downtown. So many people thought downtown Texarkana was dead, but it wasn't. Everything was closed on Sundays, so there wasn't any traffic. I think that was when most people tried to explore the small community. It was a good and bad thing. Good because that area of town was my hideout and I could be alone when needed, and bad because the people down here needed the business.

The used bookstore I liked to go to wasn't open yet and wouldn't be for another hour. I liked to get there early at least once a month to see if they had anything new. Sometimes I could find brand new books that still had the original price tag or really well kept classics. I had recently found a book of twisted Fairy Tales. It was old and the pages were stained, but it was still pretty with a maroon leather binding cover. It was one of my favorites in my collection.

I sat on the bench with animal faces painted on it, waiting in front of the bookstore, so I could finish what was left of my iced coffee. Looking around at the little shops in fascination, I noticed a new store was coming into the old pet shop where I got Legs. I wasn't sure what it was yet, but I did see boxes through the windows. I was generally not nosy, but I was curious to see what it was. Something was definitely drawing me toward the building. I felt something pulling my attention to it. I walked down the street and crossed over to the old pet shop. I could see the overhead lights were off, but there were a couple of tall standing lamps in the corners lighting up the front room. I could not really tell what the store was going to be yet, even close up. I was hoping for something unique like an old-fashioned candy store or ice cream parlor. The orange paper sign on the front glass door said "Coming Soon" in purple letters. I didn't see a name though. It did however say the grand opening would be October 29th. I decided my friends and I could come back and check it out in a couple weeks after my birthday.

Time went by faster after I started browsing the bookshelves when the store finally opened. I did find a cute little book about a girl who found a boy she fell in love with one summer, while taking care of her dad due to cancer. After a couple of hours, I left with several more books with me. I still needed more time to pass, so I walked down to the Pocket Park. It used to be a store, but the front wall was gone; in its place were iron fences and a gate. It was definitely unique, and it was hidden so there weren't a lot of people who went there. There were amazing paintings on the walls of a train and old shops that used to be downtown. There were little flower gardens scattered around. The floor was made of dark red and rusted orange brick. The small stage that sat on the left wall was made out of the same brick. A few bricks on the stage steps were engraved with names of people who created the park and founded downtown. That was one of the few places I felt as though was made for me. I had felt connected to that place since moving to Texarkana.

Before I knew it, I was halfway done with my new novel and it was time to meet up for the movie. I had Nick come pick me up at the Pocket Park. I didn't want to ride the bus. It would be crowded since it was later in the afternoon. The theater was not as busy as I thought it would be especially for a Saturday. It was still busy, but the whole parking lot was not taken up. We went straight to the food counter after we walked in. I needed food; I could really eat a lot. It shocked Nick the first time he saw me eat so much. I guess no one warned him about my appetite. I got some chili fries, some chocolate bars, and a sweet tea. "Want anything?" I asked. "No thanks, I'm not hungry", said Alexa and Nick just shook his head. Alexa's boyfriend Trevor, our friends Stephanie and Corey were holding seats for us in Room 4. They didn't want any food either.

They said they were waiting for burgers later. Halfway during the movie, Alexa and Nick both took some of my food. I growled at them playfully. I didn't mind of course, but it was fun to mess with them.

The movie wasn't as good as I had hoped. I suppose with a title like Dracula Goes to Mars, what could you expect? Next time I wouldn't look at the reviews. I would just go off the trailer, but then again, even those didn't always do a movie justice. Oh well, overall, the movie wasn't horrible. Dracula did go to Mars at the end of the movie. The rest of it was him drinking blood and hypnotizing everyone to get him there. He also died at the end. I guess he didn't realize he would burn to death or maybe that was his goal all along. It wasn't very clear.

After we all got our food and sat at our booth, we started eating like we were starving. I still got more than the guys, and teenage boys were supposed to eat a lot, ha. It was me though, I was always hungry, had been for as long as I could remember. That's why I offered to help with groceries. I swear I ate Grams out of house and home. It was weird that I could eat so much without gaining weight. I never exercised either unless you counted gymnastics. I figured I got a fast metabolism from my family, whoever they were they must've had great genes. When we finished our food, we just stayed in our booth talking for a couple of hours; too full to move.

"Alexa I plan to go to Spirit, that Halloween warehouse by the mall soon. Want to go?" I asked.

"Hey babe, I want to go to Spirit. I could help you carry whatever you get to your house," Nick said smiling sheepishly at me.

Alexa threw a fry at him. "Of course you're going to come with us goofball, you're the one who has to do the heavy lifting. Trevor, sweetie, you're coming too, okay?" Trevor just nodded. He was a guy of few words. Stephanie and Corey were in their own little world, talking about who knows what. We just left them alone. They were in that lovey-dovey stage of their relationship.

Nick dropped me off at my house a few hours later. I was relieved when I got home. I had fun that day with my friends, but I was so tired and needed some good sleep. I figured I would take a short nap for about an hour before supper. I was hoping to not have any dreams. They were messing with my head. As soon as I walked through the door, I could smell that Grams was making several sirloin steaks that night. I couldn't wait to sink my teeth into them. Mine had to be rare or I couldn't stand the taste. Too much of the meat being brown had been disgusting that last month. Lately, I had been craving a lot of red meat. It was even better if it was slightly bloody. I know it sounds weird and a little gross, but I thought it was my body changing and needing more protein. I was starving again, already, even though lunch was only a couple of hours ago. "Who knows, maybe I'm going through a growth spurt and I'll be taller than five feet," I thought to myself excitedly before drifting off to sleep.

The image of my birth certificates floated in my mind. Such a small piece of paper or two could change someone's life forever. There were two copies of mine. One was of the original; that said unknown on both the mother and father slot. The second was the amended one. Both copies had my name, Jade, but the original didn't have the last name Dixon beside it. Anna Bell Dixon and Beau Dixon were listed on the amended birth certificate. After I saw the two small blue and gray pieces of government paper, the adoption papers were next. Confirming my suspension. It seemed one thing after another had changed in my life.

Chapter Three

I couldn't believe it when I found out that I was adopted. I never thought about it; I mean, why would I? Grams confirmed it when I asked her. She was so heartbroken with tears running down her face when she told me the truth and wondered how I figured it out.

I explained what happened at the hospital. "I was told my dad died in the ambulance and my mom was barely hanging on. They both lost a lot of blood and it was a miracle my mom was still alive at all. The hospital they were brought to was small and didn't have a lot of resources. Blood being one of the main things they really needed more of. The little hospital was more of a family ran clinic. The nearest actual hospital with proper resources was at least an hour away if not longer. Medics were on their way already in a helicopter to bring more blood for my mom. I was hoping they would come in time. I couldn't lose her too. I offered to donate blood to save her, but the doctor said no, because I was a minor. I argued and yelled at him until he finally gave in and said fine and that he would let me donate. I told the nurse my blood type was AB+. The doctor looked at me with a sad confused expression.

"Are you sure?", he asked with a puzzled expression on his face.

"Of course, I am sure! I might be fourteen but I am not stupid!" I yelled, I even showed him my school id, which read that my blood type was AB+.

"Jade, it has to be a mistake. People with your parents' blood types; they can't have children with your blood type. It's not possible. Both of your parents' blood types are A+. I'm sorry but I can't allow you to donate. There is too much of a risk it could hurt your mother. Mixing blood types can even kill her."

"My school was probably wrong. The science teacher that made us do the test was sick that week. I'm sure he got the results mixed up. She can't die. You have to let me help her," I begged with tears running down my face. The doctor and his nurse wouldn't budge. The nurse told me I needed to pray and have faith. The medics would be there any minute.

The medics came in their helicopter with the right blood at last. It seemed to have taken hours, but it was less than twenty minutes. Dr. Phil, who was running the clinic, got the bullets out and had mom stable enough to be transported to the actual hospital. "It's a miracle she is still alive. She is a real fighter", he said.

I rode with my mother. I wasn't going to leave her side. I had never ridden in a helicopter before; not that I really paid much attention to it that time. I didn't even remember getting in. Too much was on my mind. Dad was gone and mom might be leaving me as well. I couldn't stand the thought of that. I couldn't lose her. She was my mom. You only get one. I also didn't understand how my blood type didn't match my parents; what was that about? It didn't make any sense at all.

My mom was rushed to emergency surgery to see if there were any blood clots or other injuries that were missed. Grams showed up a couple of hours after we got to the hospital. I ran to her, not knowing what I was going to do. So many different emotions were coming and going through my body. Mostly I felt sad and angry. It wasn't fair. What did we do to deserve my parents being gunned down? She hugged me tightly, not wanting to let me go. "Grams I'm scared. What if she doesn't make it? I can't lose her too! Dad is already gone!" Hugging me even tighter she said, "Hush now sweetie, and don't worry about that right now. Your mom is a fighter. Believe that my precious girl." As we waited in the waiting room for news, she held and rocked me as I cried. She didn't say anything else to try to make me feel better. I was glad. It wouldn't have helped. I only needed to know I wasn't alone. The smell of her perfume and the warmth of her skin helped with that.

I didn't notice that the police officer that was waiting with me left, until I saw him and his partner walk up to get Gram's attention. She walked away with them. I assumed she told me, but I wasn't really paying attention then. I couldn't hear anything or focus much on anything. My head was still spinning. I saw people walking or running around me. It was like everything was happening in slow motion. I was still trying to grasp everything that was happening. In one night my whole world seemed to come crashing down. I felt like I couldn't deal with any more loss. I wasn't strong enough.

I must have fallen asleep and so did Grams, because hours had passed when we got a small update. The doctor who was checking out my mom's injuries, said she was still in recovery in the ICU and that the damage was pretty severe. He could only hope for the best and we would have to wait and see what happened. I didn't like the sound of that at all. He was a doctor. He should be able to save her. Isn't that why he went to medical school for so many years, was to save people?

Time dragged by too slowly. Every minute seemed like hours. Grams went to go get her some coffee and me some tea from the cafeteria. I think that was more to take her mind off everything and to get some fresh air. I'm sure I was not very good at comforting her, because she was comforting me. I also didn't know what to say to her. This was her only daughter, child for that matter, which could possibly die.

The doctor came walking slowly toward me. I had moved seats since the last time I had seen him. I had to move. I was so angry and restless. I couldn't concentrate on anything. I was exhausted, but refused to go to a hotel or even go to the bathroom. I wanted to be there to make sure my mom was alright and for her to know I never left.

"Where is your grandmother honey?" asked the doctor.

Looking up at him, "She went to the cafeteria and should be back any minute now", I said in a low voice.

"Alright, would you mind too much if I stayed here and waited for her. I would like to talk to the both of you."

I nodded slowly. Even then I wasn't going to be rude. I was raised better than that. A couple of minutes later, Grams came back walking slowly. She had sore knees and looked like she was in physical pain. She was holding a white and brown foam cup in each hand. The look on Grams face was horrible when she looked at the doctor. I could tell she was trying not to cry. That look hurt me so bad. She was turning red, her eyes were getting big and her lips were trembling. I already knew something was wrong when the doctor said he wanted to talk to us, but didn't want to believe it. Grams laid the cups down on the table next to me. Her hands were shaking. She then sat down next to me and grabbed my hand, squeezing it a little. I couldn't forget the pained look on Dr. Evans face and what came out of his mouth next.

"Mrs. Flowers... Jade... I am so sorry. She didn't make it. The wounds were too severe. She had too much blood loss. Even if... Even if, she would have been here right after it had happened, I don't think she could have survived. I believe she held on as long as she could have. She was a fighter for sure. I am truly sorry. I know that doesn't mean much coming from a stranger, but you both are in my thoughts and prayers."

He stood up then from the chair across from me and patted Grams on the back as a gesture of sympathy. Then he walked off. Grams was quiet for a long time. We just sat there not moving. I think we were both in shock. It felt surreal. You see tragic stuff like that in movies and on television shows all the time, but not in real life.

Hours must have passed because there was a shift change at some point. I didn't know how I noticed the different people, but I did. When a new nurse came and asked us if we needed help, Grams broke down and sobbed. I had never seen an adult cry like that or cry so much before. I knew I lost a mom, but she lost a child. At that moment it was my turn to be there for her. I was all she had left, and she was all I had left. We didn't have any other family. Both my parents were the only child and my dads' parents died before I was born.

A few days after my parents funerals, I went to live with Grams. I was terrified. I loved her, but I was not very close to her. She came to visit for birthdays and holidays, but we never talked much. She wasn't very close to my parents either, even though my mother was her daughter. They were nice to each other, but they didn't have a close relationship like I had with my mom.

My first night there I was angry and scared. I had so much stuff on my mind. Mainly, it was one thing. I went to look for my grandmother, and when I finally found her I just looked at her sharply and asked what I had been wondering for days, "Am I... Grams, am I... adopted?"

She started to cry, sobbing actually, after I asked, but I had to know the truth. That instant I knew it. I actually was adopted. There was no more suspicion, no more wondering if I were imaging things. I felt stupid. I should have realized it sooner.

It started to make sense after a while. I had light brown hair, my eyes change from hazel to green, I was on the short side and had small feet, and my skin color even seemed to be darker than theirs were. My parents were on the tall side. My dad had dark brown hair with light blue eyes and ivory skin. My mom had light auburn hair, deep blue eyes and was pale complected, but less than my dad was. They didn't eat as much as I did. In fact, they didn't even really like the same foods I did.

I remembered the weird looks people gave us when I was younger. Everyone always made a fuss about how good we looked as a family. How lucky I must feel to have such wonderful parents. How my parents always hushed people and gave them weird looks after saying that. Everyone knew but me. I was in the dark about it completely.

We talked for hours on the screened in back porch. Well, it was mostly Grams who did the talking that night. She told me the truth about everything. "Your mother couldn't get pregnant. She tried for years, but it never happened. Your parents finally got tested to see if there was a problem. It turned out your mother wasn't fertile. Her body wouldn't produce any eggs. When she was younger she got really sick, and it caused her to have scar tissue that affected her ability to have a baby. I am sorry sweetie. I didn't want to be the one who told you all this, but I don't want to hide it anymore."

"Wow!" was all I could say.

"The bad news nearly broke your mother. She always wanted to have children. Jade, your parents weren't planning on adopting. However, your father's boss at the time was informed that a baby was left at an abandoned warehouse in New Boston. It was a little girl who was wrapped in a small blue and pink cloth blanket. There was a note in fancy handwriting that said the baby girl's name was Jade, and she was born on October 31st. The baby appeared to be healthy, well fed, and was only a few days old."

"Someone just left me there?" I asked crying. Grams looked at me with tears still running down her face. She nodded and continued on with her story.

"Your mom was stubborn. She didn't want to see you at first. She didn't want to get her hopes up, but your dad talked her into it", Grams said, as she started to smile slightly.

I didn't know what to say to her. I just nodded so she would keep talking. "It took months for all the social work stuff and legal processes to go through, but your parents loved you as soon as they saw you. Honey, your parents wanted to tell you for so long, but they didn't know how you would react. They didn't think you would see them the same way; that you wouldn't love them the same way."

I didn't see how that could be possible. I mean my birth parents didn't want me. Why else would they leave me like that? The thought of me being abandoned like that hurt so much worse than my adopted parents lying to me my whole life.

"After everything was finalized they moved away from here. They wanted to get a fresh start, so they moved to a smaller town. Your dad got a job at the local college as a law professor and had a small client base in the surrounding towns. Your mom decided to be a stay at home mom at first, but she got bored. She started doing crafts and selling them online."

"I still have some of the scented candles she made and a blue quilt with white and yellow daisies all over it. I remember she had worked for hours and hours on that thing. It was the first one she had made. She was so proud of it, so of course she wanted me to have it. I must have been four or five then." My mom was always trying to make new things to keep herself busy.

"Yes she was really proud of that quilt. She even made me one for Christmas a few years ago. I still have it," Grams said fondly.

Their lack of truth came back in mind then. "I just don't understand why they didn't tell me. How could they hide that from me?" I asked, with tears running down my face again.

"Honestly, sweetie, they were afraid whoever left you would come back and try to get you back. Your mom thought since they would be your blood relatives they might have a fighting chance, even though you were legally your parents' child by then. Your dad knew the law and he tried to convince your mother, but she didn't want to hear it. She was so afraid to lose you the first several months, that she wouldn't leave the house or you."

"It was still my right to know. I tried to save mom and I couldn't. I am trying so hard not to be angry, but I can't help it. Why did they think I wouldn't see them the same way or love them the same way? How can someone keep a secret like that, and why did so many other people know and not tell me? Why didn't you tell me? I don't understand!"

"They felt so horrible about keeping it from you. They even searched for your birth parents for the first couple years after you became part of the family. Your parents didn't have any luck honey. It's as though you showed up out of thin air. I'm sorry Jade. They really did love you and so do I. You are such a blessing to me. You always have been and it wasn't my place to say anything or anyone else's.

"Grams... Was I the reason why you and mom weren't close? She said you two used to be, but then something happened and y'all drifted apart. Now I think it was because of me, if so I'm sorry. I really am."

Grams stood up really fast then, pulled me up and hugged me tight. "Jade, you should never think that, ever. You are one of the best things to come into my life! Your mom and I drifted apart because your mom stopped talking to her family and friends because she was depressed in so many ways. I wanted to give her time to accept that you weren't going anywhere and that everything was going to be fine.

Your mom just shut everyone out and time went on."

She left me on the porch for a few minutes to make us some hot tea. When she came back she had a folder with her. She handed the folder over to me. I opened it nervously. I found my birth certificates and adoption papers. I was stunned. I knew Grams told me everything, but the pieces of paper made it a lot more real.

After we cried and hugged for a couple of hours that night after Grams told me all she knew, we just talked about everything and nothing for hours. She wanted to set my room up the way I wanted it to be with new furniture and paint. I was told to make myself at home. She knew it would be rough for a while, but she was there for me and always would be. She knew she couldn't replace my parents and she didn't want to try, but she loved me a lot and that would never change. Grams and I have been pretty much close friends ever since. She was not like other adults at all. She was open-minded, had a huge heart, and didn't talk down to younger people like other adults did.

My face was wet with tears coming out of my eyes. I had been laying in my bed for a long time then. Just thinking about the dream I had of my parents' tragic deaths and finding out I wasn't related to them by blood. I thought I was over it. Sometimes I forget to be honest. It seemed so surreal; like it wasn't true.

Some days I woke up and just knew my parents were going to be at the breakfast nook eating cereal or pancakes and eggs while wondering why I wasn't ready for school yet. Of course, I would always blame it on the alarm clock and how it was broken. They never believed me though. It was probably because my alarms were always set on my phone.

Then reality always hit me, and I was reminded all over again what happened. I didn't know what was worse dreaming about it or waking up happy and then have the truth sink in again.

Chapter Four

The week went by fast. I, of course, passed my test in biology. Not that I ever had a doubt. Alexa did well too, which I already knew she would. She had a lot of stuff to do that week for all those school clubs she was in, so I was a lone wolf for most of the week. Except for the few times I hung out with Nick, we didn't do much. Mostly I helped him with his homework or we watched some movies. It was dull because there wasn't much to do. I was ready for my birthday to come. It was going to be epic!

It was Saturday again and I was waiting on Alexa at the small park downtown. She was supposed to be bringing me a caramel frappe and some glazed donuts. I needed some sugary food bad. She was treating me as an early birthday gift. It was a tradition we had when something special was happening soon for the other person. We always gave the other person special gifts. She started that tradition when we first became friends. She gave me a blue rope-style friendship bracelet and she got a pink one. We both still wore them, even though they faded over time.

I had been waiting for an hour. I was starting to get worried, because she was never late, ever! I had been thinking about calling her to make sure everything was alright. She usually sent me a message or called if something was wrong. "Ugh, I'll give her another five minutes, if she doesn't show up, then I'll call", I said out loud to myself.

As soon as I lost my nerve and I was about to call Alexa my phone started to vibrate on the picnic table I was laying on. Of course, when I looked at the screen, it was from her. Feeling relieved I sat up to read the message she sent, hoping she had a really great explanation for stressing me out so much!

"Jade, I am very sorry. My phone died and I am just now able to contact you. I don't have enough of a charge to call you. I can't meet now. I will not be able to come to your house until later this evening. I promise I will make it up to you and bring you two frappes and a dozen donuts!"

"No worries, ya had me worried girl!! Glad ya ok... I'll go grab some food, I am starving now thanks to you... jk jk, love ya!!"

I put my phone back down. That was not what I really wanted to say to her, but I didn't want to fight with her either. She did have a good excuse at least. I really needed to learn not to freak out so easily. Laying back down, I started to read more of the book I had brought with me. I was close to the next chapter. I decided I would stop then. I had to stop at chapters in a book, if I didn't it was like being paused in time as if you had unfinished business that nagged at you. Yes, I know it was an odd quirk, but it was something that made me who I was.

Five minutes later I was done. I wanted to read more to see what happened next, but I needed to get back to reality. I decided to go down to the old pet shop to see if I could find out what was opening up. Maybe there would be a sign or something pinned up so I could tell. I was still hoping it would be something interesting like a candy store, a taco shop, or even maybe a tattoo parlor. That last one made me laugh, I could never see myself getting a tattoo. The pain was an issue and I never liked needles. It was also permanent unless you wanted to have some extremely painful laser surgery to have it removed. Nope, I was good with my body being plain. I did have my ears pierced, but that was all I needed, plus that was done when I was a baby, so I didn't remember it. I had a really low tolerance for pain.

That time the front door of the store was perched open a little and there was a purple sign that said: "Children of the Sun and Moon" hanging above it. The name didn't really tell me what it was going to be, but it did sound hippyish. The lights were on, but it was still very dim through the glass windows. I could hear some Indie dance music playing softly inside.

Peeking through the door I could see the inside had been transformed. The walls used to be dark lime green with chocolate brown trim. Now the walls were bright orange and the trim was dark purple. Shimmery purple curtains were hanging around on metal poles everywhere to make the room appear smaller and more elegant. There were a few shelves that held some candles, soaps, and what looked like herbs. On the floor were several unopened boxes that were scattered around. I could smell the scent of lavender. Looking around, I could see that there were incense sticks burning in one of the corners. I loved that smell. It was very relaxing. Maybe that is why I used lavender scented body wash and shampoo so much, it made me feel calm.

Walking inside, not being able to control myself, I looked all around the room, and I was even more enthused than when I was outside. Everything fit together so well; the walls, the curtains, the tall gold standing lamps; there were even metal dream catchers hanging on the walls. The shop wasn't ready yet, but I was happy it was going to be something truly different than what we already had or what I was expecting.

"Hello there, may I help you?" asked a young woman's voice. I turned toward her slowly because I had been caught and I was a little scared. I almost went into shock when I first saw her. She was incredibly beautiful with long wavy black hair, bright green eyes, and her skin was a light cream color. She honestly looked like an adult porcelain doll.

"I'm so sorry. I used to come here when it was another business and was curious to see what it's going to be now. Your shop is amazing. You have transformed it completely. I'm sorry to ask, but what is it going to be exactly?" I asked in a startled rush.

"It is going to be a Wicca shop. I will sell natural soaps, candles, herbs, teas, crystals, essential oils, different types of incense, and books", she said smiling excitingly.

"That sounds incredible, I have never heard of a store like this before, I can't wait to see how it looks when you are open. I'm Jade by the way, it is nice to meet you."

"Jade, that is a pretty name, I'm Lavy, it's nice to meet you as well."

"You're going to be opening in a week right? That is what the sign on the door said last week."

"I hope to, I didn't think it was going to take me this long to get everything set up. I usually have help, but I am new to this city, so I don't know anyone here yet. I'm thinking about hiring someone just to help around here part-time."

"Wow! Well, I have never had a job before but I would be very interested. I'm a fast learner and I could help after school."

"Hmm, how old are you? You look a little young. I believe you have to be at least sixteen in this state to be employed."

"At the moment, to be honest, I am fifteen but I will be sixteen a week from Monday. I would love to work in a place like this. I like that it is different. We don't have anything like this around here at all. Plus, I used to help my mom make homemade candles when I was younger, so I do have a little experience."

Lavy smiled, "You can start November 1st, the day after your birthday. I will need to pay you in cash for now. You can also have samples of some of the merchandise. I think I may change the opening date; hold off for another week or two. I want to make sure the store is ready."

"Sounds great! I can help you finish setting up. Thank you for this opportunity."

"You're welcome, thank you for offering. It saves me the time of having to look for some-one."

"I know we just met, but would you like to come to my party. It is going to be a costume party. You don't have to dress up if you don't want to though. Also, there will be a lot of high school kids and no adults, but it will be a lot of fun, I promise. I hope you will come."

"Thank you for the offer. I will think about it and let you know. I don't plan on working that day. Halloween is a special day for me and my family. Can I let you know in a few days?"

"Sure" I gave her my contact information in case she needed to reach me. I didn't know why, but I trusted her already. There was something about her that made me feel safe and that I had known her for a lot longer than a couple of hours.

She gave me a few books to read so I would know what merchandise she would be selling. "I make a lot of what I sell. I have several small gardens with different types of flowers and herbs. If I can't make it or I don't have enough ingredients for something, I order it online. It makes it easier. The best thing is everything is safe because it's all natural with no harsh chemicals", she said happily. I stayed there for a few hours longer just to talk to her. I found out a little bit about her life. Her mother died when she was young, and she lived with her dad for a long time before she left to go travel and do her own thing. I told her about my parents as well, and that I lived with my grandmother. It was nice having someone to talk to that you could relate to.

It was getting late in the afternoon. "Sorry to do this, but I have to go. I am meeting up with a friend and need to get things ready."

"Enjoy yourself."

"Thanks, I will."

"I'm happy that you will be starting soon. I could use the help, plus it was nice talking to you. You seem a lot older than you look."

"I guess if you go through what I had to go through, you wise up."

"Perhaps you're right."

"Oh, please try to come to the party. It will be a lot better if you come. There will be a lot of free junk food and of course a cake", I joked.

"I will do my best. Thank you for the invite."

I rode the bus home, I didn't want to ask Nick for a ride. He was busy anyway. He told me the previous night he had a "guy weekend" with his friends; whatever that meant. I thought I could have a girl weekend then since he was busy, but that didn't work out too well yet since Alexa bailed on me this morning.

When I walked in the door, I could smell food. Grams was cooking dinner. It smelled amazing. She was making fried chicken, biscuits and gravy, and her double chocolate cake. My stomach was starting to rumble really loud. I had not eaten all day and had just noticed then; too distracted I supposed. I walked to the kitchen and grabbed a chicken strip. It was so good. Grams looked at me, amused while shaking her head with a small smile. I laughed "Thanks", I told her, smiling back.

Leaving the kitchen with another chicken strip and a little less hungry, I went to my room. I noticed Alexa still wasn't there. If she was, my radio or my TV would have been loud enough for me to hear through the closed door. She was acting strangely that day. I did hope everything was alright with her. Opening my door, something on my bed grabbed my attention. I walked to my bed and picked up a small black box with a little blue ribbon tied around it. Where the box was I could see a small white card with my name on it. Curious, I picked it up and read what it said.

Jade, I feel like I have known you my whole life, even though it has only been for a couple of years. You are not only my best friend, you are also the sister I have always wanted. I know that sounds silly, but it is the truth. We are soul sisters forever and always. Now when you look in the box don't cry. I know how you are, I have a matching one, and I hope you like it. This is an early birthday gift for you.

Love always,
Your sister Alexa

Honestly, it was hard not to cry at what she wrote. I felt the same way she did. She was like the sister I never had. It was hard to find people you could count on for anything. Pulling myself together, I slowly opened the box, inside was a shiny silver ring with an infinity symbol engraved on the top. The design was simple but incredibly beautiful. Alexa also had it engraved on the inside: *Jade and Alexa sisters forever*. Seeing that made me cry. It was sweet and now I knew why Alexa was late. She was leaving the gift for me and she knew we would both cry like babies if she gave it to me in person. What would I do without her? I truly have no idea.

After dinner, Alexa sent me a message saying that she couldn't spend the night. I was a little disappointed, but maybe it was for the best. It had been a long day and I needed sleep. Before bed Grams and I played Trouble. I was always on the blue side and she was always on the red. We played a few rounds. She won the first two and I won the last. Trouble was her favorite game. I think she liked the bubble popper the most.

Grams also made us banana splits with my favorite toppings of hot fudge and caramel syrup, whip cream, and extra bananas. We sat on the couch and watched an old black and white TV show. It was about a crazy lady who was always up to something. She was either scheming to be in her husband's production or getting in some type of trouble with her neighbor. I loved spending time like this with her. I may not have had a girl's night with Alexa, but I had one with Grams, which was always better.

♡

Lavender was playing in the small clearing I saw everyone dancing at before. She was so little and full of life. Her dad and mom were sitting on an old broken log looking at her and smiling. The pointed ear woman looked sad, and so did the man sitting next to her. As much as I wanted to stay and watch little Lavender, I was too curious to know what was wrong with the couple. I walked over to the log to hear what her parents were talking about.

"Kegan, I have to go. You have known this was coming for months. She will have you to protect her. I will come back to you my love, I promise", the lady said with a few small tears running down her face.

"You say that as if you know for certain, my wife. How can you though? You can't see the future; you don't know what dangers await you. So many of our kinds are dying due to this horrible war. I can't bear the thought of losing you."

"I have faith in the greater power. He has led me to you and has brought us this far in life. You should have faith as well my love. I know it is not easy, but without faith, we have nothing really."

"Jewel... I can only say I'll try for you. I promise I will take care of our daughter and try to believe you will come back to us. I would rather that I be the one going instead of you. I am supposed to be the one who protects us, I am a Guardian, and this is what I was born to do; to protect!"

"Hush now. Lavender can see that we are upset. She doesn't need to worry. She is a strong girl, but she needs both of us as she grows up. If I am to return unharmed I will need to know that you will be strong for all of us and not worry so much. I am a warrior of my people as well; we fairies are strong people. They also need me for healing. No one has the gifts I do"

Kegan smiled at that and told Jewel she was right and he knew it. Males weren't the only gender who could protect the ones they loved. A mother's bond with her child was one of the strongest bonds of all time.

Lavender came running up to them just then. They both held her for a long while, telling her how much she meant to them. They looked like a happy family. Looking at them made my heart hurt. I was happy for them, but I felt so alone and so lost.

Time jumped ahead quickly. I could see Jewel leaning down and saying goodbye to her daughter. They both were crying. Lavender was begging her mother not to leave. "I promise I will be good and not get into any *trouble. Please don't leave mommy." The pained look on her mother's face was awful. "My sweet girl, I am not leaving because of anything you have done. I need to go and help our people. I promise I will return to you, no matter what", she explained to the child. After kissing her daughter goodbye on both cheeks, she stood up and turned to Kegan, who looked just as heartbroken.*

He grabbed her into his arms and held her tight. His eyes were glowing even bluer than they did the last time. He was trying hard to look brave, but he wasn't doing a very good job at it. Jewel looked sad but proud. She knew she had to be strong for her family, even if it meant leaving. She kissed Kegan softly on the lips and told him "our hearts and souls are one, I will return to you my love, I promise this, one day I will return."

She turned away, grabbed a large brown pouch, then threw the strap from the bag over her shoulder. She left her house abruptly and walked to a small group of women. It was the same women who were dancing with her that night around the fire. A few moments later, some men walked up to them. They looked like the women. The men had pointed ears and their skin also shimmered with different colors, but each one was slightly different. They were all fairies I assumed. The men were just as beautiful as the women.

A few of them had similar pouches like the one Jewel did. Others had different types of weapons. I could see a couple of wooden bows with a colorful arrow and others had long sticks that looked like staffs with sharp ends. They all appeared to be warriors. A few of them even had dark marks painted under their eyes. Looking at them, well studying them really, Jewel seemed to be the one in charge of the group; like she was their leader.

I followed them down through the path in the forest, but instead of going to the clearing, they were going a different way. They headed through a darker set of trees, these looked twisted and angry. I could feel an evil presence surrounding all of them like they were watching me as I walked.

Jewel stopped about a mile into the creepy trees. Everyone got in a circle and held hands. They all closed their eyes, and then Jewel started saying words I didn't understand. As she went on and her voice became louder, the ground started to shake and dirt from the ground was being lifted into the air. It started to spin around them getting faster and faster with every second until it shot behind me and made a loud noise sounding like thunder.

I didn't want to turn around. I was scared of what I would see, but I knew I needed to. When I finally got the courage to look, I could see that out of nowhere a cave had appeared. The entrance to the cave was black and felt cold. Jewel and the other fairy warriors walked up to the entrance and stopped. Jewel lifted her hand and touched the blackness. When she did, it rippled. It looked like clusters of blue and white glowing light swirling around. There was still a blackness surrounding the edges of the light, encasing it. Jewel then walked through the light; then disappeared. After she was gone, one by one the rest did the same thing. After each warrior walked through the portal, black hole, gateway, whatever you wanted to call it, it went solid black again. Each time someone else touched the blackness, different colors appeared, the colors matched their souls. I wasn't sure how I knew that, but I was sure that was it. After the last one went through the portal, it was quiet, as though no one had been *there a few minutes before. I walked up to get closer to the blackness, I did the same thing the others had done. I touched the blackness with my hand, and I could feel its energy. It didn't feel good or evil, but it did feel extremely powerful. When I touched it the blackness turned blue and white like Jewels, but brighter. The colors were swirling slower than they had for the others. I drew my hand back, getting scared, the blackness came back. When I tried to turn and walk away, I felt something grab me and pull me into the darkness.*

I set up and screamed, I felt so scared. I didn't hear the door open before I felt arms around me. "Everything is alright honey, you were having a bad dream", I heard Grams whisper with her soothing voice. I calmed down, after realizing she was right. It wasn't real. It was only a nightmare. Nothing was after me. I was safe, I was home in my bed.

Chapter Five

I had been wearing the infinity ring Alexa gave me, ever since I found it on my bed. The first time I saw Alexa I cried. I couldn't help it. Then, of course, she cried just as much as me. That got us strange looks from our boyfriends. "You two are being such girls", the boys said in unison. We glared at them, "we're sorry", said a startled Trevor. Nick then piped in "yeah, babe we were just joking."

I walked away from them, and Alexa followed. I thought I would let the guys stress for a little while. There was no reason for the rude comment. As we walked, she showed me her ring. It was identical to mine except hers says *Alexa and Jade sisters forever*. "I love it, I said pleased. We both had them on our right-hand ring finger. It was crazy how much we thought alike sometimes.

"Hey, yesterday I heard on the radio that a carnival is coming to town", she said.

I got genuinely ecstatic, "you know we have to go, right?"

"Of course, that is why I sent you an email already with all the details. You can read it later in your study period. You don't want to be caught on your phone."

"Yep, your right. Last time it was taken away for the whole day. It was awful", I sighed dramatically.

I wasn't attached to my phone that much. It was nice to be connected to the world though. I didn't care much for social media. I mostly used my phone to talk to Grams, Alexa, and Nick, oh and of course to read books. I had several hundred on my e-book app.

Study period finally arrived. I sat in the back of the library in the corner. I liked privacy, and my spot was hidden from everyone. I took my phone out of my pocket to check the email Alexa had sent me earlier.

I had never been to a carnival and always wanted to go to one. The description in the email of the one coming to Texarkana was like the ones I have read about in books and had seen in movies. There was going to be trapeze dancers, stilt walkers, fire breathers, knife throwing, food and game booths, a petting zoo, and other attractions. I never read about petting zoos being at a carnival, but I loved them, so I knew we were going to have a great time!

I asked Grams if she wanted to go, but she declined. "Jade, sweetie, I have to go out of town for a couple of weeks. I will be leaving tomorrow afternoon. I am sorry sweetie, but I will not be here Monday for your birthday."

"Oh, where are you going", I asked trying not to sound upset.

"Well, there is an old patient of mine who is in serious trouble in Granger, Texas. It is a life or death type situation. I am the only person they will talk to; I am the only person who can help. I hope you understand. If it wasn't really serious I wouldn't leave you."

"Go ahead and go. Don't worry about me. I will be fine, it's okay," I said with a fake smile on my face. I was a terrible liar and I knew it, but Grams seemed to have believed me. I didn't want to make her feel worse than she already did.

She felt so bad, she took me to go buy the car I wanted the next day. I told her she didn't have to, and I knew I was supposed to wait until I was sixteen. She explained it wasn't right for me to have to wait due to her being away. It was only six days until it was my birthday anyway. I smiled and gave her a tight hug and said thank you about a hundred times. I think my excitement made her feel a little better about leaving. I was glad she was only going to be gone for a couple of weeks.

The good news was I could go get my drivers' license on Monday and I would already have a car. I called Nick to have him go with us, so I could drive the car home. I was right the car was more my size than the trucks. It felt great being behind the wheel of a small car. The bug still needed work, but Nick said he would get his friends to start working on it that Thursday afternoon so it would be ready by Monday. They could work on it at the school's auto shop and get extra credit. It also wouldn't cost me anything. That was one of the reasons why I liked him so much. He really did care about me. I didn't even mind that he was also helping me for extra credit. He was smart, but his grades weren't the best.

The past few days dragged by. It was finally Friday and the carnival was the next day. It felt like it took weeks for the carnival to arrive.

Maybe I was a little more excited than I should be, but oh well. The event was going to be at the fairgrounds. It was the only place big enough to hold it and all the people who were going to be there.

It was hard to go to sleep that night. It was weird being in the house alone; I heard strange noises all the time. The wind would make a branch hit my window or the floor would creak like someone was walking around. No one else was in the house, the alarm was on and the doors were locked. I was just being paranoid. I had felt that way since Grams left, I didn't want to stay with anyone because I didn't need a babysitter. Turning on music to put me to sleep worked great, just like it had for the previous couple of nights. It helped mostly because it drowned out all the weird noises.

I have been awake since six in the morning and have already drunk three iced coffees. "That could explain why I am so hyper", I thought, laughing to myself. I was ready to go and have been trying to keep myself distracted for hours. The first admission wasn't until two in the afternoon and time was passing by slower than usual it seemed.

I tried something new with my hair: I put it in a french braid starting from the top left of my head circling to the bottom right. That way the end of the braid would fall off my right shoulder. I think it turned out pretty cute, even if it did take me an hour to get it right. I was also wearing some new jeans with black stars on the back pockets and a t-shirt I bought myself for the special occasion. The shirt was black with a blue crescent moon on the front and had my name on the back in blue letters. I had it made at a store in the mall that creates customized shirts. I was really starting to like the moon symbol from my fairy warrior dreams. Plus it fit with my new job at Children of the Sun and Moon.

I also got my costume done last night for my party. Yes, I was still having a costume party for my birthday. I generally didn't do costume parties but this was a special year and I loved Halloween and dressing up. I got inspired and made myself a fairy costume. It took me about a month. I couldn't wait to wear it, I think it turned out really well. No one knew what it was. I had kept it a secret. I was hoping no one else dressed up like me. Oh well, I thought the more the merrier.

The doorbell rang. I went to the door and peeked through the peephole, I smiled at who it was. As soon as I opened the door, Nick leaned down and kissed me, then gave me a small box. I invited him in and told him to go to the living room, so I could go put on some shoes. I walked back to my room really fast to put on some socks and black sneakers. I was sure we were going to be walking around a lot so I wanted to make sure I was comfortable.

When I came back to the living room, Nick was on the couch waiting for me and staring at me as I walked toward him. He smiled when I met his eyes, "you're so beautiful, I hope you know that." Blushing bright red, I replied with "thank you and you're not looking so bad your-self." I sat beside him and opened the small box he brought with him. Inside was a blue Volk-swagen Beetle Bug keychain to match my car. Loving it, I kissed him on the cheek. "This is amazing, thank you!"

We left my house a few minutes later and made it to the carnival within twenty minutes. I couldn't wait any longer. We arrived close to 2 pm. There were a lot of people there already, but I didn't care. Nothing was going to ruin this for me. I have been to plenty of fairs with thrill rides, games, and lots of different food trucks, but nothing like this. Getting out of the car I was in total shock, the scene in front of me looked exactly how movies have shown what a circus should look like.

There were two large bright red and white tents in the middle of the field. Around the large tents, there were several smaller blue and green striped tents, food carts, and game booths. We parked further back to make it easier to leave when it was over. I walked extremely fast, practically running to the ticket booth. After getting our tickets, Nick finally made it to where I was. I knew he wasn't as excited as I was, but he could have seemed a little more enthusiastic. We walked through the entrance gate, the view was a lot better than I had first seen. This carnival was bigger up close. There were a lot more tents and food carts than what I saw at the car.

The first thing I wanted to do was to get something to eat. I was starving and who could resist carnival food. I needed something that would fill me up and I needed something tasty. Nick spotted a taco stand, we walked over and I got four huge fully loaded Mexican style Tacos for each of us and a couple of bottles of water.

These were so much better than the Tex-Mex kind. After we finished eating, we decided to walk around to see what all the attractions were.

In the center of the main entrance, was a sign that said fascinating acts would be showing at six that evening. We had plenty of time to see everything, I was thrilled! The first thing we wanted to check out was the house of mirrors, even if the outside was kind of creepy. The mirrors were in a pop-up storage building instead of a tent. It had large yellow eyes with black slits painted in the top corners that said: "Come and see the Mirrors of Illusion". The walkway was red and so was the curtained door. From far away it looked like you were walking into a mouth. The room was dark inside except a few strobe lights hanging from ropes around the mirrors. Of course, these were the ones that made you look wider, thinner, taller, shorter, and made your head look like a bubble.

Nick got bored so I let him leave. Even though they were fun to me, he didn't find them amusing. He had been to carnivals before so all this wasn't new to him. After he left, I looked in all the mirrors again, loving how they

made me look weird. When I was about to leave
I noticed one I hadn't seen before, it was behind some of the mirrors, hidden away. Curious, I walked over to it, this one was different
from all the others. It had a silver border where
the others all had black borders. The mirror
didn't change my appearance at all, staring
back at me was just simple Jade. Confused, I
looked at the mirror closer, thinking I may
have missed something. The longer I stared at
it, the more I realize it was just a normal mirror. Feeling stupid, I started to walk away, but
then, I saw it light up out of the corner of my
eye. When I turned back toward it, the mirror
looked normal like it had a moment ago. I
started to walk away again to leave but saw the
same light again. This time when I turned back
toward the mirror, it was still lit up. It had a
soft white light illuminating from it. I stood
there just staring, after a little while my features began to change: my eyes looked like
snake eyes, but my irises were blue, my teeth
were pointed, and I looked healthier, stronger,
and powerful.

I closed my eyes to clear my vision, when I
reopened them the mirror was showing just me
again, no alterations. Laughing to myself, I fig-

ured it was some type of trick with a projector. "I think that is pretty neat", saying out loud to myself, a little embarrassed.

I left through the exit, to find Nick with a few of our friends. Alexa was with Trevor of course, and Stephanie was with them, but Cory was home grounded. He snuck out of his room to go see Stephanie that past week and was caught. He said he would do it again though, to see his girl. I thought it was sweet, but his parents, not so much.

The next stop on our little adventure was to the House of Unusual Beings. The sign intrigued me for sure, so of course, we had to check it out. We all walked into the blue tent. It was dark in there as well, with only small old lanterns hanging up. There were several small sections separating all the "unusual beings". The first one was a Bearded Lady who was maybe in her early twenties. She had thick blonde hair all around her face, arms, and legs. Her eyes were golden yellow and her teeth looked really white and canine-like. She didn't seem mean; sadder than anything. She was in a rusty metal bar cage that she could sit or lay down in, but not do much else. I felt bad for her, but that was probably part of her act, to get more people interested in the wolf lady. Her costume was realistic, the contacts, canine teeth, and hair looked so wolf-like.

I walked past her, I couldn't look at her anymore even if it was all an act. She was really good at making me feel bad. The next one was a big bald guy who could swallow snakes with his mouth, then release them from his nose. No thanks, moving along. The third room was full of animals with two-headed turtles and snakes in tanks and some small furry animals with extra limbs in cages. Their colors were off, they were brighter than what they should be. I walked by that one fast too. That wasn't my type of entertainment.

Finally, the last one was a large tank with two women in it. They both had fish tails, like mermaids. "Wow, these people are good with costumes", I said to myself. I was impressed. The mermaids looked so real; the dark-skinned one had a purple tail with purple scales going up in patches on her arms. It also looked like she had gills on the sides of her neck. The other one was light skinned and her tail was dark green. She had scales and gills in the same places as the first one. Their wet hair matched the color of their fish tails. I was not sure how they made their costumes so real looking, but they did. Both of them were swimming around slowly back and forth. I walked closer to them. I couldn't help it. They were so amazing looking. When I got to the stop rope, that was about two feet from them, the one with the purple tail popped her head out of the water. I took a step back a little startled. Her eyes were solid black except a small orange ring around the edges of her thick black pupils. The fish contacts were neat, even if they did freak me out a little.

The others were probably still at the snake swallowing guy or looking at the strange animals. After a few minutes of looking at the "mermaids", I decided I should go find the others. I was ready to move on from this place. Stephanie was at the animals, she looked amazed. She probably knew that they didn't live long just like I did. She was a big science nerd. Alexa, Nick, and Trevor were staring at the snake guy in fascination; to me, it was still gross. I loved snakes and reptiles, but not putting them in my body, nope, I was good.

I finally dragged everyone away from the weird display; it took some coaxing. I got everyone a snow cone for finally leaving as a treat. I told them what I saw and that I was upset and needed to chill out for a few minutes. All of them told me they didn't see a lot of what I did. The bearded lady was a young woman who had a long beard around her face and really long hair and the mermaids were just two women dressed in some tacky costumes. They did see the snake guy and the strange animals but they didn't look sick; they looked healthy and normal.

I looked back at the Unusual Beings tent and people who were walking out were smiling and appeared to have enjoyed it; maybe it was just me. I pushed my feelings away and ate the rest of my cake flavored snow cone. "I'm going to have a good time and not worry about it; I'm sure it's all in my head", I thought to myself. I didn't sleep well last night; too many weird dreams about people turning into animals, that was probably causing me to hallucinate.

"Jade, let's go check out the petting zoo. It will be fun", Alexa said cheerfully. "Awesome, let's go, anyone else want to go", I asked. No one else wanted to go with us, they wanted to people watch instead. I kissed Nick and walked off with her. The petting zoo was on the other side of the circus, so it took us a few minutes to get over there. We talked about my party tomorrow evening. She was excited and couldn't wait to dress up and see my costume. I agreed with her. My birthday party was going to be awesome!

We reached the petting zoo. It was in a fairly large tent. There were about 10 stalls: some had horses, sheep, goats, and chickens, the usual stuff. The more unique animals were the zebras, camels, llamas, capybaras, owls, and parrots. There was even a couple of large sulcata tortoises. A few people were getting to ride some of the horses and camels in a round enclosed gate outside the tent. I couldn't do it. I was not good with heights even if it wasn't that far from the ground. We did get to feed the animals some grain stuff which was awesome! We had to use a small shovel so we didn't get bit. There were even signs that said, "Animals Have Teeth, They Can Bite, Watch Out!" I thought it was funny and obvious, but some people don't think, I guess.

It was finally time for the main event of the circus. The time passed by really fast. We went to the other tents with different booths, games, and more food carts. I won a few stuffed animals, but I gave them away to a few little girls I saw trying hard to win something. I bought a few scented candles and a small black and blue dreamcatcher from one of the craft booths. They were handmade and beautiful. The candles were pink with orange flowers mixed in to the wax. They smelt amazing. The people behind the booths as well as all of the people who were working at the circus were dressed up in costumes and makeup. Some of them had strange contacts to change their eyes, some of their skin was changing colors depending on the way they turned, and I swear I saw one of them have large black wings, but when I looked again they were gone. Maybe there was something in the food, I didn't notice anything odd until I ate something first. However, no one else seemed affected. Maybe it was just lack of sleep and my mind was playing tricks on me. It could be a side effect of all the dreams I had been having lately also. Yes, that was most likely it. Maybe the dream catcher I got would do its job and make the crazy dreams stop.

After entering the really large tent we sat down at the bottom of some bleachers. The metal bleachers were circling around the entire tent except for a few small spaces for exits. There were a lot of lanterns hanging around on ropes at the top. These looked to be battery operated instead of with a real flame. It still had the same dim lighting though.

Loud introduction style music was starting to play grabbing everyone's attention and silencing them. A man was walking into the center of the arena. He was scruffy looking. The man was about six feet, a little muscular, his skin was dark brown, his eyes were almost black and he had black hair that was braided to the scalp. He had a limp as well but it was not that noticeable. He welcomed everyone with a raspy voice and said everyone should enjoy the show. When he walked away toward one of the exits I swear I saw his hair turn into snakes and they moved a little. I blinked and when I looked at him again, he was normal. I felt that I was losing my mind. I also needed to lay off the coffee, maybe it was time to give up caffeine.

Focusing on what was happening, I watched the trapeze artist flying through the air doing different twists and flips. They swung freely from one person to the other. There weren't any nets to catch them, and I couldn't see any cords holding them up. I hoped they didn't fall because I didn't see how they could survive it. The dancers were flawless though. They did their act with ease.

When the dancers finished, everyone stood up and applauded including me. I was relieved they were alright. The next act had a small car that came driving to the center of the tent. When it stopped, twelve clowns came out of it and started doing tricks. A few of them were juggling axes and swords, some were doing back flips around the jugglers, others were doing the normal clown type stuff. They were making balloon animals, giving them to kids in the crowd and spraying each other with water from the yellow and green flowers on their shirts. The crowd seemed pleased with all this. I guess I was too a little, at least some of it seemed safe.

The clowns left after they finished their tricks. As soon as they exited, a tiger, panther, lioness, and cheetah walked in on large chains. Everyone around gasped with surprise. There were large muscular men holding on to the chains. The animals appeared to be calm and not aggressive at all, and they all looked to be female. A few of the circus workers set up large rings and bars for the animals to do tricks with. One by one the animals were let off their chains and did their routines. They were rewarded with "good girl" and a pat on the head.

There were supposed to be a few more acts, but I was getting restless and I kept thinking about the weirdness I was seeing there. I told the group I needed some air and they didn't have to come with me. I made up an excuse that I needed to go the restroom and wanted privacy for that. Nick and Alexa let it go and told me to be careful.

The cold crisp air felt amazing. I felt better as soon as I was out of the tent and alone. I saw a booth that was selling drinks. I didn't want anything this place made, but I figured a bottle of water couldn't hurt. After getting a water, I gulped it down hoping it would refresh my body and make me not feel so tense. A little while after being there I had been feeling off, but I didn't tell anyone. I didn't see the point to worry them.

I walked back to the tables I was at earlier with Nick and decided to climb on one and lay down for a bit. It felt nice to have a cool hard surface under me and just look up at the clear night sky. The stars and moon were not hidden behind any clouds and there wasn't a lot of city light there that was blinding, so I could actually see them.

"A beautiful view is it not", asked a raspy voice. That made me jump up and almost fall off the table. The dark man with the braids was standing in front of me. He looked completely normal. His eyes weren't mostly black but dark brown with normal irises. He was dressed in dark jeans and a white circus t-shirt.

"Yes it is", I said sharply.

"Please forgive me, I didn't mean to startle you young one. I just saw you over here alone and wanted to make sure you were alright."

"I'm fine, thank you. I needed some fresh air and didn't feel like walking around."

"I understand. I have seen you here all day. I am sure you must be exhausted."

"You... Have you been watching me? To be honest that is a little creepy."

"I apologize young one, I didn't mean for it to appear that way. I noticed that you are soon to be one of us", he stated as he turned around and gestured with his hand.

"What do you mean one of us and why do you keep calling me young one?"

"Surely you know what I mean, surely you know what you are? It is going to happen soon, your birthday is soon, isn't that correct?"

"Yes, but how do you know that? What do you mean know what I am?" I asked practically screaming. I'm going to go back to my friends now, I would say it was nice to meet you, but I don't like to lie."

I ran back to the tent where my friends were. When I looked back, the creepy guy wasn't there or anywhere that I could see. I decided not to tell anyone what had happened. I already felt crazy; I didn't need anyone to confirm it. There was no need to make me feel even more insane. I was sure I just needed a good night sleep to forget all about this. In two days I would be turning sixteen and everything would be alright; I was sure of it.

Chapter Six

I didn't have any dreams last night. I hung up
the dream catcher in the middle of my bed
frame. I guess it did its job. I was feeling a lot
better today than I was yesterday. A good
dreamless night's sleep was what I needed. I
got out of bed and did my normal routine. I
brushed my hair and teeth, changed out of my
night clothes, and looked at myself in the mirror. I saw the same girl I always did; nothing
had changed. I decided to ignore the creepy guy
from yesterday; he didn't know me at all.

Alexa stayed the night with me last night.
She stayed over because she was worried about
me. She also wanted to help me get ready for
the party tonight. She was still asleep in my
bed, snoring softly. I have tried to tell her she
snores, but she doesn't believe me. I thought
about recording her several times but decided

against it. If someone did that to me, I would be really angry.

I left my room and headed to the kitchen to find some food. I didn't eat last night when I got home, still stressed about everything I saw or thought I saw. So, I decided to eat a large breakfast. I was making pancakes, bacon, eggs, fruit salad, and some fresh orange juice. Yes, this meal could feed an army, but I invited Nick and Trevor over so they could help with setting up for the party. The extra food was their bribe.

By the time I got done fixing all the food, the guys showed up and Alexa was up and ready for the day. We ate and talked about where to put the decorations and food tables. The party was going to be in the backyard which was huge and fenced in for privacy. We were also at the end of the block. The neighbors weren't close so we could be loud, without worrying about the police being called.

We spent hours setting up blue and purple lights around the fence. The lights were from the Halloween store I went to last week. We also hung up fake bats, spiders, webbing, and a few skeletons under the lights. I had the guys put a black coffin in one of the back corners of the fence. The coffin was open slightly revealing a skeleton with glowing red eyes. I rented a smoke machine as well, to put beside the coffin to make the ground look foggy. We also laid out a few foam gravestones on the opposite side of the fence from the coffin. It looked amazing, I loved Halloween and the decorations I got to play with.

Trevor set up a table for the stereo and party favors Alexa and I picked out. We got blue, green, purple, and orange glow necklaces and bracelets. We also got googly eye sunglasses, skeleton bone sunglasses, masquerade masks, magic wands that held glitter liquid, rubber snakes and bugs, vampire teeth, and of course lots of candy.

Alexa set up the food and drink tables. She had the organization skills, so I let her have at it. We had a little bit of every kind of finger food and snack food. A lot of different sandwiches, chips, snack cakes, cookies, vegetable and fruit platters. Not to mention the drink table that held the different types of punches, sodas, and waters.

After everything was set up and I approved, I went to my room to change into my costume. Alexa followed me. She had her costume in a dress bag hanging in my closest just like mine.

I took mine in the bathroom so I could get ready, and Alexa changed in my room. After putting on my costume, I did my make-up. When I was done I was quite pleased. Alexa told me a few minutes earlier that she was done and I needed to hurry up. She was ready to see me. I opened the door slowly and she screamed; in a good way!

"You look beautiful, I'm so jealous!" she exclaimed.

"You're being ridiculous! You look beautiful, like a Greek goddess", I said laughing playfully.

She was dressed in a long white dress that came down to her ankles. The dress had one sleeve on the right and nothing on the left. She was wearing white strappy sandals. Her hair was done up in a fancy braided bun, with a few strands of curly hair that hung loosely on each side of her face and on the back of her neck. She had a little makeup on, light brown eyeshadow and very pale lip gloss to make her lips look shiny. She really was stunning, and she looked so innocent.

I walked to the mirror and looked at myself. I was dressed in a short midnight blue silk spaghetti strap dress that had thin dark purple glittery trim at the bottom. The top of my dress had the same glittery trim except in the middle there was a silver crescent moon to match the color of the glitter. I had classic fairy wings on to match my dress. The wings were made of thin mesh material the same color purple as the trim on my dress and outlined in midnight blue. My makeup looked like what I usually do except I had glitter above my eyes and a little on my cheeks. My lip gloss was dark pink, instead of clear like I usually wore. I felt pretty and my costume turned out exactly how I wanted. We walked into the living room and got whistles from the guys, which made us giggle. After staring at us for a few minutes, they left to go change into their costumes.

I went back outside and looked around again. It was getting darker. I sighed a little. I felt a little bad. I spent a lot of money on the party and material for my costume; at the same time I didn't care, I was only going to turn sixteen once. Grams offered to help, but I told her no of course. She did enough for me already. I missed her a lot, she hadn't been gone long, but it felt like forever. I really wish she was here, but I understand she had to help her friend.

She called me when she got to her friends a few days ago.

"Jade, honey it's worse than I originally thought. I can't give you any details right now. I am alright. I miss you sweetie. Alexa has your gift from me. I hope you like it."

"Grams, it's so good to hear from you. I miss you a lot too. Please be careful. I hope you get to come home soon. I am sure I will love it; you have great taste."

"Sweetie, I don't know when I will be able to come home. It may be a little longer than I originally thought."

After staying silent for a minute or two, I responded, "I understand, take your time. I love you, be safe please."

"I am sorry honey, I love you and miss you dearly. I will be safe, I promise. Good-bye Jade."

People started showing up close to five. It was a school night after all and everyone had curfews. The party was going to stop at nine. I thought four hours was long enough. It was a birthday party after all, not a normal high school party. Everyone who showed up brought me a gift. I told everyone who was invited they didn't have to, but no one listened. I invited about forty people, and most of them came. I didn't want to make it too big but wanted to invite a lot of people I knew and spoke to regularly even if they weren't in my circle of close friends.

After everyone showed up, I had Trevor put on some dance music. I didn't like to dance, but other people did. I walked around and talked to my guests for a while. When a slow song came on, Nick dragged me to the side where everyone else was dancing. He put my hands on his shoulders and placed his hands on my waist. He looked very handsome. He was dressed in a black tux and his hair was slicked back with hair gel. The way he was looking at me, made me blush. I smiled up at him, he leaned down slowly and kissed me on the lips. "You look beautiful tonight. Jade, I am happy you're in my life. I have never met anyone like you before, and I never thought I would. I think you are very special!" Blushing more, I replied "thank you". I wasn't sure what else to say to him.

A little while later Lavy showed up to my party.

"I sent you a text message letting you know I was coming but didn't get a response back. I thought you wouldn't mind if I showed up", she explained.

"Oh, I am so sorry. My phone is in my room. I don't have any pockets in this dress."

She smiled, "I can see that. You look amazing. You look like a real fairy!

"You look great as well. I'm glad you came!"

She was dressed in a short black dress and had a red velvet cape tied around her neck. She was holding a little wicker basket and a large paper bag. I didn't think the bag was part of her costume so I offered to let her keep it in my bedroom. She took me up on the offer and followed me to my room.

"Your gift is in the bag, but I'll give it to you later. It's for your eyes only."

"Oh, thank you. Of course, you didn't have to get me anything. You already gave me a job that I get to start this week."

"You're helping me by taking the job. It's your birthday. I wanted to get you something. Sixteen is a special number. You go through a lot of changes when you hit that age."

"Ah, yes so I have heard. Hoping I grow taller and I stop getting acne when I stress", I said laughing

She winked at me, then we walked back outside to everyone singing the standard Happy Birthday song to me. Alexa and Nick knew I didn't like that song but had everyone sing it anyway. It made me feel like a preschooler. "They are going to regret this later", I thought a little evilly to myself. As soon as the song was over, Alexa brought my cake out. I didn't get to pick out my cake this year; Alexa did. We made an agreement that we could pick out each other's sweet sixteen birthday cakes. I was a tad bit nervous, to be honest. She knew me better than anyone but still, this was a huge deal. The pink box was very large. It had to be to feed everyone. She laid it on an empty table Trevor brought out. When she lifted the lid, I started to cry. It was spectacular. It was a large rectangle. The cake was a bright midnight blue, a little lighter than the color of my dress. There was a gold crescent moon in the center of the cake with silver and gold stars all around it. The wavy border around the cake was gold with specks of silver glitter. At the top in curvy writing was "Happy Sweet Sixteenth Jade". It was exactly what I would have picked out for myself. I gave her a hug, "This is perfect, and you did a great job. Ah, I don't want to cut it. It's too pretty!"

After I reluctantly cut the cake, I started to open gifts. I got a lot of books about vampires, werewolves, witches, and all the other type of supernatural creature stuff I liked. I also got a few gift cards and money, some hippy jewelry, a few t-shirts that were definitely my style, and I even got a new purse. I swear Alexa must have sent an email or something to everyone that said this is what to get Jade. I loved her. She really was one of the best people I knew. Lastly came, the gifts I had been waiting all night for. The first was from Nick. It was a shadow box he made himself. It was made of dark mahogany wood with stained Plexiglas on the top and sides. The top had black roses in all four corners with green vines with pointed smooth leaves that connected them all. On the sides were black rose petals that appeared to be floating down to the bottom. I opened the lid, it was mostly empty except for one thing that was in the middle. There was a small skeleton key taped to the bottom with a tag tied to it in black thread. The tag said, "You have the key to my heart and always will, love Nick". I smiled at him and kissed him on the check. I didn't know how to respond exactly. I cared for him deeply but I knew I wasn't in love with him.

Next was a gift from Alexa; well a second birthday gift. This one was in a rectangular blue gift box with a black ribbon tied around it in a bow. I opened the box, inside was a vanity plate for my car. It was custom made for me. My name was in the center with a blue tarantula on the top right side. "It's Legs!" I squealed. Everyone laughed at me, but not in a mean way. "Thank you! You know me so well. I love it!"

The last gift was handed to me by Alexa. "Grams gave this to me before she left. She was sorry she couldn't give it to you in person." I held a black velvet jewelry box in my hands. I opened the lid slowly. I could see a silver chain link bracelet inside with a cross in the middle. The cross had a small blue gem in the center. It was simple, but incredibly beautiful. Alexa told me that it was with me when I was found as a baby. "Grams said it was from your birth mother. The note that was with you when you were found said not to give this to you until you turned sixteen. Grams found it in a safety deposit box that was your parents; both the note and the bracelet were in a sealed bag." I looked at Alexa and started to cry. I walked inside telling everyone I needed a minute. After a few minutes alone, Lavy came to check on me.

"Are you alright? What was that about, if I may ask?"

"This is something from my birth mother. I have never had anything of hers before", I said holding up the bracelet.

"Your birth mother? You're... You're... adopted Jade?"

"Yes, I thought I told you when we met. I'm sorry, I figured everyone knew already. It's not really a secret."

"There is no need to apologize. That explains a lot."

"What do you mean explains a lot", I asked a little too sharply, not meaning to, this was a lot to handle.

"I have met your grandmother, you look nothing like her is all. She seems to be a very kind lady and cares for you deeply", she said not being fazed by my rudeness.

"Yes, she is. I have lived with her for a couple of years now. She is the best for sure. Blah, okay, I'm fine now. Enough with all the sad talk! Let's go enjoy the rest of my party!" I wiped my tears away and looked in the hallway mirror. I looked fine, just a little pink in the face.

After I stopped feeling sorry for myself, the party went great! It was like nothing ever happened. All the guests had a lot of fun and all my friends loved Lavy. I knew they would. There was something about her that made you like her instantly. When the party came to an end, everyone else left, except Alexa and Lavy, who stayed behind to help me clean up. Nick and Trevor had to go, due to their curfews. Alexa could only stay for another hour at the latest. She had a lot of club stuff to do in the morning before school.

It didn't take long to clean up since I had a few large trashcans by the gate. Most people threw their trash away already. I didn't deal with the decorations though; I could put them up tomorrow since I was skipping school anyway.

"Hey, I think I am going to go, the clean-up appears to be done", Alexa said looking drained of energy.

"I'll talk to you tomorrow. I'm going to crash soon. I'm exhausted. You need some sleep too. Be safe. Thanks for all your help", I said as I walked her to the door.

Lavy could tell I was not feeling well. I am sure I looked rough.

"Do you need to lay down, maybe get some sleep? I can stay with you to make sure you're alright, and this way you're not alone while your grandmother is out of town."

"Thanks that would be really nice of you, if you don't mind. I'm feeling nauseous. It may be all the junk food I ate."

"That's what friends are for", she said smiling at me.

It was after eleven, I wanted to stay up until midnight at least, to welcome my birthday, but I was starting to feel worse. My stomach hurt and I felt like I was running a fever. It came on kind of fast. I really hoped I was not getting a stomach virus. That would not be fair when my birthday was so close. No one else seemed sick earlier, so maybe I really did just eat too much junk food at the party. I decided to take Lavy's advice to go lay down. I went to my room, Lavy followed.

"You can sleep in my bed or Gram's room down the hall if you're worried about me vomiting on you."

"I'm not worried about you, Jade. I'll stay in here tonight with you. This way I can watch over you in case you need anything. You're not looking too well.'

I changed into some night clothes, and I gave Lavy some as well. She was taller than me, but I had some of Alexa's clothes that would mostly fit her. After getting out of my fairy costume and washing off the makeup I felt a little better, more human anyway. I still felt hot and nauseous. I was starting to think, that is what food poisoning felt like, and it sucked!

I got into bed. Lavy then brought me a cold rag and put it on top of my head. I gave her a small smile and thanked her.

I must have drifted off to sleep because I woke up in severe pain! I was sweating a lot, my stomach hurt more than it had ever hurt before, and my mouth was throbbing. The right part of my upper back was on fire. I felt like my stomach was being twisted in knots, the top of my gums felt raw like there were thick needles poking out of them. I didn't know what hurt more. I thought I was going to die; I was more than sure that I was! The world was definitely coming to an end! I didn't know what I had done wrong, but I was being punished severely!

"I am sorry for whatever I did wrong. I will do my best to be a better person. Please, someone, make this stop", I prayed to myself.

My whole body was on fire, my veins felt like they had acid running through them. I was trying to scream, but nothing was coming out of my mouth. I couldn't even open my eyes all the way. "Oh my gosh! I'm paralyzed, I can't get help! I am going to die alone and in pain for something terrible I did, whatever it was." I could feel myself crying, at least I thought I was crying. My eyes felt watery under my eyelids, I also thought I felt teardrops running down the sides of my face. It could have also been sweat coming from my body. It was hard to concentrate on what my body was doing exactly, everything hurt in some way or another.

The pain finally started to ease up, after what seemed like several hours. I was still burning up but my stomach didn't hurt, my gums were sore, but I didn't feel like my teeth were being yanked out of my mouth. My shoulder felt warm, but not burning hot like it was before. I wanted to try to move, but I was scared I wouldn't be able to. Starting off small, I wiggled my toes, "yes they are moving", I thought to myself. Next, I moved my hand, it moved, lastly I opened my eyes slowly. My vision was different. My ceiling was too bright. It was white before but now the white paint was screaming at me. The sun was already up and the natural light was making my head hurt and eyes burn. "Ugh, I think I'm going to be sick again!" Trying not to vomit, I slowly rolled over to my side, and I leaned my arm down to touch the floor. When my hand touched the cold wooden floor, I tried to ease off the bed. I thought if I could make it to the bathroom I would be fine. I needed to make it to the shower; I needed to feel cold water spraying me.

Dragging myself on the floor I saw two feet come in front of me. Then before I knew it, I was in my bathtub, submerged in cool water. I didn't remember getting undressed, but I didn't care. The water felt so good and it smelt like citrus. The bathroom lights were off, but there were a few candles around so I could see a little. The low lighting wasn't hurting my eyes and the water was helping me feel better slowly. I didn't feel hot anymore, but my mouth still felt sore. The warm feeling on my shoulder was gone though. I thought when I got out of the tub I could put some medicine on my gums. That should help.

My stomach was starting to make a grumbling noise. How I could possibly eat right now was beyond me. There just wasn't anyway. I was planning to ignore my stomach. If I ate anything I was sure I would not be able to keep it down.

I slowly dunked my head in the extra soapy water trying to get the gross feeling off of me completely. As soon as my head was fully submerged, I heard footsteps coming to the door and the bathroom door opening. I slowly set up trying to not get sick again. I turned my back to lean against the back of the tub, pulled my legs against my chest and closed the shower curtain.

I opened the curtain a little to see Lavy walking toward me. At least, I thought it was Lavy. She looked different now. She still had on the same clothes that I loaned her the night before, but her skin was shimmering! Her skin shimmered slightly with tents of orange and purple! Her hair was still dark and her eyes were still the same bright green. Her hair was now braided and hanging on the side of her shoulder, but I couldn't stop staring at her ears. Her ears were now pointed, like an elf!

"Hello Jade, how are you feeling? You had a rough night, do you remember anything?"

I just looked at her wide-eyed and nodded. "I remember being in a lot of pain and feeling like I was going to die."

"Yes, that is usually how the transition feels. It was the same way with me when I turned sixteen long ago."

"Transition? What do you mean, am I dead? I must be dead or am I dreaming?" I asked almost screaming.

"Sweet girl no, you are very much alive and awake mostly. I will explain everything to you in just a little while. I want to wait until I know you're alert and can understand me. Here, I brought you something to drink to make you feel better. It will help I promise."

Freaking out because of what she looked like and because she sounded like a crazy person, I simply nodded and said okay. She handed me a plastic cup that was warm and smelt sweet. I asked her what it was, and she told me something to ease my stomach. I took the cup hesitantly and drunk slowly. As soon as the liquid hit my mouth, my body felt like I was being energized. I practically gulped all the contents down. It was dark red and thick but tasted really good. She took the cup back from me.

"Thanks, that was good."

"You're welcome."

"Lavy, um how did I get in the tub?"

"After the water was ready, I put you in the bathroom and told you to undress and get into the tub. I didn't think you would feel comfortable if I had helped you with that part."

"You're right, thank you for everything."

"You are most welcome. I'll wait in your room while you are in here. Take your time though. No rush."

A few minutes later I was feeling a lot better than I had last night. After getting out of the tub and drying myself off, I looked around and noticed there weren't any clothes around for me to wear. "Blah", I thought. I wrapped the towel around me, thankful that I was little and the towels were really big. I opened the door and walked to my closest slowly trying not to look at Lavy. I was sure I was hallucinating earlier. I looked around my room though, because I couldn't sense anyone in the room. She wasn't here. Sighing with relief, I walked over to the mirror on my door to see how horrible I must look. To my surprise, I looked amazing. My skin looked flawless. It was not slightly pink or uneven looking, my eyes were brighter and my lips looked pinker. Whatever she gave me must have been a super strong energy drink!

I started to walk back to the bathroom when I glanced back and noticed a blue mark on my right shoulder where my skin was burning like fire the night before. I thought I was seeing things at first, but I wasn't. There was a mark on my shoulder. It was a blue crescent moon with three small blue stars on the side of it. That made me think about what else was hurting me last night. I was sure I was crazy but I had to check anyway. I turned to face the mirror, I opened up my mouth slowly. I didn't see anything at first, so I went closer to look, just for my peace of mind. Slowly descending from the top of my mouth were two long sharp pointy teeth, between them were four smaller pointy teeth. I screamed, then everything went dark.

Chapter Seven

"Jade... Jade... Can you hear me?" asked a concerned soft voice. Opening my eyes slowly, I could see a blurry Lavy leaning over and staring at me. She hadn't changed since I saw her in the bathroom. She still had the same shimmery skin and pointed ears. Trying to focus on my surroundings to make sure I was seeing correctly, I blinked a few times.

Lavy stood up and offered me her hand; I took it, shaking a little. When I was on my feet, I walked to my bed to sit down and stare at the floor. I needed a minute to think and process everything that was going on. "Okay, so I have a tattoo on my shoulder, I have a new set of teeth, Lavy is a fairy, I think, and I am not dreaming", I screamed to myself.

"Jade, sweetie are you okay? I know this is a lot to handle, especially if you were raised in the human world. I am here for you, and I will help you with whatever you need. I know this is probably a shock for you; it would be for me."

I lifted my head so I could look at her. I was trying very hard not to yell at her. I could tell she was worried, but how could she possibly know how I felt. I didn't even know exactly. I did know I was angry that was for sure, and I had questions and I wanted answers!

"What am I now? I know I am not a human anymore."

"You are what you call a vampire. There are other words for it, but that is the most common one used now."

Trying to process what she just said, it confirmed what I thought, well not exactly. I thought I may have been possessed by a demon. At least I knew for sure I was different now, but that wasn't what I was expecting at all.

"You said earlier I wasn't dead, is that true?"

"Yes, you are not dead. Vampires are not like what you see in the movies or read about in books now. They are alive; they have beating hearts and they breathe."

"Do I have a soul; will I go to hell when or if I die?"

"Yes, you have a soul, everyone does. It is your choice whether to be good or evil. As far as hell, I can't answer that. There are so many beliefs in the world. It is up to you to choose what you want to believe. You do die at some point, but we live a lot longer than humans."

"Will garlic or a cross hurt me?"

"Those are both myths; neither will hurt you. Garlic will give you bad breath but gum, a mint, or mouthwash will help that. You can touch a cross or any other religious object. We all have our own different faiths. Again, what you probably know about vampires isn't accurate."

"Do I need blood?"

"You do need blood, but that is not all you need. You also need other foods. You can eat what you have always eaten, except you just add blood to your diet. The blood energizes you and helps you heal faster. You do not have to drink blood from a person, but you can't drink dead blood. That is blood from a dead person. You can drink animal blood, but I heard its gross and it doesn't help as much as human blood."

"Why am I like this, who made me this way? Was I bitten by a vampire, did they give me their blood to change me?"

"You were born this way. No one bit you and you didn't drink anyone's blood to become this way. All of us who belong to the Shadow Realm go through the change when we turn sixteen."

"My birth parents were like me?"

"Yes, they had to have been. That is why you are what you are now. Again, I know this is a lot to take in. There is a lot more you need to know, but I think you have heard enough for now."

"What are you exactly?"

"I am a fairy or fair folk."

"The cup you gave me earlier in the bathroom, was that blood?"

She sighed and said yes. She told me I needed it after the transition. I could have waited awhile and not drink anything, but I would have become weaker. She didn't tell me what it was because she knew I wouldn't drink it. Honestly, I thought I was going to be sick. I asked her to leave me alone for a little while. I needed to digest everything she had told me. It was a lot to deal with.

When she left, I laid on my bed and stared at the ceiling. I had no idea what I was going to do. Stuff like this wasn't real; it couldn't be. So many thoughts were going through my mind. I needed blood now to survive, because I'm was a vampire. However I could go into sun light and I was not dead. There was the human world and the non-human world. Lavy was a fairy and somehow knew I was going to transition. I needed to know how she knew. I also needed to stop feeling sorry for myself. It may not have seemed real, but it was.

I got up and went to go find Lavy. She needed to explain to me about how she knew about me, and why she didn't tell me. Maybe I wouldn't have believed her until it happened, but she still could have mentioned it.

After I got dressed, I left my room and went to go look for her. She was at the kitchen table eating some berries and looking at her phone. She doesn't look human anymore, I wasn't sure how I missed it before. Besides the shimmery skin and pointed ears, her hair looks different. It looks shinier; that kind of shine you don't get from any hair products that I know of.

She must have heard me walk into the room because she turned toward me and smiled. I smiled back. I knew she wanted to help me. I knew I was scared of her and of myself, but right now she was the only person or thing that could help me. I took a deep breath and walked up to her.

"How did you know I was going to change, and why didn't you tell me before now?"

"I didn't know until late Saturday. Elias had told me after seeing you at the circus because he was worried about you. He could tell you didn't know anything about the Shadow Realm, your past, or what you were going to turn into. He was sure you were turning into a vampire, but there was something different about you. However, he wasn't sure what. He knew I moved here and thought I could look out for you. We keep in touch because I have recommended creatures to his circus."

"Hmm."

"His circus is a like a safe haven for the Shadow Realm; a place where creatures go, if they don't have anywhere else to go. Some are there for a type of community service, because they are on probation for a small crime."

I told her I was seeing things there that didn't make sense to me at all. I told her about the hairy girl, the weird animals, and the mermaids. I also told her about Elias hair, and how it moved. She told me that Elias being a gorgon means he has snakes for hair and he can sense things about people from our world and the human world. The hairy girl is a shapeshifter, and well the mermaids were just that, mermaids.

She told me that all the fairy tales and myths are true. I asked about zombies. She laughed and said no, that is probably the only thing that doesn't exist. I had so many more questions, but I was interrupted by a phone call.

I answered and it was Alexa crying. She was actually sobbing. It was hard to understand her. I got a few words from what she said: died, no blood, and body. Freaking out and trying to stay calm, I asked her to slow down. So many thoughts were running through my head; first of all, who died. If she was crying that hard, it must have been someone we were close to or her at least. After telling her to take some deep breaths so I could make out what she was saying, I finally understood the person that died or was killed was Ms. Silvia.

I didn't care for the teacher, but I didn't want her to die. I hung up with Alexa telling her I would come to her house soon. I told Lavy what she told me. She went pale then and looked scared. I asked her what was wrong, but she told me she would have to explain later and that she had to go. Before I knew it she was gone; she just went, poof. She was there talking to me, and then she wasn't. She vanished into thin air!

Not wanting to add to the list of things I was worried about, I ignored the disappearing act. I would ask her about that later. I would add it to the long list of questions about the new life I had. I went back to my room to put on shoes, grab dark sunglasses, and to make sure I looked human again. Besides my new tattoo and fangs, I did. The new addition to my skin was covered up with a t-shirt, and my new fangs weren't showing anymore. It took me a few minutes and concentration to make them ascend into my gums. I had to try my hardest to hide this from everyone, especially Alexa. She would know something was different about me.

I made it to Alexa's house about thirty min-utes after she called. I tried to reach Nick, but he didn't answer his phone. He was probably still at school, and his phone was most likely on vibrate. I sent him a quick message, asking him to call me as soon as possible. He didn't like Ms. Silvia, but he wouldn't want her dead either. Plus his dad was a cop so maybe he had news about what happened.

I walked through the front door. Her family never left the house locked, so pretty much anyone could walk in. She lived outside the city, so they didn't worry too much about people breaking in. Alexa was on their old brown couch crying. Her face was red and blotchy, and her hair was a mess. I went to her and hugged her, asking what had happened, and how had she found out.

She couldn't answer me. She has never taken death well; not that she was ever around it much. Her brother Alexander was there trying to comfort her, but he was not great at it. He is about six years older than her, he doesn't look anything like her, probably because they shared the same mother but not father. Alexander's or Alex's dad died when he was young, their mom remarried a little over a year before Alexa came. Alex had light blonde hair, is taller than six feet, and was really tan. You could say he was the stereotype beach boy.

I looked at Alex, giving him a look that said to talk.

"Alexa found out at school. She was in the main office and was copying papers for some club this morning when she overheard the principal talking to a detective about a body. The body was found on Saturday night, and they couldn't find anyone to come claim it. The police searched through personal belongings found on the body, a school faculty identification card was found. The name on the card was Kristina Silva, which stated she worked there. The detective went on to explain that the body needed to be identified to make sure it was the same person. He said he couldn't give all the details, but the deceased had no blood in her body, and it appeared there were several small puncture wounds on several places of the deceased."

"Wow", is all I could say.

"Alexa wasn't supposed to hear that conversation, obviously, but Alexa has great hearing. After she heard about the body, she left quickly, because the two men had stopped talking. She was worried they would know she was able to overhear them. She came straight home and told me what she heard before she burst into tears."

"When did all this happen?"

"A little over an hour ago. It hasn't been confirmed one way or the other, if it was her or not."

I knew I needed to reach Nick. He must have heard something. I was sure his dad wasn't the only detective around, but surely he knew something; he had to! This was scary!

I tried to call Nick and text him so many times that day but never got a response. I thought maybe his phone died or maybe he broke it. There had to be a good reason why he was ignoring me. He might have even been grounded and not allowed to talk to me. Surely, if something was wrong, his dad would have let me know. I'm sure he had my number or if he didn't he would have come to talk me in person, or something. It was hard not to think the worst.

Alexa finally calmed down early that night, her mother was working a twenty- hour shift at the hospital so she couldn't be there to help me with her. She was also an ER nurse like Grams. That's how Alexa knew about me when I first moved here. Her mom has known Grams since Alex was born.

We still didn't know if it was for sure Ms. Silvia or not. Not knowing was stressful and annoying. There wasn't anything on the news yet, and Alex said there probably wouldn't be until after ten that night.

By the time the news came on, Alexa was asleep. She had worn herself out. Channel 12 news confirmed it was Ms. Silvia, and more details were released that she was found at the entrance of the Grimm hotel downtown. Her neck was broke, she was drained of blood completely, and she had several sets of puncture wounds on her arms and legs. There was also a piece of skin cut from her forearm, probably taken for a trophy. The news stated there hadn't been a death like this in over sixteen years. The thought of someone dying like that made me sick; no matter how mean they could be.

I had to excuse myself to go to the bathroom. I felt like I was going to vomit. When I got to the bathroom, a smell hit my nose that was so intense, my fangs were starting to descend. I'm not sure how I knew, but I knew it was the scent of blood that had made it happen. It was possible it was from me remembering subconsciously about the blood Lavy gave me earlier that day. I suddenly felt hungry; my stomach hurt and my mouth was watering for blood. I needed it. I went hunting to see where the smell was coming from, and I found a used band-aid in the trashcan with dried blood on it. When I went to pick it up and wanted to lick it; I knew I had a problem. I ran out of the bathroom, grabbed my stuff and left. I had to go somewhere else, anywhere else. I just needed to be alone. I needed to get a grip.

The only place I could think to go was Children of the Sun and Moon. I had a key that Lavy gave me to let myself in if needed. It didn't take me long to get there. It could be because I was speeding. Thankfully there weren't a lot of cops out. I also knew downtown would be deserted this late at night, even if a murder happened. It was close to midnight, and I was sure that the cops wanted daylight to get whatever evidence they needed. After unlocking the door and going in, I called Lavy frantically to explain what was happening to me.

"I'm scared, I was at Alexa's house trying to help her when I heard the news confirm the body that was found was my teacher. I felt sick so I went to the bathroom, and that's when a smell hit me and my fangs descended. I found an old bloody band-aid and I almost licked it! I am now at your shop. I am really scared!"

"Jade, it's okay, this is normal for your kind. You're hungry. You didn't feed much earlier. I gave you a small portion of what you needed. For that, I am sorry sweetie, I should have given you more blood, but I was planning on watching over you for a few days and give it to you moderately. Too much can affect your thinking and cause you to be uncontrollable."

"What am I going to do? I don't have any blood, and I don't want to hurt anyone, I don't want to drink it from anyone; I may have a little animal blood from frozen meat at home, I can drink that, would that help me?"

"Look in the back room I use for storage, there is a black mini fridge, you will find two bags of blood. Jade, only drink one. It will be hard, but you don't need to overdo it. At first, it will be hard to control your thirst, but you need to. I will be there soon. I am in a meeting now and can't leave. I promise, I'll be there as soon I can."

After hanging up with her, I went to the storage room and got out one bag of blood. I couldn't smell it before, but as soon as I opened the refrigerator door I could. The blood was cold. At the time I didn't care, it was so good. The hunger went away, I felt my body wake up and become more energized. After draining the bag dry, I wanted more, but I was trying to listen to Lavy.

I went outside. To get some fresh air. I didn't notice before, but the night sky looked different. It wasn't simply flat black with a white moon. It was brighter. The sky was glossy with several different shades of black and dark blue. The moon was more silver than white, and the stars looked like huge twinkling lights, instead of little specs in the sky. The wind was blowing and I could hear it rustling leaves around me. I could hear the stray cats scampering in the basements of some abandoned buildings. Scents from all over were surrounding me; the strongest were various flowers and death.

Besides the smell of death, I smelt blood. It didn't smell fresh, but it wasn't dried up. It smelt a little rotten. I didn't want to see what it was alone, so I waited for Lavy to show up. Trying not to freak out, because it was probably nothing at all, I took deep slow breaths and went back inside.

The way things looked and smelled to me was a lot to take in. I mostly had come to terms that I was a vampire, even if they were supposed to be made up. Everything is sharper and stronger, even my emotions seemed to be intense. I felt like my whole body was more than alive; it was electrified. It was probably from the blood, I just drank. I wasn't sure why the blood Lavy first gave me didn't make me feel that way.

I felt somewhat normal at Alexa's. Maybe it was because I was weak, or it could have also been I was more worried about her than me.

My mind was still working overtime, even more after drinking more blood. I still had so many questions about my kind. Could I do anything special? What was the Shadow Realm like and what other creatures are there? Also, was I part human? If Elias said there was something else about me, besides me being a vampire, could my mother have been human? Is that why she had given me up? Did she think of me as a monster?

I didn't have time to think about it too much. Lavy materialized a few moments after I started to think about my birth mother. I was on the verge of tears, but stopped as soon as I saw her. She had seen enough of me crying and feeling sorry for myself. I didn't want her to see it again. I didn't want to seem weak, especially when she appeared to be strong and in control of what she was.

"How are you able to disappear and reappear in thin air?" I asked. I had to know.

She smiled and answered, "It is an ability that fairies have. Each race or species has certain abilities and being able to transport one's self to certain places is a fairy's. However, we can only transport ourselves to a place we have been to before. We have to be able to visualize a place accurately. When we go somewhere, we leave a print of our aura's there, so we can return if needed quickly. The print allows us to have a connection to it. We don't have to do this with every place. We can pick and choose if we like a certain place."

It made sense mostly. Before I forgot, I told her about the smell of death outside. I explained it didn't have a small smell but a large one. I didn't want to check it out by myself, because I was scared and wasn't sure what it was. She looked worried after I told her. The same look she had early that day after I told her about Ms. Silvia. I asked her about where she went. She told me she went to a meeting to talk to other Shadow Realmers. They talked about the murder and how it looked like a vampire attack. A witch who works in the morgue was there and told them she was a reaper. Of course, I had to ask what a reaper was. She told me a reaper was a human with a special ability to see the Shadow Realm. Reapers mostly run in families, but there are a few who just have a connection with our world. Not all humans with the sight were reapers, mostly it was humans who were scared and thought we were monsters or evil. When I asked how they knew Ms. Silvia was one, she told me she had the reaper mark, a small black dagger with a snake twisted around the blade. That sounded creepy to me. She said it was a tattoo they got to show they were a member of that cult. The skin that was missing was where the tattoo was, but the mark was imprinted into the bone.

So much was happening; a lot of scary stuff to process. Not only were there supernatural and mythical creatures, including me, but there were also reapers.

Trying not to let it get into my head, I went with Lavy to find the death smell. She told me we had to. She couldn't smell the way I could, so she needed my help. It wasn't too far. It was about a block over down the road. The closer we got the stronger the smell was. I was getting more afraid the closer we got. We finally reached the smell at the old Union Supply building. It was an old grocery store that has been deserted for decades. It was more of a warehouse. The gray paint was peeling off, all the windows were boarded up, and there were weeds growing up all around it. The place looked fine during the day, but at night it was creepy. There was a dim street light that was turned on, which was casting shadows on the building. I had to remind myself, I was a vampire. I am supposed to like the night, nothing was supposed to scare me. I was stronger than I was when I was human, nothing could hurt me, nothing! That small pep talk helped me for maybe a minute.

We walked around the old grocery store looking for a way to go in. The smell was definitely coming from something inside. We had to figure out what it was. After making a few laps around the building, we finally noticed a thick piece of plywood that looked to be leaning against one of the windows, instead of being nailed to it. I went to see if I could slide it to the side, so we could get in. The piece of wood slid easily. It wasn't heavy at all. I was happy to be a vampire at that moment. When I was human, there was no way I could have moved it.

After turning on the flashlight on my phone, I went in and Lavy followed behind me. It was dark and packed full of boxes with junk in them. There were also loose papers, boards, and broken shelves everywhere.

We went slowly. Even with the flashlight and my better eyesight, it was hard to see. I tried to focus more with my sense of smell instead of my sight. It was working. The smell seemed to be coming from everywhere. I closed my eyes, trying to focus more, and the scent of death and blood got stronger. The smell of blood was getting to me then, so I tried to ignore it but it was hard. I knew I needed to focus, but my stomach and fangs didn't want to cooperate. My stomach grumbled and my fangs descended. That was going to be a problem I was going to have to try to focus on after we figured out what was going on. Taking deep, slow breaths, ignoring my hunger, I continued to walk and almost tripped over something.

When I ran the light over whatever it was that I almost tripped on, I screamed. The last thing I was expecting was an arm that looked to be ripped off its body. What made it worse, was that there were two legs next to it. All of the body parts were bloody and smelled horrible. They have been there for at least a day. I continued to walk. I could smell the scent of death and blood further away. It didn't take but a couple of minutes to find the rest of the body. It was next to an old deep freeze. I saw the second arm, and the back with the head still on it. The bones were sticking out and there was so much blood and gore, I felt sick. In the middle of the back of the body or what was left was a black dagger with a snake around it. Lavy went to the body to turn it over since it was face down. When she did and I saw who it was, I broke down, crying and screaming, it... it was Nick, my Nick.

Chapter Eight

It had been a couple of days since finding Nick ripped apart. Lavy said it was a shapeshifter attack of some sort. Well, that's what it appeared to be. She said it is highly unusual the way these murders happened. There are rules we had to follow; we can't expose ourselves to humans unless there is no other option. We can't kill humans for fun. If we do, we must make it look like an accident or clean it up. We can't use our abilities to gain wealth or steal from the human world. Those were a few. There were more but we would discuss them later.

There wasn't a funeral for Nick. There was a memorial service for him though. His body was too far damaged, and his dad was having a hard time handling the death. I went to the service at their small local church, but I didn't want to. I felt betrayed and angry. He was a reaper. He was hunting my kind. I wanted to know if he knew about me and if that was why he dated me. Lavy did tell me she didn't know how she missed him being a reaper, usually, people from our world could sense the humans that were, but she didn't sense that about him.

I also wondered if that was why Ms. Silvia hated me so much. Did she know? Lavy explained that reapers don't know if you're from the Shadow Realm until you've changed, but they had an uneasy feeling around you.

I did find out Nick's dad wasn't a reaper, but his mom probably was so that was how he had the sight. She didn't come to the service because she was out of the country is what Nick's dad said. She had some important job she couldn't get away from. I felt bad for him. He was miserable; losing your son would do that to you. At the service, he smelled like alcohol. He was acting strange too. I didn't know what to say to him, so I gave my condolences and left him alone after that.

Grams came to the service, but she could only stay for a couple of hours, she couldn't leave the person she was helping for too long. It was so great to see her and I needed her then. Of course, I didn't tell her about anything that had happened to me that past weekend. I didn't think I ever would. I didn't want her to be scared of me. She was open-minded, but I don't think she would have been that open minded.

Of course, Alexa and my other friends were there. Alexa was more upset than I was, but she also didn't know what I did about him. I did my part and cried and said I would miss him. Not all of the crying was an act. I would miss the way he showed he cared about me, even if it wasn't real. He had been a good actor that was for sure.

I did look over my car really well with Lavy's help to make sure there wasn't anything wrong with it. Nick had worked on my car, I wanted to make sure he didn't do anything faulty to it. It all appeared to be normal, but I didn't know a lot about cars, so I had Lavy take it to a repair shop, to get it fully checked out. It came back fine. There weren't any issues with it. She told me she took it to a person from the Shadow Realm and explained the situation to make sure they looked at everything. It didn't cost me too much; not that it would have mattered if it had. I was attached to my little Bug. I would have paid pretty much anything.

I skipped school that week after finding Nick. I didn't want to be around anyone. I had a lot to think about, and I didn't need any more stress. Grams didn't need a lot of convincing. She told me that I deserved a break. I had a bad ordeal happen to me, and she knew I could make up my school work. She also told me she was going to have to stay with her old patient for a couple more weeks. She hated to leave me but she knew I would be fine. She could get the neighbors to check in on me. I told her it wasn't necessary. I could take care of myself and if I needed anything I had money, plus I had Lavy who could help watch after me. Grams was a little taken back by how close I had gotten to Lavy, but after talking to her before she left again, she was thrilled for me to have an older friend.

Lavy stayed over at my house the first few nights. I didn't want to be around anyone but her. Mostly, it was because she understood what I was going through. Besides the painful change I went through, I found out I was being hunted by my boyfriend. Also that he was murdered by someone from the Shadow Realm, and I didn't know why exactly.

She did help me learn a little about what I could do as a vampire. I was stronger, that I already knew, but I was a lot stronger than I thought I could be. I could lift my car! Also, I was fast, I could run fast. I didn't test that ability out yet, but I wanted to. I wanted to wait until I could go somewhere more secluded. I didn't want anyone to see me. I didn't care to bring attention to what I had become. One amazing ability was hypnotizing, entrancing, or whatever you wanted to call it. I could control what people thought or did with my mind. I could do this to creatures in the Shadow Realm, but it worked better on humans; their minds were weaker. I really couldn't wait to try it, but I had to find a test subject. The next time I saw Alexa, I was going to try it!

A couple of weeks had passed since Nick's memorial service and nothing much had changed. School was the same, except it was gloomy. The shock of what happened to Nick and Ms. Silvia was still fresh. It was hard to go knowing everything I did. It was more of an adjustment for me though, more than anyone else. I had to make sure to have blood with me at school in a dark bottle because of the cravings.

It was getting a little easier to control my fangs. I still wanted blood a lot. Something new did happen to me: my eyes started to glow blue when I was hungry for blood. The hungrier I was the brighter the glow. Lavy helped me get a mini fridge for my room and helped me get blood bags for a few days. She said she would take me to meet someone that could help me get more blood when I needed it that Saturday. It was Wednesday, so I only had to wait a few more days. I was anxious to meet more people like me. So far I had only met Lavy, but I was trying to stay more to myself than be social then. Alexa didn't notice I was avoiding her. She was keeping busy with school clubs and presidential duties. I knew she wanted to forget what had happened recently, so I left her alone. We both needed time apart and to adjust, even if they were for different reasons.

The rest of that week dragged on. I wanted Saturday to hurry up. I knew there were other people like me since the transition, but I wanted to meet them already. I met Elias, but I didn't know he was a Shadow Realmer. I thought he was a creepy guy that was stalking me. We waited until it was close to sunset to leave the store; we closed up early that night.

We hadn't gotten a lot of business since the store opened. We knew it was because of the deaths downtown, but eventually, everything would go back to normal and business would pick up.

We didn't have to go far for the Shadow Realm main hang out. It was the Grimm Hotel. I didn't know why it surprised me. The hotel was huge! On the outside, it appeared to be run down and ready to be condemned. If you focused on it, the roughness went away and the building looked newly built, even though the hotel was almost a hundred years old. It was built out of mostly dark rusty red bricks that made up the top five stories. The two bottom stories were made out of cream colored bricks. The front had three arched windows that held thick glass doors. When we walked closer to the front of the building, we walked through some type of force field. It felt like a strong energy that was pulsing. The energy had a slight white hue to it, so you knew it was there.

"Wow that felt weird."

"There is a barrier to hide the hotel away from humans. The energy makes them uncomfortable so they stay away. It also makes the hotel look abandoned. A high powered witch owns the hotel so it can't be sold or torn down; this way if Realmers are in Texarkana they will have a place to go."

The inside of the hotel was unbelievable! The first floor was bright, the walls were white, the floor was made of silver-gray marble, and the lights on the ceiling were small flat circles that fit into holes in the ceiling. In the middle was a large bar. There were a few bartenders helping out people with drinks. Around the bar were tables and chairs that people were eating at. Some of the stuff they were eating I wasn't sure about, but everyone was showing who they were. They didn't look human. I saw vampires with their fangs out, creatures with wings, and shapeshifters who were mid-transformation, and witches. Lavy had been explaining to me what creatures were in the Shadow Realm and what they looked like. We didn't go over a lot of them, but the ones that looked the most human. She said I would have to see the others for myself and go from there.

Each floor was different. The main floor was a restaurant and bar for everyone. The second floor was for spa rooms. The third floor was for movie theaters or stages for plays. The fourth floor was for the dancing rooms. There were quite a few with different styles of music. The fifth floor was a training center or gym, and the six and seventh were guest rooms if you wanted to stay. The inside of the hotel was twice the size the outside showed it to be. Lavy told me that The Shadow Realm doesn't abide by human physics; our boundaries and rules were different. What you can imagine could probably be done, but you had to be careful. Sometimes the consequences weren't worth it.

I let Lavy go find her friend who could help me with blood. I walked around for a while, I didn't stand out, I actually seemed invisible, which was nice. After an hour, I got tired and wanted a break. I went back down to the first floor to go get something to eat. I'm sure if I wasn't supposed to eat anything there, Lavy would have told me. My appetite changed a lot since my transition. I was not as hungry as I used to be. I figured it had something to do with the blood I drank. It gave me more energy than food.

I sat in a booth in the corner and checked out the menu. The menu was digital and had several categories. It depended on what species you were. I had clicked on vampire and there was a list of human blood types, animal blood and organs, pure human plasma, there were even ages of blood. Something that made me shiver was virgin blood, I passed. I ordered some A+, a burger, and some fries, from the waitress. I wasn't sure what she was. The top part of her body was a woman and the bottom half was a deer. Her skin was golden and her eyes were all black. She didn't have any pupils. Her hair was long and white. She spoke English well, though. I even told her so, she laughed a little, telling me she spoke many languages.

When I got my food, I started eating immediately. Lavy hadn't come back to find me yet, but I'm sure she was fine. She knew this world better than I did, and I knew she could take care of herself. I ordered another glass of blood and had it halfway gone when Lavy showed up with two guys. One was definitely a vampire; the other was a shapeshifter. I could tell because his eyes glowed yellow. Lavy introduced the vampire as Boston. He looked the same age as Lavy around twenty-five. He was light skinned with red hair and green eyes. After she introduced him, he told me he worked at a blood donation clinic and was able to get blood for the right price. I asked him about pricing and he told me I could have a monthly subscription for a couple hundred or just call him when I needed it. Depending on what was available, the cost varied. It was first come, first serve without a subscription. I told him I would pay for the monthly subscription, and I wanted to be able to quit anytime, it felt wrong taking from a donation clinic.

I was able to choose what I wanted so I got A+ and AB-. I didn't want to feed from any humans if I had a choice. That would be my last resort, and of course, they would have to agree. I did try animal blood from a pig after I first turned, and it was horrible. It tasted stale and fatty.

"Our friends appear to be rude. I'm Falcon. It is nice to meet you Jade", said the shapeshifter as he extended his hand to me. He was cute, close to six feet, and he looked to be of Native American descent. He had short spiked black hair and had muscles. He looked a little older than me, about eighteen. His eyes stopped glowing after we started talking. They turned to his normal eye color of dark brown. "It is nice to meet you as well", I said blushing while I shook his hand. He didn't notice; that was a good thing.

Nick had just died. I didn't need to think about another guy being cute. It wasn't right. Even if it was a fake relationship, it was too soon to look at another guy in that way.

Falcon and Boston stayed with us for a few hours. I think Boston has a crush on Lavy, but he seemed shady to me. Lavy didn't seem interested in him, and I was relieved. I couldn't imagine anyone being good enough for her. She was genuinely a nice person and wanted to help people. I felt protective of her, but I didn't need to judge Boston. I didn't know him and look at what happened with Nick. I thought he was a good guy and he turned out to be some crazy person who hunts people from my world.

It started to get late and I wanted to go home. Lavy left with me and walked me to my car at her shop. When I got home, I took a shower and crawled into bed. I needed some sleep. It was fun seeing other creatures from the Shadow Realm, but there were so many things I didn't recognize. This whole new world was going to take some getting used to, that was for sure. When my head hit the pillow, it didn't take me long to fall asleep.

ဢ

I stared at a beautiful girl who was climbing a tree. She had light brown skin, dark brown eyes, and long black hair. She was wearing a short sleeve dress made out of animal skin that came down to her knees. Her dress was light tan, with dark blue feathers hanging off the bottom and around her neck was a blue stone tied up with rope.

When she got to the top of the tree, she took off her dress and hung it on a branch. In the top middle of her back was a blue crescent moon with two stars on the side. The stars had six points instead of five, just like mine. The girl started to change forms. She started to get smaller; her arms became wings with brown, black, and white feathers. Her feet changed into talons, her mouth and nose became a beak, and her eyes went from dark brown to black. I could hear her bones crunching as she turned. When she was done she was a falcon, a beautiful bird. After the change was complete she flew away.

The next time I saw her. She was tied up. Her wrists were tied behind her back. There were thick ropes tied around her ankles that were connected to a large rock. An elderly woman was standing in front of her looking terrified. She was scared of the girl, but I couldn't understand why. I felt a connection to the girl. She had a pale blue aura with white surrounding the edges. There wasn't anything dark or evil about her. She was pure.

Behind the scared woman was a cliff. I could hear water rushing underneath it. What were they going to do to the girl?

"Jahana, great tracker and hunter of our people, you are being condemned to the sea, because of your demon mark. We know that you are causing this plague that is consuming all of our people. Your death will be the end of it. Farewell girl and your demon", said the scared woman.

The girl didn't speak. She didn't look scared at all. She was ready to die. She knew she would come back one day, and that destiny wasn't done with her yet. A man walked up to Jahana, picked her up and threw her off. I screamed but no one heard me. The people that were watching, that I didn't see until now, were shouting with joy. They were pleased with themselves.

"Well done Chief Aruna, Elder Diomedes will be quite pleased. Remember that you have *done a good deed," said a light-haired middle aged man. That man was human, whereas everyone else was not. There were maybe thirty other people there, but they were all shifters, just like the girl.*

That was the second time I had that dream. I didn't know what it meant but it scared me. How could that girl's people kill her? She was one of them. How could they think she was evil? She wasn't. The older man was evil, but not her. Her people were blind and stupid!

Before I could think much about it, the doorbell rang. Wondering who would come to my house without letting me know had me worried. I had to remember I wasn't helpless, I was a supernatural creature. I should scare people, not the other way around! I walked to the door as quietly as I could, peaked through the peephole in the door and saw that it was Falcon. I cracked the door open slightly, a little stunned he would show up at my house. Also, how did he know where I lived?

"Good morning sunshine, how are you this lovely morning?" he asked.

"What are you doing here? It is eight in the morning on a Sunday!"

"Well... I was trying to be nice and bring you some breakfast. I saw last night that you like to eat. That is not a bad thing, of course. It makes you healthy, and not like human girls who complain if they eat salad. Ah, sorry. Okay look, I was trying to be nice and see if we could eat some food and talk."

"First how did you get my address? Second what kind of food? And third, what were you doing watching me eat last night?"

He smiled then. He was the one blushing that time. He told me he got my address from Boston. Breakfast was chicken and cheese crispitos from his favorite gas station. Before I could politely reject them, he asked me to trust him they were really good. I invited him in and we went to the kitchen to eat. I was still in my night clothes, but I didn't care. The guy saw me drink blood. That was worse than this. He was right the food was really good. I was glad he brought a lot of them because I ate six.

"I am sorry about your boyfriend. I heard that he was killed. There is an investigation going on in our world to find out who did it and why. If I find out anything I can let you know if you want", he said out of nowhere.

"News travels fast huh? Honestly, I'm not sure I want to know exactly what happened with Nick. He is gone, there isn't anything I can do to change that.

He looked at me with a sad expression on his face and nodded.

"What else do you know about him?" I asked looking away, trying to avoid eye contact.

"I know he was a reaper and you didn't know. I know his dad isn't, so I doubt he knows. I know that you cared for him a lot and were hurt by him. I am sorry about that. I am also sorry that you had to go through the transition not knowing what was happening. It was hard for me. I still remember the pain, and that was two years ago. I knew it was coming though, my parents told me. I think you're doing great considering that our world is completely new to you. I am here if you ever need me. I just want to throw that out there."

"Thanks, I guess Lavy filled you in huh? The change was painful. I thought I was dying, or that I was being punished for something I had done. I prayed it would stop, and after several hours it finally did. That is when I realized, I had fangs and I looked different, but the same still." I didn't want to tell him about the mark.

There wasn't a reason to. I felt I should hide it, so I did.

"There is something else. Your old boyfriend's dad is looking into his death. We need you to convince him to stop. We don't want him to be in danger. That could get him hurt or worse. We don't need any more attention drawn toward here. The elders need to stay where they are."

Chapter Nine

"Who are the Elders? What do you mean, worse than hurt? How am I supposed to stop Dan from investigating Nick's death? That was his son and he is a cop."

"The Elders are like the human government, but smaller and only for the Shadow Realm. If he goes snooping around, he may be killed. There are a lot more reapers now than there have been in decades. Too many of them will draw the Elders here. They would want to know why this city is drawing them in. At the moment, no one knows why. If they do come, we want to have answers for them. The Elders aren't bad; however, they are strict with their laws. They are also very old."

"How old are they?"

"Some are several thousands of years old. We age differently. Once we hit the human age of twenty-six, we stop aging until a year before we die. When it is our time to die, we age rapidly to appear the age of a human in their eighties or nineties. Everyone is different in the aging process, just like humans."

"That is insane that we can we live that long! That explains why I haven't seen any older people from the Shadow Realm! Everyone looks to be in their mid-twenties. I feel that there is so much to learn; I don't really know anything."

"You will figure out all our secrets. I am happy to answer any questions you may have."

"Thanks, Lavy said I can make humans do what I want them to do, kind of like mind control. Maybe I can persuade him to stop investigating. I don't want to lose anyone else or there to be any more death."

"You are a vampire, so yes you have the ability to compel humans. I am a shifter, so I don't. To compel a human, you make eye contact, focus on your thoughts, and tell them what you want them to do."

"Okay, I'll try it when I can. Can you shift into anything?"

"No, shifters can only shift into one animal. When we turn sixteen, we change into our spirit animal. Every shifter is different, each family member can shift into the same animal or something completely different."

"What do you change into?"

He smiled at that, "I transform into a panther."

"Do you only transform during the full moon? Can you transform whenever you want? Do you have control over yourself when you do?"

"No, yes, and yes, unless I am in animal form for too long. Then the animal instincts become stronger and try to take over. If we go a few days without changing back into our human form from being an animal, we lose our humanity in a way. The freedom of not having the worry of being human is amazing. So I have heard. I don't stay in animal form more than a day or so"

"Does it hurt, when you transform?

"Yes, my body is being changed into something different than my human form. I can feel my muscles stretch and bones break while I change. The change is a lot better than it used to be. You adapt to the pain and sometimes enjoy it."

"Fascinating! Will I ever get to see you transform, or is that too personal?"

Before he could answer that his phone started to ring. He walked off into the living room to take the call. I threw our trash away, washed my hands, and grabbed a bottle of water from the fridge.

"Sorry to do this, but I need to leave. Extra hours at the car shop I work at became available. I could use the money."

"No worries. Thanks for the food. I hope we can talk more soon. I have more questions about this new world I'm in."

"I have your number, I'll call you."

"It's a date. Oh, not a date. Blah, you know what I mean."

"Yes, I know what you mean." He walked up to me then, smiled and kissed me on the cheek, then left.

I was too stunned to move. I was sure he was just being nice, or teasing me about that whole date comment. "Get a grip Jade, you don't need any boy drama right now', I told myself.

Needing to get out of my head, I got dressed and drove outside the city limits. It was Sunday. Most people who lived out there would be at church. I knew there was a cemetery I could go to that had wide roads I could run some laps in. It was secluded; a lot of trees and bushes were hiding it. I thought this would give me a great opportunity to test out a few of my new skills. Plus, I wouldn't get caught.

I drove through the rusted tall metal gates with large letters that said Rhondo Cemetery. I could see all the gravestones. Some were old, some were new, and few had flowers. I always had liked to look at the oldest ones. It also sadden me to see that so many barely lived twenty years. So many people complain about getting older, but they don't understand how much of a luxury that actually is.

The old army tank and cannon were still in the same places that they had always been. The tank on the left, right behind the entrance and the cannon in the center of the cemetery. Behind overgrown vines was an old small, abandoned church. So many horror stories have been told about it. There were nuns who were slaughtered, small children who were trapped for weeks, and the list goes on. If you looked through the windows it looked torn apart some. The pews were broken, there wasn't an altar any longer, and there was dust everywhere. Of course, most of the windows were broken. There also wasn't a way to get in. The front door had a padlock on it that had rusted with age, and the windows were too small to fit through.

I didn't come here often, even though it was peaceful. I wasn't a fan of death, and this re-minded me of so much that I had lost. I pulled my car to the side to hide it behind a large tree. Getting out of the car and looking around, I could see the wide dirt roads I remembered and the freedom that came with this place. I needed to run. I needed to have a clear head. I looked around to make sure no one was there. I didn't see anyone, but I also listened for heart-beats. I heard none, but my own.

I wasn't sure how this worked. I knew I could control my strength. I thought I would crush everything I held, but that wasn't the case. It was actually easy to control it. I was hoping the same thing for the speed. Lavy told me to follow my instincts, and they would guide me. I hoped she was right. I felt stupid doing this, but I had to learn sometime.

I started to walk down one of the paths, then started to jog until I was in a run. I started at a slow pace, normal human speed. Then I felt a rush of energy pass through me, and I went faster. All my surroundings were going by so fast, but nothing was blurry. I could still see everything so clear. I ran ten laps within a minute. When I stopped at my car, I felt invigorated. I wasn't out of breath, I felt alive! I wanted to run again, so I did. I spent an hour running. I never got tired or out of breath. The more I ran the more alive I felt.

After I finally stopped, I laid on the ground under the tree where I parked. The leaves and branches hid the sun from my eyes, so I didn't need sunglasses. The light still irritated my eyes though. I was told it was because my eyes could focus more on everything around me now than I could when I was human. That made sense. After my transition, I could see everything. I could see each piece of grass on the ground, the individual thread work in a blanket, droplets of rain on a window. Everything I saw was enhanced, the colors were even different, they were more vibrant than before. Seeing at night was not as difficult as for a human, but I didn't have weird night vision like you see in the movies.

I didn't stay much longer before I got a call. It was Alexa. She wanted to meet up with me. I told her she could meet me at my house. I needed something to eat anyway. I drove back home. When I arrived, she hadn't made it yet. I thought it would be a good time to drink a blood bag. It had been several hours since I had any. When I looked in the mini fridge that was in my room it was empty. I forgot I was out and was waiting for my order. "Boston needs to hurry up," I said to myself annoyed.

I dragged myself to the kitchen looking for meat. I hadn't gone grocery shopping for food since Grams left. That needed to change. We had some bread, milk, and a few canned goods. Nothing that looked appetizing. I checked in the freezer and saw frozen hamburger meat. If it was thawed I could eat that. At the thought of not having blood, I felt my eyes change and my throat tighten. I needed some soon. I was told that my body would start to adjust soon and I wouldn't need it as often. I could eat more human food, and that would keep me alive, just not as energized.

I looked in the mirror in the hall, my blue snake slit vampire eyes were looking back at me. I had a little trouble getting them to go away. That was another reason to have sunglasses. I didn't want anyone finding out about me. I didn't want to put them in danger. It wasn't like I could just disappear and cut everyone out of my life. Too many questions would be asked then, so I had to hide what I really was, even if it was hard. A little while later the doorbell rang. It was Detective Smith, Nick's dad. He looked rough and smelled of whiskey. He looked worse than the last time I had seen him.

"Hello sir, how are you today", I asked trying not to sound over concerned.

"Jade, dear, I am hanging in there", he said in a low voice. His words were slurred as he spoke.

"That is good to hear. I know you have had a hard time lately. I am still sorry about what happened."

"You were such a good girlfriend to Nick. He loved you. I know kids your age shouldn't be in love, but he really was with you."

"Yes, he was always nice to me". I did my best to hide my disgust about his son and act sympathetic. He was out of it, so I didn't have to try hard.

"You must be devastated, as well, since you are the one that found him."

"It was awful. I am still recovering", I said sounding distraught.

"How did you know he would be there? That is something I can't figure out."

"I didn't. I was exploring the building. I know it was wrong. I was curious about the building and have been for a while. I like the history of the downtown area"

"Curiosity killed the cat", he laughed.

It was obvious he was still drunk. I invited him to get some food in his stomach and some hot tea. Hoping that would sober him up. I also wanted to talk to him about the investigation. He needed to be more alert. That way I could tell how much he actually knew.

I made him some chicken noodle soup and provided some saltine crackers. I wanted him to eat something he could keep down. I also gave him some herbal tea. I didn't like the stuff, but Grams did. He ate it all without complaint. Besides looking rough from not showering or shaving, he also looked thinner.

"Any luck with finding out what happened?"

He looked up from a now empty bowl and gave me the oddest look. "Not really, mostly getting bad information and conspiracy theories."

"Sorry to hear that. What do you mean conspiracy theories?" I asked, giving him a small smile.

"The usual stuff: cult related, serial killer, and then you have the crazy theories of monsters."

"Wow"! I tried to sound alarmed, without sounding like I really believed any of it, especially the monster part.

"Technically I am not allowed to work on the case, but what people don't know, won't hurt them", he joked.

I knew I needed to do something, but wasn't sure what. I didn't want to push him too hard for answers. I didn't want him suspicious.

"What do you think happened? I have tried to think of something, but it's hard to think about it. Who could do something like that?" I asked, hoping to get him to talk more.

"I honestly don't know. Obviously, monsters are out. Monsters aren't real unless you count sick and twisted people in the world. I am leaning more toward a cult."

"That's scary! I didn't know cults were real. I thought they were only on TV. A way to scare kids to listen to their parents and be careful with what crowds they socialized with."

I know I sounded naive, but I had to. I hope he bought it. I wasn't a good actress and I knew it. I had always been bad at lying. Everyone who knew me knew it as well. Think Jade, think, I told myself. He was still a little tipsy. He didn't know about the Shadow Realm. He thought it was just humans being twisted. At that moment, I knew what I needed to do, even if I had never done it before.

"Mr. Smith, can you turn around and look at me. I have a question and I need a straight answer."

He turned around slowly and faced me. His eyes looked hazy. I hoped this would still work. I looked into his eyes and concentrated hard. At first, nothing happened. I felt dumb, actually. I reminded myself to stay focused. I was a vampire! I have seen vampires do this on TV. I was sure I could do it. I tried again, instead of trying too hard, I tried to relax. I felt the same energy I had earlier when I was running start to fill my body. I started to feel a connection to his mind. It was weak, but the more I pushed toward it, the stronger it became. He looked frozen as if he was trapped in his mind. He was staring back at me and not blinking.

"Mr. Smith?" He nodded slightly. Good, I thought.

"I need you to do something very important for me, can you do that?"

"Yes."

"Very good, tell me the truth about what you think happened to Nick."

"I think Nick may have been involved with a cult."

"Why do you think that?"

"He started to act strangely a couple of months ago. He was secretive."

"How was he secretive?"

"He would sneak out a lot and get strange calls from people I didn't know."

"Do you know what the calls were about?"

"Mostly about hunting. He wanted to go hunting for something."

"Do you know what he was wanting to hunt?"

"No, when he thought I was listening, he would hang up."

"Did you try to talk to him about it?

"When I did, he got angry. I thought it was him being a teenager."

"Do you believe in the supernatural?"

"No, that stuff is make-believe; a scary fairy tale."

I was relieved. He didn't have a clue. I didn't want to mess with his mind too much. I also didn't want him to get hurt. I thought of a quick plan that would help me save his life and to get rid of him at the same time.

"I need you to leave town. Find another city to go to. You want to do this because living here hurts too much. There are too many bad memories here. Moving away is what Nick would have wanted you to do."

"Yes, moving away would be good."

"You should move away from this city in a week. Whatever needs to be done, do it and go. Don't come back to Texarkana. This place is not good for you. Do you understand?"

"Yes."

I pulled myself back from his mind. As I did, I felt the energy I was using to compel him drift away. I hoped that had worked. I took a deep breath and moved away. After a minute, he seemed to be himself again, but more sober.

"Jade, thank you for the food. I think it is time for me to leave."

"Oh okay, it was nice of you to visit. Will I see you again soon?"

"No. I mean, I need to leave the city. I think it is time for me to move on. Nothing is here for me anymore. Nick would have wanted me to move on and not be drinking like I have been."

"I understand, you're right, moving away may be better for you."

He left after that, five minutes later, Alexa showed up, and I told her about Nick's dad showing up. How he smelled of liquor, and how he is going to move away from here. She wasn't surprised and agreed it may be the best thing for him to do.

Since there was no food in the house and I wanted to eat, I ordered some take out. It didn't take long for it to come. We ate until we were full, which for me was still a lot, especially with not having blood in my system.

Since I bought food, Alexa said she would do dishes. It was only a couple of plates and forks, but she insisted. We didn't have a dish-washer, Grams never got one. She always thought hand washing was the best way to go. I never argued. Maybe, it was because I never had to do the dishes. She always took care of the housework. I missed her a lot. It was weird her not being around. The house was too quiet, just a little longer and she would be home again.

There was a crash sound from the kitchen then followed by the smell of blood. The salty scent hit me hard. I could feel my throat tightening. My eyes were focused. I heard Alexa's heartbeat speed up. Before I knew it, I was in the kitchen, she was pinned to the wall, and I was about to suck the dripping blood from her cut fingers. That's when she screamed.

Alarmed, I looked at her and forced myself backward. "Get a towel!" I yelled. She obeyed after she stopped screaming. She stayed as far away from me as possible, eyes wide, and mouth open like she wanted to say something or scream more. I wasn't sure which.

I took slow deep breaths from my mouth, trying to calm myself. I didn't look at her. The fear on her face from before made my heart ache. How could I blame her though? I tried to drink her blood. I closed my eyes trying hard to focus. I needed my fangs to disappear, my eyes to go back to normal, and for the thirst to leave me. I could do it, I could control myself! I was stronger than this! After a little while, I was me again. However, when I looked back up to where Alexa had been, she was gone.

Panicking, I called Lavy. She was there in a couple minutes. She appeared out of nowhere. It was still going to take a little while to get used to that. I explained what happened with Alexa. I wasn't worried about telling her what happened with Nick's dad then.

"Do you think she will tell anyone what she saw?" Lavy asked.

"No, she wouldn't do that. She would think she was crazy first and no one would believe her. Mental disorders run in her family."

"I am glad she won't say anything, but I will keep tabs on her to make sure."

"Please don't hurt her. She needs time to comprehend what she has seen. I will give her a couple days and try to talk with her."

"No harm will come to her, I promise."

"Thank you, oh I took care of Mr. Smith, he will not be investigating anymore."

"What did you do, should I be worried", she asked jokingly.

"I compelled him to leave Texarkana and never come back."

She looked at me stunned. I gave her the whole story about what had happened when he came by. She was impressed that I was able to do it. It took vampires a lot of training to be able to make a strong connection. I blushed when she gave me praise. "It felt right," I told her. I also told her about me running and how it made me feel alive.

"Falcon came by today, also. He told me he could shift, which I already knew, but he also told me what he can shift into."

"Did he? He must trust you. From what I am told he is reluctant to tell his secret, even if it is someone from our world."

"He told me about the elders as well, how they are the government type of our world."

"That is correct. They are the ones who set our laws and come up with punishments if we do not follow them."

"I hope I don't have to meet them. I know they aren't necessarily evil, but I have a feeling I shouldn't get on their bad side."

She smiled at that and nodded her head. She left after she thought I had calmed down from the Alexa ordeal. I wanted to go see Alexa as soon as Lavy left, but I knew I needed to give her time. I hoped she wouldn't be scared of me or hate me. I couldn't believe I almost hurt her. I needed to make sure I never went a long time without feeding again, especially for the next few weeks. That whole experience could have been avoided. Lavy told me that Boston would be stopping by later to give me my order. He couldn't come soon enough. I needed blood, I was sure running and using compulsion was the reason I needed more so bad. If I didn't get it soon, I was afraid I may really hurt someone. I couldn't live with myself if I did that.

Chapter Ten

It has been three weeks since Grams left. I needed her home. I was having a rough time. Besides Nick dying and betraying me, Alexa was avoiding me, not that I really blamed her. She wouldn't return my calls or text messages. When I went to her house, she had her mom or brother tell me she wasn't feeling well. Trevor was avoiding me as well, so I stopped going to school after the Alexa thing, not that it really mattered. Thanksgiving break started and a lot of my friends were gone for the holidays visiting family. This year had gone by fast; Thanksgiving is next week. I hoped Grams was back by then. I wanted a normal holiday. Plus, I just needed to be around her.

It had been about a week since I last saw Alexa. Lavy had checked on her a few times, and of course, she never said anything about me to anyone. I knew she wouldn't. Besides the fear of people not believing her, she wouldn't betray me. If the situation were reversed, I wouldn't betray her either. I wish she would talk to me to let me apologize and explain. I was afraid she would never talk to me again.

I called Grams. I didn't tell her what was going on with Alexa. She had enough to worry about. I just needed to hear her granny southern voice. She always cheered me up!

"Hey, honey. I was just thinking about calling you. I have some great news."

"Great minds think alike. What's the great news?"

"I am coming home tomorrow honey. The lady I have been helping is doing a lot better."

"That is the best news ever. I miss you being here. I'll make sure to go get groceries before you come home. I have missed you so much. I'll take us out to dinner as a treat too, wherever you want to go!"

"That is sweet honey. We can go to my favorite buffet place. We can also eat dessert first. I will be leaving early in the morning, so I can beat the rain that is supposed to hit."

"Sounds like a plan. I am glad your patient is better. Grams please be safe. It's getting late.

You need to get some rest before driving. I love you. See you tomorrow."

"I will honey. You get some rest too. I love you as well. See you tomorrow sweetie."

I was ecstatic she was coming home! I had to clean the house; not that it was dirty. I just needed to do something to keep myself calm, and to keep my mind off of everything else. I wasn't due to work at the Wicca shop for a couple of days. I had worked there non-stop for the past week. I was stocking and organizing more than anything else. Lavy told me to go home and take a few days off. "You may be a vampire but you still need teenage girl time."

It took me a whole thirty minutes to clean. I didn't even use vampire speed. I went slowly, but there wasn't much to do, except my laundry. It was around nine when I got done. I decided to go grocery shopping. It would kill a couple of hours. I didn't have anything better to do, and the store was open until midnight.

I grabbed the prepaid card for groceries and headed to the store. I got the usual stuff on the weekly grocery list. I also got some extra stuff to treat us. Of course, I paid for that. I got Grams her favorite pecan log rolls. She can't eat them too often because of her diabetes, but I figured she deserved a treat. I got me my favorite as well, peanut butter cups. Chocolate and peanut butter is one of the best food creations.

I got back a little after midnight. I went extra slow at the store. By the time I unloaded all the groceries, I was actually tired. Relieved, I went to bed and didn't wake up until my phone started to ring. Groaning, I rolled over and grabbed my phone off the nightstand. I realized I forgot to charge it. It barely had half a charge. I didn't recognize the number, so I ignored it. After the call ended, I noticed I had two missed calls; now, three missed calls from the same number. A minute later, the same number called.

I answered it reluctantly. I hoped it wasn't a telemarketer. I knew I could easily stop the calls, but still.

"Hello", I asked groggily.

"May I speak with Jade Dixon please", asked a gravely sounding voice.

"This is she", I said alarmed. Flashbacks of my parents drummed through my mind. That sick feeling I had back then came rushing back.

"Are you related to a Carol Ann Flowers?"

"Yes, ma'am. She is my grandmother. What is this about please?"

"I am Nurse Betty, and your grandmother is in the ICU at Granger Memorial Hospital right now. She was involved in an accident. The doctor would like you to come here. We found your name and number through her insurance company as the emergency contact."

"What kind of accident was she in?" I asked starting to cry.

"I can't go into the details over the phone. Once you get here we can talk about it. Please get here as soon as you can."

She hung up with me a minute later after giving me the address to the hospital. I called Lavy right after, asking her to go with me. She appeared a couple minutes later. I changed quickly, brushed my teeth, but skipped brushing my hair. I put my hair in a messy bun as I was walking to the car and then put a cap over that.

Lavy programmed the address into her phone's GPS. I had to let my phone charge on the way up there. The drive to Granger was quiet. I didn't want to talk, and I'm sure she sensed that. I kept telling myself Grams would be okay. I knew the ICU was for critical people, but she had to be fine. It was probably something minor, but due to her age, they didn't want to take any chances. I was sure that was it.

I had to stop for gas along the way. I should have filled up when I was at the store last night but didn't want to bother. I was regretting that now. Lavy told me I should eat, but I didn't have much of an appetite. I felt sick to my stomach. I was trying to fight the emotional pain I knew I would feel soon.

We arrived at the hospital a few hours after the call. We did hit some bad weather, but it didn't faze me; however, it made people drive slower and more dangerous than usual. That was another good thing about being a vampire; better vision in rain and reflexes. When we parked, the rain had stopped. We walked into the main entrance, and I could barely get out the question about where the ICU was at the front desk.

"On the third floor", the receptionist said.

We went to the third floor using the elevator. The dropping feeling elevators gave you made me feel worse. It dinged three times; then stopped. The ugly metal doors slid open slowly revealing a circular counter holding fake plants. I assume it was to make the place more cheerful. After walking out of the elevator, everything started to go in slow motion again. It was just like when I was at the hospital with my mom. I went to the nurse's station. There were four nurses there looking at monitors and doing paperwork.

"Ex... Excuse me, my name is Jade Dixon", I said trying hard not to cry.

"Awe, yes we have been expecting you. You talked to Nurse Betty on the phone is that correct?"

"Yes, I was told my grandmother, Mrs. Flowers was involved in an accident. I wasn't told what type of accident. Can I see her please?"

"Let me see if I can reach the doctor. She was wanting to talk to you first."

Nurse Maddie, according to her name tag, reached for the phone, pressed a couple of buttons, then put the phone against her ear. It only took two rings for someone to answer. I overheard the conversation. Another perk of being supernatural.

"Hello", said a low voice.

"Jade Dixon is here. You said you wished to speak with her."

"Thank you for notifying me. I will be there momentarily."

She hung up the phone after that. I looked away so she wouldn't think I was eavesdropping.

"Doctor Riker will be here soon. You can have a seat in the waiting room", she said, while gesturing to the right with her hand.

The waiting room wasn't empty. There were a few people sitting in chairs, looking at magazines or looking at the news on the television hanging on the wall. I didn't bother to sit. I needed to stand. I walked over to the windows. The blinds were open to let some of the sunlight in. Lavy followed me. I was glad she was there. I really needed someone there, even if they were silent. Knowing I wasn't alone helped me a lot more than I thought it would.

Roughly ten minutes later, a lady in a white lab coat came up to me and introduced herself as Doctor Riker. She had a lovely round face, thick light brown curly hair, and a pleasant voice. People like her stood out from others. Maybe it was because she had a strong personality.

"I'm glad you were able to make it so quickly. I didn't want you to hear this over the phone. I am afraid it's not good news."

"Honestly, I figured that already. Can you tell me what happened please?"

"Mrs. Flowers, your grandmother was in a bad car accident. She was hit on the driver side of her vehicle by a drunk driver. She is currently in a coma. Her injuries are severe. She hit her head, and there was a lot of bruising to her brain. I am sorry to say, but I don't think she will wake up."

She wasn't rude about what happened; just straightforward. It took me a minute to comprehend what she had said.

"Why don't you think she will wake up?" Lavy asked.

The doctor looked at me, and I nodded my head that it was fine to answer.

"Due to her age and how severe the injuries are, it just doesn't seem likely. I am sorry about this. The brain injury is the worst. Her other organs are in bad shape as well. Her heartbeat and kidney functions are not looking good. The fact that she has diabetes doesn't help. The way things look right now, I would advise you to say your goodbyes."

"When can I see her?" I asked. I wasn't hiding the tears then. There wasn't a reason to.

"You can see her now if you like. I'll have Nurse Maddie walk you to her room. Your friend can wait here. We have a policy: family only in the ICU rooms."

I simply nodded. I didn't want to argue. I wanted to see Grams. I wanted to spend as much time with her as possible.

The nurse led me through two double wooden doors that opened automatically after you entered a special code. After walking through the doors, the air seemed different. It had the faint smell of death. We walked down a long hallway; dim lights in the ceiling lit the way. Grams was in room 313.

I opened the door slowly, not knowing what to expect. Lying in a hospital bed, a thin blanket pulled up to her chest, was Grams. Her bruised arms were lying flat beside her. Her eyes were closed as if she were sleeping. There were tubes coming out of her nose and arms. A couple of IVs were next to her bed with clear liquids in them. Monitors with black screens were making green and white squiggly lines going up and down. They also made annoying beeping noises. I couldn't stand hospitals.

"I'll leave you two alone", the nurse said, before she shut the door.

I walked over to the bed, looking at Grams. Her face was bruised at the top, and the rest of her face was pale. I sat down in the chair beside her, grabbing her hand, to feel her touch. Her hand was cool. Not warm and full of life like it usually was.

I sat there for an hour or so. I didn't move or saying anything. I just looked at her. The same nurse came back in to check on her.

"Jade, is there anything I can get for you?"

I shook my head because I didn't trust my voice. There were still tears in my eyes. When the door closed, I closed my eyes focusing on Grams. I didn't know how I knew what to do but I did. I opened my mind, pushing toward hers. It took a little effort but I managed to do it.

I created a beautiful green park. The sun was high in the sky with a warm breeze blowing around. A picnic table covered with food and drinks was in the middle of some shade, created by a large red oak tree.

My mom was in a purple sundress that made her hair stand out. She had the biggest smile on her face. Grams was chasing a little girl with light brown hair that was in pigtails.

"Jade, come to grandma. Come on sweetie."

The little girl ran to her. Grams scooped her up and gave her a big hug.

"I love you Grammy".

"My sweet girl, I love you too."

"Mom, Jade, Y'all need to come eat before the ants get it", said my mom playfully.

I watched as they ate, laughed, and talked. I got closer to the table, so I could soak in the images of the women there.

The scene changed. My mom was a lot older and so was Grams. We were all in my room at Grams. I was getting ready for my senior prom. I was wearing a long flowing light blue dress. My hair was twisted in a braided bun, with a lot of loose spirals hanging down from my face. Both mom and Grams were gushing over how beautiful I looked. "Stop, you two will make me cry. That will ruin my makeup", I told them while laughing.

The smiles on their faces made my heart melt. The two best women I have ever known were standing right next to me. That was the best feeling in the world. Even if it wasn't real. They pushed me out of my bedroom door.

"Your date has been waiting in the living room for you for an hour", my mom said. "Ugh, I hope dad didn't give him the third degree. I really like this guy." I walked into the living room and saw Falcon, looking handsome in a black and white tux. Grams and mom took too many pictures, but it was worth it to see the light in their eyes and huge smiles on their faces.

Changing to a different scene again, I was in a church. I was standing behind two closed wooden doors that had green ivy and white flowers all around them. I was wearing a spaghetti strap white silk dress that went down to my ankles and holding a bouquet of white and pink lilies. Grams was there in a light pink dress holding a cane. My mom and dad were on the other side of me. My arm was looped through my dad's. It was my wedding day. The doors opened, and my dad walked me slowly to the altar. I could see all my friends and their families in the pews. The classic wedding song being played on the piano; it was like a princess fairy tale.

I came back to reality before I had to show a groom. I wanted to show Grams big moments that she would have missed, even if they were all made up. I wanted to let her see me. She

was like a mother to me after mine had died.
When I was in her mind, I felt her pain. She
was hurting so bad. She knew her body was
shutting down, but she didn't want to leave me
alone. I knew I needed to tell her she could let
go. I knew I would be fine, even if that wasn't
entirely the truth just yet.

Before I got the chance to connect with her
mind again, there was a knock on the door.
Nurse Maddie told me I had a visitor, and that
she would like to talk to me. I glanced at my
phone and realized hours had passed since I
came into Gram's room.

"Grams, I will be back soon. I love you." I
kissed her head and left the room. I walked
back to the waiting room with the nurse. I was
shocked to see who was there. Alexa ran up to
me and hugged me.

"Jade, I am sorry about Grams. I got here as
soon as I could", she said while sobbing.

"What are you doing here?" I asked in a low
voice.

"Lavy called Alex and told him what happened. I didn't answer my phone when she
called. I am so sorry. I should have."

"Okay."

"Can we talk alone in private?" she asked.

"I can't leave Grams alone. I need to be with her. She isn't going to make it through the night."

Lavy walked up to me then. "Jade do to the nurse what you did to Nick's dad." It took me a second to register what she was saying. I could compel the nurse to let them in with me.

I walked up to the nurse's desk. The nurse Maddie looked at me. I stared into her eyes, feeling the energy of my mind connect to hers.

"This is my sister Alexa and our cousin Lavy. They would like to go see my grand-mother with me now."

She simply nodded. Both of them followed me and the nurse back to room 313. "You can leave now and thank you", I told the nurse.

I opened the door again. Grams hadn't changed from when I had last seen her a few minutes ago. I was hoping she would miracu-lously wake up and be alright. They followed me into the room, not saying anything. They just gasped at how broken Grams looked. I went back to the chair I was at before and grabbed Gram's hand.

"What do you want to talk about? I asked Alexa.

"It can wait. Just know I am here for you, no matter what", she said crying soft sobs.

"I need both of you to let me concentrate then. She is in a lot of pain, and I'm going to let her know she can let go and move on."

They both looked at me with sad eyes and nodded. I went into Grams' mind again. This time I talked to Grams directly. No fake memories of what could have been, but I did make her forget she was in pain. I also created her back porch for her. It was a warm summer night and the stars and moon were shining brightly. She was sitting on the porch swing, gazing up at the sky.

I walked up the backstairs. She turned toward me and smiled. "There you are, my sweet granddaughter. I was just thinking about your senior prom with that nice young man that was your date. Then about you being the most beautiful bride, I have ever seen. Your dad walked you down the aisle. He looked so handsome. I can't remember the groom, though. Oh well, that day was all about you anyway."

"Hi, Grams", I said trying hard to hide that my heart was breaking.

"Honey, what's wrong? Is this about a man?" she asked, winking at me.

"I wish that were it. I have to tell you something. I just don't know how."

"Alright, what is it? I can take it", she mused.

"There is a lot; but first, you were in a car accident. You are in the hospital right now in Granger, Texas; not far from where you were staying. The doctor said you may survive a week if you're lucky. Your body is too damaged for you to get better. You're going to die", I said in a low rush.

"No, I'm not. We are at my old house sitting on the back porch. I can see it with my own eyes, honey. Are you feeling alright sweetie?" she asked a little confused.

"Grams, I am controlling what you are seeing right now, but not what you are hearing. I wanted you to be somewhere you loved and somewhere you felt at peace.

"Let's say you're not off your rocker and what your saying is true. How are you doing it?"

"Please don't hate me. I... I'm a vampire." I was born this way. I am not dead, though. My heartbeats, I breathe, I feel; everything is just more intense than when I was a human. I am still the same Jade that I have always been.

There is just this whole other supernatural world. All the myths are true. Well, most of them", I said in a rush.

"That doesn't surprise me", she confessed, with a slight grin on her face."

"You don't hate me then? You believe in vampires? You don't think I'm crazy?"

"Honey, I could never hate you, no matter what you are. Of course, I do! There are too many unknowns not to believe in the, what did you call it? The supernatural world? That explains a lot about some of the people that came into the hospital over the years. So many remarkable recoveries or strange deaths that didn't make sense."

"Grams, I love you so much. I am happy to hear you say that. I thought you wouldn't love me anymore; that you would think I was a monster and hate me."

"Jade, listen to me. You are my granddaughter and I believe God created you in his image. You may be different, but that was God's plan."

"You think God created supernaturals?" I asked stunned.

"I believe he created everything for a reason. We all have a purpose in life. Just because you are different doesn't mean you're bad honey. I believe you are going to do wonderful things in your lifetime sweetie. There is a plan for you. I can feel it in my bones."

That was a big reason why I loved Grams so much. She had a huge heart and didn't let the world's insecurities or judgments affect how she thought or felt about anything. She was strong and independent and had her faith.

"Grams I... I came to tell you goodbye as well. I don't want to, I really don't. But your body is in so much pain. I can feel it all. Your body is shutting down quickly. I am doing my best to take the pain away from you, but it's draining me. I am growing weaker with every minute that I try to make you feel okay. I want you to know that you can let go and be at peace. I will miss you so much, but I don't want you to suffer anymore. Just know that you have helped me so much these past couple of years. You have made me grow into a strong person. I love you more than you know. Thank you for everything."

"I love you too sweetheart. You are looking sort of tired honey. I am so sorry. I am doing this to you. I will let go, sweetie. You don't need to suffer because of me. Remember wherever

I'm going honey, I'll be watching over you. I love you, my precious granddaughter. No matter what, I will be with you always, my sweet Jade."

"Always", I replied.

I was rushed back to the hospital room. This time; it was because there was nothing to connect to. Grams was gone. Lavy turned off one of the monitors. It was making that horrible dinging noise. The same stupid noise you hear on TV when someone dies. This time, though, it was real. No matter how much I didn't want it to be: it was still real.

I stayed in the seat next to Grams' body. It was hard to think of her just being a body. Her soul was no longer in it. There was no heartbeat, no life force; it was only a shell. The smell of death lingered in the room, even after she was dragged out of the room a little while later. I was told that I needed to leave soon. Someone could talk to me about funeral arrangements or whatever type of service I would like.

The thought of me arranging Grams funeral made me sick. I went to the bathroom in her hospital room and vomited in the toilet until there was nothing left to come up. I had officially lost all my family then. I was alone in the world. I felt selfish at that thought. Grams was the one who had just died. I prayed she was at peace. She deserved that much.

"Jade, we need to leave", I heard Lavy whisper at the closed bathroom door.

When she opened the door, I looked over at her and nodded. She grabbed my hand and led me to the elevator. I somewhat acknowledged that Alexa was following us. We went down to the first floor and walked to my car. The passenger car door opened. I was told to sit down. I obeyed with no hesitation. It was hard to think about what was going on. I don't even remember who told me to sit. I somewhat heard Lavy and Alexa talking in the background.

"Alexa, will you stay here with her? I'm going to go back in and see what needs to be done. She needs you more than anyone else right now."

"Of course I'll stay with her. Go do what you need to do."

I am not sure how long I waited in the car before Lavy came back with paperwork. Alexa got out of the driver's seat, so Lavy could get in. We drove to a small bed and breakfast. Lavy checked us all in. When we reached our room, I went to the bed and laid down. I let myself cry for hours. I let the pain of losing her, my parents, Nick's betrayal, everything bad that happened to me in my life go. I was tired of the hurt, I wanted it gone. When I felt numb and no more tears came, I just laid there being quiet.

I finally sat up, because I was tired of feeling sorry for myself. I could feel eyes on me, I looked over at Lavy and Alexa who were staring at me like I could break any minute. I got off the bed and walked to the bathroom. I turned the shower on, stripped, and took a hot shower. Washing with whatever soap and shampoo was in the bathroom. I needed to wash the tears, sadness, and anger away. I stayed in the shower until the hot water ran out. I dried myself off and put on one of the bathrobes. I left the bathroom feeling better than I had in several hours. My friends were sitting on the floral couch still, they hadn't moved since I went to the bathroom.

"I need food and blood."

Alexa looked at me bewildered. "I'll take care of both", Lavy said. "Thanks", I said smiling faintly at her. She nodded, then started looking on her phone.

"After we eat, we can talk. Okay, Alexa?"

"Okay", she whispered.

"Food is on its way, and you can drink blood from a vein in my wrist", Lavy informed me.

I looked at her confused. "Don't worry. It has pretty much the same effect as a human, but it's sweeter." "Thanks, I need my energy up. I have a funeral to plan."

Chapter Eleven

It had been two days since Grams died. I didn't have to make any arrangements really. She had it set up already. It was all in her will. The funeral was at the small yellow brick church on State Line that she had attended. She had been a member there for at least thirty years. So many people came. There wasn't an empty pew in the whole building, and people were standing in the back, barely able to fit. She made a real difference in people's lives.

Of course, people came up to me and gave me their sympathies. I didn't know any of them, but that didn't seem to bother any of them. Apparently, Grams bragged about me to everyone, so each person said they felt like they knew me.

The event was exactly how she wanted it. Simple and southern. She was placed in a cherry wood casket with an antique white lining. She was wearing her favorite Sunday dress. It was a floral pattern dress she had bought in the 80's. Her old Bible laid beneath her hands on her chest. She had a few arrangements of white daisies in the corners of the church. There was a picture of her and my mom from years ago, in front of the casket. Her favorite hymns were playing from the sound system in the back of the church.

A few people made speeches about how she had made a difference in their lives. Each time someone talked, they looked at me. It made me feel uncomfortable, but the service wasn't about me; it was about her. I tried to avoid eye contact with people. My emotions were all over the place. I was worried what I would reveal.

All my friends were there with me; supporting me. Lavy and Falcon even came. Lavy, I expected to come, but not Falcon. It was a nice surprise. He didn't say anything to me. He just nodded and stayed close to me. During the service, Lavy and Alexa sat on either side of me, comforting me. It was nice to know I wasn't alone, even if my family was gone. I realized, then that my friends were my family, even if we didn't have ties by blood or legal documents. We all loved each other like family.

When the service was over, I stayed for the dinner. I wasn't hungry but didn't want to be rude. The day dragged on, but no one left me alone with the strangers at the church. I was planning to help clean up but was told I could leave. I had enough to deal with. After thanking everyone for their support, I left.

Grams wasn't going to be buried until the next day. I was the only one who was going to be there. That part was for me to say goodbye to her one last time. The funeral was for everyone else.

I woke up bright and early that next day, ready to be with her one last time. I watched as she was placed into the ground. Her casket getting slowly covered with dirt. It didn't take long for it to be completely covered. When I was alone, officially I placed a yellow rose on top of the dirt patch and stared at the spot holding Gram's lifeless body.

"Grams, I am going to miss you. You were more than family to me. You were everything I had left. I want you to know that I will be fine. I am a big girl, and I know I can take care of myself. You have more than helped me with that. I want to thank you for the house. It was an amazing thing for you to give me. I wanted to let you know, I can't stay there. The house reminds me so much of you. It hurts too much to be there without you. I am sure you will understand. I don't plan for it to go to waste. I know you are watching over me in Heaven with mom and dad. I am happy you're not suffering anymore. I will do my best to move on, but it won't be easy. I promise I will never forget you. I love you and always will."

I said what I wanted and left the small cemetery in Fouke. I didn't plan to return for a while. I got in my car and drove for a while. I wasn't staying at the house. I hadn't since Grams died. I was staying at Alexa's. I didn't want to be alone, and Alexa and I had things to work out. For the most part, I believe we did. The night Grams died, Lavy left us alone for a while, so we could talk.

"What do you want to talk about?" I asked. I was sure I knew what it was about, but I wanted her to start. I needed to know what she was thinking without my influence.

"I'm sure you know. It is what I saw before. What I saw you do. I have been thinking of the

possibilities of what it could be, but only one really made sense. Even if it is crazy."

"Tell me, what did you come up with?"

"Don't laugh. I think you're a demon or vampire. I know that sounds crazy, but you came out of nowhere. You were strong enough to stop me from moving, and you tried to drink blood from my cut fingers. Also, you told Lavy you needed blood a little while ago. I know that sounds insane, but that is what I think."

"If it were true, that I was a vampire, would that matter?" She looked at me wide-eyed. She was starting to realize it was true.

"You still appear to be the Jade I have always known. You seem different, though. You seem stronger and your features are flawless. I don't mean to sound rude, but you are incredibly beautiful now; like magazine photoshop model beautiful. You even smell differently. You have a naturally sweet scent. To answer your question, no it wouldn't matter. You scared me before, but you stopped yourself from hurting me. I believe you wouldn't hurt me. I trust you. I have always trusted you. No matter what you're my sister. I am sorry I ignored you before. I didn't know what *to think. Then with what happened to Grams, I took it as a sign that I needed to be around you."*

"I am sorry about that. I went a few hours without blood and used a lot of energy that day. That was a mistake that will never happen again. I couldn't stand myself if I hurt you or anyone else. There is so much I want to tell you. First I am a vampire. Apparently, I was born this way. Before I can tell you more, you have to swear you won't tell anyone about me or any of what I am about to tell you. You can't even tell Trevor. I want you in my life, but if you can't keep this secret, I can't be in your life."

"I won't tell anyone, I promise. I need you in my life. You're my best friend. It doesn't matter what you are or what you eat. Please don't leave. You can tell me anything. You know that. Tell me everything. It will stay with me, I promise."

"Good. Humans aren't supposed to know our secret. I told you I am a vampire, I drink blood, but I'm not dead. I am very much alive. My heart beats, I breathe, and I eat human food. That whole myth that a vampire drinks your blood, you drink their blood, and then

you change: it's a lie. Those are just stories made up for the movies to make them more interesting, I guess. The night of my birthday party, well technically at midnight. I transformed into this." I showed her my eyes and fangs."

"Your eyes look like blue snakes eyes, and you have more than two fangs. The eyes look awesome, but um the fangs, look scary. Sorry, but they do."

"Yes I know", I said smiling at her. I went through what the Shadow Realm call a transformation. It was extremely painful. I felt like I was on fire from the inside out. I thought I was going to die. It lasted several hours. When it was all over, I wasn't human anymore. I needed blood. The thought of it was gross, but it tasted amazing the first time.

"Okay, that is gross, but continue."

I laughed at her. "Also I have a tattoo. I haven't shown anyone this, not even Lavy. I pulled the robe off and showed her the mark.

"That is beautiful", she said while touching it.

"It was there when the transformation was over. I have a feeling no one else gets marks *like these. I don't want to say anything yet. Too much is going on right now."*

"I understand. Your secrets are safe with me. I promise."

I believed her. I knew she would never betray me. She truly was my sister. "I have super speed. I can run really fast. You know about the strength. I can also control people's minds. Mr. Smith left town because of me. I compelled him to leave, for his safety. He was getting too close to Nick's death and how the Shadow Realm was possibly involved."

"What do you mean too close to Nick's death? What is the Shadow Realm? This is the second time you have mentioned it."

"First, the Shadow Realm is where every mythical or supernatural creature is from. You have the human world; then, you have the Shadow Realm. Second, Nick was killed because he was a reaper. A reaper is a human with the sight to see people like me for what we really are. They kill my kind, even if we aren't bad. I think he was dating me to get close to me because he knew I would change into what I am. He was killed because he was hunting realmers or supernaturals."

"Jade, I am so sorry. I couldn't even imagine that about him. He seemed to genuinely love you. That must have been so difficult for you. I am sorry you couldn't tell me sooner."

"I am sorry you got dragged into this crazy new world of mine. All the myths are true, well except there are no zombies. I asked already", I said laughing.

"Alright, good to know; no zombies. Is Lavy a vampire too?"

"No, she is a fairy. It is hard to explain what she looks like. She is one of the most beautiful creatures I have ever seen. She has pointed ears, her skin shimmers shades of orange and purple, and her eyes are unnaturally bright green."

"Wow!"

"I think you have enough information for now. I think I have told you the short version of mostly what has been going on and about the supernatural world."

"Jade, one last thing. Please don't use mind control on me or compel me, whatever you want to call it."

I looked at her, she was serious. "I won't, I promise." I hoped that was a promise I could *keep. I didn't want to lie to her, but I didn't want to lose her either.*

Not long afterward; Lavy came back to the room bringing clothes and food. Alexa just stared at her, trying to see what I saw when I looked at her.

"I guess you two had a good talk huh?" Lavy asked.

"Yes!" Alexa and I said in unison, then laughed at ourselves.

Ever since then, I felt more comfortable with myself. I felt a lot better now that I wasn't hiding anything from Alexa. I had been staying with her a couple of days then. Thanksgiving was coming up. I was invited to stay with her family as long as I wanted. I was grateful for that.

I hadn't been back at the house much during that time, except to get clothes and store blood. I knew I needed to figure out what I wanted to do. I couldn't live with Alexa forever. I decided after the holiday, I would get my GED and get emancipated. I also wanted to get the rest of the money that was left to me.

Besides leaving the house to me in her Will, Grams had a couple of different life insurance policies as well. She had set it up where I could be sixteen and have it, just in case anything happened. That was nice. I wouldn't be getting it until the week following Thanksgiving, though. That gave me some time to come up with a plan to make myself legally an adult. I was afraid social workers would come around because I was still a minor. I didn't think it would be too hard to go in front of a judge. The biggest concern the system would have was a way to care for yourself. I had that part covered. Legally, if I got my GED, I wouldn't have to stay in school. I could even take a few online college courses if I wanted to. I was sure that would give me brownie points if I mentioned it. If I had any trouble, I could always compel them to grant me what I wanted.

I know I needed a change. There was no point trying to stay with my old life. I wasn't human any longer. I didn't want to live in Gram's house. I didn't want to be in school. I needed a fresh start.

Thanksgiving was fun for the most part. We had the usual meal with turkey, potato salad, cornbread dressing, ham, and, of course too many desserts. Everyone ate too much and then complained because they ate too much. It was nice to be surrounded by a loving family.

Lavy and Falcon didn't celebrate Thanksgiving. I thought that was odd, but didn't say anything.

The next week I went to take my GED. That didn't take much. I had to take some assessment test, which only took a couple of hours. I thought it would be more complicated than it was. I was relieved when they said I passed.

The following day, I drove to Dallas where the insurance company my parents used resided. I did have to compel a few people there to do what I wanted. I had more money than I thought I did, originally. When it was all said and done, I wound up with a little over five hundred thousand dollars, and that wasn't including Grams money. I created a few different secret accounts for the money to be placed in. You never know when you might need to disappear.

The last couple of weeks I felt like I was being spied on. I ignored the feeling, because who would be watching me. No one knew about me. I was sure I was just imagining things.

The second to last thing on my list of things to do was to get emancipated. It was a little harder than dropping out of school. I had to provide my GED certificate, and show that I had an income. I had to provide one of my bank statements that showed I had several thousand dollars saved up. That account was the one Grams had helped me set up. I also had Lavy come with me to show that I was employed.

The judge told me that I would need to find a place to live. I showed him the deed to the house that I owned now. He didn't need to know I wasn't planning on living there. I had yet to figure out what I wanted to do with it. After a couple of days of me providing information, I was finally legalized as an adult.

All I had to do then was find a place to live. I didn't want to live alone. I wasn't used to that. I shared my concern with Lavy one day when I went to work.

"I can move in with you if you want. My place is too small, and I have a month to month lease, so it won't be a hassle to leave."

"You wouldn't mind? That would be awesome. I really don't want to live by myself."

"I think it would be great, especially with you being new to the shadow world."

"I agree. We can start looking for a place now if you like. I can pay the rent and utilities, and we can split the grocery cost."

"Thanks, but I would rather us split everything we have to pay. The shop is doing really well, and I have investments that bring in money for me."

"Sound's good. I prefer an apartment. I think it would be easier upkeep. Maybe a loft down here close to the shop."

"We could move into the Grimm. You would be closer to more people in the Shadow Realm and get to know more about the environment. However, humans aren't allowed there, unless they are providing services for vampires or other realmers."

I shuttered a little at that, "I'd rather not live there. There is a loft that just became available a few days ago. It is across the street from the Grimm, and Alexa could come over."

"Alright, we will check it out and see if we like it."

"I have the number. I'll call and see when we can look at it."

We were able to see the apartment that day. The landlord was thrilled. He was honest and told us someone had died there recently from old age and no one wanted to rent it. The pain of Grams death came back to me, but I pushed it down. I needed to move on. I reminded myself that she was in a better place.

The loft was large and spacious. Everything was open except the bathrooms. The bedrooms were up narrow flights of stairs on opposite sides of the loft. The living room was the first room you walked into from the front door. Then, to the right was a dining room, followed by a large kitchen. One bedroom was off the living room and the other was off the kitchen. Under each bedroom area was a small bathroom. It was nice. We wouldn't have to share. The walls were painted a pastel green and the floors were hardwood all around. There wasn't any carpet, not that I cared. The place seemed perfect for us. Open and free.

Lavy looked at me and I nodded. "We'll take it", I said happily. We were handed a key each. Now we just had to furnish the place. Lavy was going to bring her stuff from her old apartment, but I had to go shopping. I decided to leave my stuff in the house. I wanted a new start in life, so that meant a change of scenery, including furniture. I did take my books, mini fridge, clothes, and bathroom stuff. However, I left all the furniture I got when I moved there. I also brought Legs of course. She stayed at the house while I was at Alexa's. Her mom loved me but didn't care for my pet.

It was going to be nice to have a place of my own choosing. I was going to be able to be myself here and not have to hide what I was. That thought made me happier than I had been in days. I didn't have to be scared or cautious.

Chapter Twelve

It has been a little over a month since I started living with Lavy. Nothing out of the ordinary has happened lately. No new bodies have been found. I haven't had any bloodlust outbursts. That is probably due to me feeding on blood more often. I also have been crazy dream free, which has been great. The dream-catcher I had was doing its job.

The apartment was looking nice as well. We painted it to match our own style. We agreed on antique white for the living room, dining room, and kitchen area with some ivory white trim. Something to brighten up the place. Our bedroom areas were our own to do whatever we wanted. Mine was a dark blue-green color. I decided to get a dark brown wood bed, dresser, and desk. I kept my room simple. There wasn't any pictures anywhere or any fancy decor. I did, however, upgrade Leg's terrarium. She was placed into a small sliding door one that had plenty of hiding places for her. She appeared to be a lot happier with it. I also had some book-shelves lining the back wall of my room. Lavy's room was bright orange with purple flowers and green vines hanging on the walls. It was quite unique. It matched her skin tone really well.

Christmas came and went. I wasn't really in the mood for celebrating. I did get my friends a gift card each to their favorite stores. I didn't want to shop, but I figured they would enjoy buying themselves something. Of course, they all gave me something. I didn't want them to, but they didn't listen. Alexa got me a blue rose that was encased in glass. Lavy gave me a book about our world, it was more like a journal, ti-tled "Index of Supernatural Mythology". Lastly, Falcon got me self-defense classes for a couple of months. "You need to know how to protect yourself. You can never be too careful", he said grinning at me. I thought it was different, but it could be useful. My first class was coming up the day after New Year's. I was a little excited. I didn't know how to fight if I ever needed to. The ability to defend myself the human way could be better than me showing my fangs and growling at an attacker.

New Year's was a day away. We decided to have a small party. More like Lavy decided to have one.

"You need to get out of your slump. I know it has been rough lately, but you're strong. You can't keep working and not have a social life."

"I have a social life. I get out."

"Working at the shop isn't a social life. You barely see Alexa anymore. I know you don't go to school anymore, but you can do something. You can go to the Grimm and meet some people from our world."

"Fine! After the holidays are over, I will be more social. Let me just get New Year's out of the way. It will be a new year and everything will be better."

"I have a great idea! Let's throw a New Year's party. We can invite other realmers and you can socialize with them here. That way you don't even have to leave the apartment."

I tried not to get irritated. I knew she was only trying to help. I tried to push the hurt away of losing Grams and not having her around for Christmas, but it was so hard. She loved the classic Christmas; a large tree, a lot of food, and gifts early in the morning. She also liked to sing Christmas carols.

"If we must, you're doing all the planning and inviting though", I said a little more rudely than I meant to.

"Great, do you want Alexa to come? I can make sure everyone else that comes is on their best behavior." She ignored my harsh tone.

"Sure, just warn her that people from our world will be there."

"Will do, I will take care of the food, decorations, everything. All you have to do is show up."

"Deal".

She was a lot happier then. That made me feel a little better. I didn't have to do anything at all. The food, drinks, music, decorations, and invitations were all done by her and Alexa. She even got me a dress to wear. It was a short sleeve black dress that came down to my knees. I wore it with black ankle boots.

The party started at ten. Elias was one of the first ones to arrive. I recognized him instantly. This time I could see him for what he really was. He was a gorgon with black eyes and snakes for hair. Looking at him didn't turn me to stone. "They can turn you to stone if they choose to, but you don't become stone by simply looking at them", Lavy explained. "Good to know." I avoided him, it was still weird he knew what I was going to be before I did.

Boston came. Of course, he came mostly for Lavy. It was sort of a date for them. I didn't want them together. I didn't think they would work. He was fine for doing blood orders, but I had an uneasy feeling about him. I still thought he was shady, but it's possible it was just me.

A few more people showed up. I didn't know any of the new-comers. There were a few fairies, vampires, shifters, and witches, like the first time I went to the Grimm. I was disappointed there weren't any trolls, goblins, leprechauns or mermaids present. Those were a few creatures I wanted to see more of. Mermaids didn't always have fins and gills. They could transform themselves into appearing like humans if they chose to, but only for a day or so. Leprechauns weren't the guys in green plaid that brought you a pot of gold if you found them at the end of a rainbow. In the book I read about them, they were barely four inches tall and they granted wishes to the deserving.

I noticed the vampires who came to the party had yellowish-green eyes instead of blue.

I didn't notice that the first time I saw more of my species, and Boston hadn't shown me his vampire eye yet. Yellow-green was the color they were supposed to be according to the journal Lavy gave me. I didn't say anything to anyone. I figured no one would notice mine if they appeared. I didn't understand why I didn't notice before when I went to the Grimm for the first time. I supposed it was because it was all new to me, and I wasn't focusing on people; more like taking everything in.

The witches were the same. They appeared completely human. You only could tell if they were a witch because of the energy you felt from them sometimes not even then if they could cloak themselves. I could tell who the shifters were because of the way they smelled. They didn't smell bad. It was a forest type scent.

The fairies were pretty obvious: beautiful men and women with pointed ears and shimmery colored skin. Lavy stood out from all of the fairies. She was the most beautiful one. I have gotten used to her not looking like a human. She always had the pointed ears, shimmering orange and purple tints to her skin and her eyes were always bright. It was amazing how the human world didn't see what I did. At the same time, it was nice to have a secret that not everyone knew about.

Around eleven-thirty, Falcon showed up. Right before he arrived, Trevor came by for Alexa. She invited him but didn't tell him about our special guest. He would only be at the party a little after midnight. I was sure he would be safe. Everyone promised they would be good. They knew humans were present. The part about Alexa knowing the truth was left out, though, no one needed to know that.

Alexa and Trevor stayed close to the front door talking among themselves. Falcon followed me to my room. There weren't any walls, so we weren't entirely alone. I didn't want to be alone with him anyway. Ever since the date comment and Grams funeral, I felt a little awkward around him. I didn't want any boy drama. I was still trying to figure out the whole Shadow Realm world and being a vampire thing. I was getting used to the idea more, but I still woke up surprised at what I was and what I could do.

"Hello, I haven't seen much of you lately."

"You saw me at Christmas", I said smiling shyly.

"That is true, but it was only for a few minutes. I feel like your avoiding me, but I can't figure out why."

"I'm not avoiding you. I have been busy lately. The whole Grams dying, the funeral, dropping out of school, getting emancipated, and working. A girl stays busy."

"I am still sorry for your loss. I'm sure it still hurts. However, the rest of it was over weeks ago. Did I do something wrong?" he asked sounding a little hurt.

"No, it's not you. I have been in a funk lately. I still feel like all this is new to me and it scares me. I don't know everything I should know about our world or what I am exactly. I... I also feel some... something that I shouldn't."

"Feel what?"

The party started to count down then for the New Year. Ten, nine, eight, seven. They kept going. I was looking at Falcon when the counting started. I turned away, grateful that we were interrupted. Everyone screamed, "Happy New Year!" Falcon turned my face toward his and kissed me. The kiss was warm and soft. I felt a shock of electricity when he kissed me. "Happy New Year", he said, sounding out of breath.

He left right after that. The party continued on for another couple of hours. I was too occupied with my thoughts to continue to be social. All I was thinking about was what does the kiss mean? Why did he run away? Did he regret what he did? I hoped he didn't regret it. I didn't. It felt great, it felt right. Nick kissing me never felt like that.

A week had passed since I had last seen Falcon. It was hard not to think about him. He hadn't even called or sent me a text message. I didn't want to be one of those girls who waited around for a guy. I was better than that. I had more self-esteem than that. I was actually starting to get irritated at him. It was rude to ignore someone. It was fine if he wasn't interested. I thought it had to do with my age. I needed to focus on something else and not him.

The self-defense classes were exactly what I needed. I was already in my second class feeling pretty good. The first time I went it was more of an introduction to the teacher and everyone getting to know one another. The class was filled with only humans. There were more men there than women, which was a surprise. I knew I was being prejudiced thinking only women needed to protect themselves.

During the second class, we were working in pairs. One of us was the attacker, and the other was the victim. Then we would switch. We learned the basics. First thing was to yell "Back Off", and push back at your attacker. I felt silly yelling at someone who didn't deserve it, but I got over it quickly, because I was learning how to protect myself, without revealing what I was. The next thing was to stomp on the attacker's foot, turn around if you could and punch them in the nose or kick them in the knee. Whomever the attacker was at the time during class had protective gear on, so they wouldn't get hurt. We took turns in fifteen-minute increments. The class was an hour long, roughly. At first, it seemed like a long time, but it went by quickly.

When class was over, everyone said goodbye to each other and to the teacher. I was one of the last ones out, because I wanted to change out of my sweaty clothes, but didn't want to change in front of other people in the women's locker room. I didn't want anyone seeing my tattoo. Plus, I was a private person. I didn't want any stranger seeing me naked or close to it.

When I left the teacher and my partner that evening were talking. I left without saying anything. I didn't want to be rude and interrupt them. I started to walk to my car that was a block down from the gym. As I was walking, I felt a strange presence following me. When I turned around nothing was there. I started walking again, but the uneasy feeling of someone following me became stronger. I tried not to get alarmed. I was trying to convince myself it was probably nothing.

"Hello, there little girl. You smell nice", I heard from behind me. I looked behind me and there was a man there. At least I thought it was a man. He was tall, maybe a little over six foot. His skin was blood red, and his hair was black and spiked. He had yellow eyes the color of lemons. I turned back around and started walking faster to my car.

"Come on little lady. Don't be like that. I only want to talk to you, and to get to know you a little bit."

Feeling curious as to what he was, I stopped and turned around slowly. "What is it that you want?"

"I am trying to figure out what you are, baby. I can feel your magic and it's strong. I have never smelled anything like you before; not in my four thousand years of being in this world..."

"I'm a vampire. I thought that was pretty obvious", I snapped, annoyed. I felt myself change to show my vampire features, my fangs were showing and knew my eyes were glowing a little.

"No baby, you are something else entirely", he said smirking.

He was getting closer to me as he talked. The closer he got, the more I felt a pull towards him. He started to transform himself into a human: a cute human, who was tanned, had blonde curly hair, and blue eyes. He kept flickering back from his red self to his human self.

"What are you?" I asked, feeling dazed. I could tell he was working some type of magic on me. He was trying to get close to me, but I wasn't exactly sure what he was planning to do.

"The man of your dreams little lady." He was only a few inches away from me then. Once he stopped right in front of me, I felt paralyzed. My mind told me he was evil, but my body wouldn't listen or move. He put his hands on my shoulders to hold me in place. He stared at me. I felt him trying to control what I was thinking. I fought it as best as I could, but it was no use. After he knew I couldn't move at all, he opened his mouth, and inside were two rows of silver razor sharp teeth. The teeth were circling his entire mouth and in the back of his throat was a circular slimy black tentacle, that had saliva dripping from it. It was coming out of his mouth towards me.

I tried to step back, but I was still stuck. Starting to panic, I forced myself to relax. I was strong, and I could fight whatever this thing was. I concentrated on making myself move. I looked deep within myself and felt the energy coming forward. It wasn't like what I felt before. This energy was stronger. My body started to feel electrified. The thing in front of me noticed something was up too. The disgusting tentacle thing drew back into his mouth. He took a step back slowly from me. His eyes were looking at me questionably. I was angry. I didn't know what he was trying to do to me, but it wasn't sanitary.

I felt my hands lift up toward him. A jolt of power pushed toward him. I didn't see anything come out of my hands, I only felt the power. He fell to the ground, shriveled up, and then disappeared. Before he disappeared completely, he released a foul smell. It was like a rotten animal corpse that had gotten ran over a few times.

No one was around when it happened. It felt like it lasted hours, but it was only a couple of minutes. I was glad it was late at night. It was also in the middle of the week, and most people were at home getting ready for work or school. When I went to look at where the creature had been, nothing was there, no trace of him.

I ran to my car as fast as humanly possible and went straight home. I went over the speed limit. I was in a hurry. I didn't get pulled over by a police officer, thankfully. Not that it would have mattered really, I could have compelled them to let me go.

As soon as I was safely in my apartment. I brushed my teeth and gargled a lot of mouthwash; then, took a shower. After what seemed like an hour in the shower, I got out and put on fresh clothes. I went to my Supernatural Mythology book. I didn't remember seeing that red thing in it before. I was sure I hadn't missed anything but wanted to double check. My mind had changed some, but losing my photographic memory wasn't one of them. I was right. It wasn't in the book. I knew that every supernatural or mythical creature being in this book was a long shot. Only the most common creatures were. I needed something that explained the not so common creatures.

Also, why do people from the Shadow Realm keep telling me about myself? First, Elias told me I was one of them. He was surprised I didn't know. Now this creepy demon looking thing said I was more than a vampire. "More than a vampire, what does that mean"? I asked out loud. Not that anyone would answer me. Lavy was out on a date with Boston. I didn't want to influence her judgment about him, so I kept my opinions about him to myself. There was probably more to him than meets the eye.

"More than a vampire, probably means your special or something", said a small little squeaky voice.

"Who said that?" I asked, looking around. The apartment was empty. I was sure I would have heard someone come in.

"No one else is here girly, only you and me".

"Who is there? Are you a ghost or spirit?"

I heard a small chuckle, "Of course not silly."

"Then who are you? Where are you?" I asked as I continued to look around my room and downstairs to the rest of the apartment.

"I am sitting on your dresser in the glass box."

I walked over to my dresser, I saw only Legs. "I only see my tarantula."

"For someone who is supposed to notice things you're being clueless right now. Look down. Do you see me looking up at you?"

"Legs?" I asked a little stunned.

"Bingo sugar plum".

"How are you talking to me?"

"I'm using English words to communicate with you."

"I got that, but how? You're not supposed to be able to talk. I shouldn't be able to understand you."

"You are a vampire with special powers. Your eyes glow blue, which isn't normal for a vampire, not to mention all the crazy stuff you have seen since your transformation; and yet you question how I can talk to you?"

"Good point, but I think this is the strangest."

"If you say so."

"I do. Why haven't you talked to me before? Can all vampires talk to animals?"

"No vampires cannot talk to animals. You are different! Only witches can talk to their animals. They are called their familiars."

"Oh, then shouldn't you be a black cat?"

"That is a dumb stereotype. We come in all forms."

"Wait, I am not a witch. I am a vampire."

"You are both! Your magic just took a little longer than normal to show itself to you."

"I am a vampire and a witch? How is that possible?

"You are a hybrid Jade, you are one of a kind. You're stronger than a normal creature from the Shadow Realm."

"How do you know this about me? How do you know about the Shadow Realm?"

"I am over a thousand years old. The Shadow World is where I came from too. I have been waiting for you for centuries. I have learned a lot during that time about different species. I may be small, but I am quite intelligent"

"How have you lived so long?"

"Magic."

"This is crazy!"

"Really? You have known something is different about you since you turned. You have felt it, even before you turned. You saw glimmers of our world. You are the one who chose to ignore them."

Legs was right. I saw the warnings. I didn't think it was real. I thought I was crazy, but I wasn't. I knew I was special. I couldn't fight it any longer. I knew without a doubt, I was a hybrid and that scared me.

Chapter Thirteen

I laid in bed all night thinking about being a hybrid and about the fact that Legs could talk. I was afraid. I didn't know what that meant about me. I hadn't been at this whole supernatural thing long, but nothing has ever been mentioned about a mixture of species. I was worried I was a freak of nature, more than I thought I already was. I wasn't sure if there was anyone else like me in the world. I knew I needed to talk to Lavy, but wasn't sure how to bring it up. I was scared she would reject me. The only way to find out was to talk to her, even if it was going to be hard.

I had to wait for her to wake up. She didn't get back until really late from her date with Boston. She seemed happy and to really like him. It's possible I misjudged him. The shop wasn't due to open for a couple more hours, so I let her sleep.

I needed something to do to keep my mind busy. Reading wasn't an option because that would require me to think. The apartment was clean, I never cooked, and all my laundry was caught up. I decided to do something I was dreading, but I was tired of waiting for him to come around.

I sent Falcon a text. "Hi". I know it wasn't epic, but I had to start somewhere. He didn't reply back immediately. I was scared he was ignoring me. I didn't know why I cared so much. Maybe it was because he was one of the few people I knew who understood what I was going through, and who had been through it more recently. I was also slightly attracted to him. Ugh, I was such a girl.

"Hi". That was all he sent me. I had to remind myself that was all I sent him.

"How are ya?"

"Fine, you?"

"Um, good. Haven't heard from you in a while. We ok?"

"Yeah, why wouldn't we be?"

"Idk, thought you may have been mad at me or something."

"You didn't do anything to make me mad."

"That's good... so you're not avoiding me?"

"Nope, just been busy lately."

"Think maybe, we can hang out this week?"

He didn't respond for twenty minutes. I was starting to get worried. I wasn't sure what I did wrong. I wasn't rude or anything. I was curious to see why he hadn't talked to me lately. I thought he liked me. Why else would he have brought me food that morning, went to Grams funeral, and been a friend to me instantly? Also, why did he kiss me, why did it feel the way it had? Maybe it was that New Year's thing, to kiss someone at midnight. I hated feeling confused about a guy. The whole teenager thing was complicated.

"Sure, Sunday will work. I would like to go for a drive. I want to show you something."

"Great, what do you want to show me?."

"It's a surprise."

Sunday wasn't that far away. Maybe I would get some answers then. I had to keep my mind occupied, otherwise, I would stress over our time together. It was never this way with Nick. He was always upfront with his feelings. Although, that could have been an act. Why did I have to have issues with guys? Alexa had a great relationship with Trevor, so did Stefanie and Corey. I hoped I wasn't destined to have trouble with guys for the rest of my life. I had enough to deal with.

I decided to get some food. I went down to the kitchen and got a toaster pastry. I loved the unfrosted strawberry kind. I also got some milk that I stuck in the freezer for a couple of minutes for it to get colder. I loved it when it was close to frozen. I sat at the bar in the dark and ate. My vision was slowly getting better in darkness. Of course, it was always better after I drank blood. After I was finished eating, I was still hungry. I was finally full after I ate two muffins, a cereal bar, and a large bowl of cereal. I figured I was stress eating. Oh well, it all tasted good.

I was starting to get impatient waiting on Lavy, but I didn't want to wake her up until the alarm went off. Since I was still in my head stressing over things I couldn't do anything about, I decided to go for a walk. I changed into some sweat pants and t-shirt, grabbed my phone and headphones, and left the house to go walking. The sun was high in the sky. There was a chill in the air, not that it bothered me. It felt great against my skin. I have been warmer since the transformation. I ran hotter most of the time like I was my own heater. I liked it, I didn't have to bundle up like I did when I was human.

I walked down to the Pocket park. It looked the same, except the flowers were dead. I knew they would come back when it was spring-time though. The park made me feel safe. I walked through the gate and felt at home like I always did. I took the view in, the paintings, the stage, the tables, the door at the end, and the two windows. I looked back over to the door at the end. It had faint swirling yellow lines in the doorway, which weren't there before. The swirls were so faint that they were almost invisible.

I walked over to the doorway. I didn't want to go through it because I felt the power. There was energy bursting through that felt like it was pulling me toward it. It was similar to what I felt in my dream about Jewel. It was a portal of some kind. It wasn't the same kind that was in the fairy land. This one didn't feel cold. It felt welcoming. This was something else I wanted answers to. Where did it go? Was it safe? Had it always been here? I examined it a little while longer before leaving. The energy's strength never changed and neither did the colors of the portal.

When I got back home Lavy was awake and ready to go to the Wicca shop. She was at the breakfast bar eating eggs and some fruit.

"Hey, where have you been?"

"Needed to go for a walk, couldn't sleep. Needed to clear my head."

"Okay, I got worried."

"Sorry to worry you. I only meant to be gone for a few minutes. Next time I'll leave a note."

"Thanks. Everything alright?"

"Yes and no. Let me take a quick shower then we can talk. Okay?"

"Sure, no problem", she said. She looked a little more worried than when I came home. Next time I wouldn't mention I needed to talk to her about something, then go do something else first. I didn't like it when people did that to me.

I took a shower as quickly as I could, got dressed, and looked in the mirror. The reflection of myself stared back at me. I didn't look any different, but I felt different since last night. I felt the power coursing through my veins. Not just the enhanced hearing, vision, or strength. I felt power deep inside me. My whole body was vibrating with energy like something had been awakened in me. I felt hyped up like I had been shocked by an electric current.

I had to figure out how to explain what I was feeling to Lavy. She was awake and she knew I needed to talk. I needed to be a big girl and face my fears. I could handle this. It probably wasn't even that big of a deal. I was sure I couldn't be the only hybrid around. They may not have been very common, but surely they existed. Right?

I walked with Lavy to the shop. I didn't say much on the way. I was trying to gather my thoughts, and figure out the best way to say it. I finally decided to just say it. Whatever happened, it would be alright. We walked into the shop, after she unlocked the door, turned on the lights, and made sure everything looked cleaned and organized. She then turned the closed sign on the front door over to show we were open.

After getting up my nerve, I blurted it out.

"Lavy, I'm a hybrid. Legs told me so last night. She said she is my familiar and I am a half witch. I think she may be right. I feel this power coursing through my body like an electrical current. Also, I think I killed something last night. I am not sure what it was. It was a man, he had red skin and strange eyes. He kept flickering back and forth from his red self to a beautiful man. When he got close I felt like I couldn't move. He also had this gross black tentacle thing come out of his mouth. I got scared and felt a rush of energy come out of me. He was pushed back and then he disappeared, like poof."

"What?" she asked looking at me wide-eyed.

"Do I need to repeat it all again? It was hard enough to get all of that out the first time. The way you're looking at me now, I don't think I should have told you anything."

"No, no your fine. Give me a minute."

"Um, okay."

"First, you were attacked last night by some creature? Are you alright? I know you're alive but are you okay?"

"I think so for the most part. Do you know what it was?"

"Yes, I am surprised you're alive, to be honest. The fact that you killed it is amazing. Even people who have been trained have had trouble killing them."

"Okay, what is it?"

"It's called an Incubus. They are half-demon and half human. Those are the male gender of the species. They are attracted to creatures with a lot of power and um, virgins. They suck their life force out. It is what you think of as a soul"

"Half demon and half human? Wow. So they are like hybrids? What is the female gender of them called?"

"No I wouldn't call them a hybrid exactly, they are a mixed breed but they are more demon than human. The female version is called a Succubus. They do the same thing as the males, but they are better at it, from what I'm told."

"Crazy, so a human actually mates with a demon willingly?"

"Not exactly, some do, but demons can take on human form and others take the human forcefully. The mother who gives birth rarely survives. If she does survive, she often goes insane. Males who mate with demons, tend to die after mating."

"Is there more than one type of demon?"

"Yes, but they produce the same form of mixed breed. The stronger the demon, the stronger its offspring."

"Crazy." Not only are there vampires, shapeshifters, witches, and everything else. There are also demons now. "Are there angels too?" I had to ask. It was about time I figure out what really existed.

"Yes, there are angels. They sometimes mate with humans as well, although it's not very often. The female version we call Seraphs and the male version we call Cherubs. They are mainly known as Nephilim."

"Wow! I don't know what else to say, but wow!"

"Legs talked to you? How?"

"Um, yeah. After the incident with that Incubus, I came home freaking out, and she spoke to me. She told me I was a witch, well half of one, and that she is my familiar."

"Wow!"

"Yeah, I know. She told me I was a hybrid. That my power had taken a while to surface itself. That is why she hasn't talked to me before. Is it possible? Do hybrids exist in our world?"

"Not that I know of. There hasn't been any in thousands of years. Supernaturals can't mix. That is why most of us don't care for birth control."

"Can't mix? So a vampire and a witch can't have a child or a witch and a fairy?"

"No, it's unheard of. Hybrids are more of myth or legend in our world. It is something in our genetics. We can't mix with other species. We can only mix with humans, and, of course, our own race."

"Why only with humans?" I was really interested in this. What was so different about humans than us?"

"Humans don't have magic in their blood, they are bland. Everyone from the Shadow Realm has some sort of magical blood. They may not all have the same power, but we all have some sort of ability or abilities."

"Do the half-humans ever go through a transition?"

"Yes, but they don't until they turn twenty. They also don't live as long as we do. Pure breeds can live for several thousands of years. We only know we are close to death when we age drastically. In our final year, we look to be in our eighties or nineties if we were human. Mixed breeds live a quarter of that if they are lucky. They also don't have the full strength or power as that of pure breeds."

"So a human can mix with anything: a vampire, shapeshifter, fairy, witch, and they will eventually get some type of power or ability? Falcon told me about the age thing. Which is crazy."

"Yes, after the transition, if they survive, they will get some type of ability. We all look human until our transition. The most popular mixed breed with humans is a vampire. We call them guardians. They have close to the same strength as a vampire, but don't have issues with sunlight and don't need blood. They can't compel anyone, and they don't have half the speed as that of a vampire does "

"To make sure I am understanding clearly, we all look human until our transition, then we look like whatever our parents do, even the half-breeds? Pure breeds can also live thousands of years, but half-breeds not as long?"

"Yes."

"What happens if a half-breed mixes with a pure breed, will that child take after the pure breed parent?"

"Yes, it's hard to make sense of, but a half-breed can't pass on any magical traits of itself to the child. It can pass on appearances, but not abilities. Me, for example, my mother was a pure breed fairy, but my father was a guardian when I was conceived. I didn't get any abilities from him. I don't need blood and I am not super strong. I am pretty much pure fairy, except my wings aren't as big as hers."

"Your father was a guardian? Did something happen to him? You have wings?" This was a lot to process, but I wanted her to continue.

"He went through a ritual to become a full vampire. It was hard for him to do that, but he wanted full strength to find my mother's killer. He had to sacrifice something for him to become a pure breed. He also had to take on the thirst for blood, problems with the sun, and live longer than he expected."

"What kind of sacrifice? Why would living longer be an issue?"

"He can't have any more children. He said since my mom died, it wouldn't matter. He doesn't want to live forever. He wants to live and die like he was supposed to originally."

"I am sorry about your mother, how was she killed?" I felt bad for asking, but I wanted to know.

"She was stabbed in the chest, then her wings were ripped from her body", she said, as a tear was running down her face.

"That is awful, I am sorry. If I had known, I wouldn't have asked."

"No, it is good to ask questions. How else will you find out the answer? Back to your other question, yes I have wings. They are just hidden most of the time."

"Can I see them?"

She laughed at that. "Okay, now?"

"Sure, if you are up to showing me."

She went to the front door and locked it, turned the open sign to say closed, then walked to the back room. I followed her. I wanted to see them. Fairies actually had wings. She turned on the light, turned her back toward me, and then took off her shirt. Her back was just as beautiful as the rest of her. It shimmered with orange and purple tints. Slowly coming out from her back out of two slits were two wings. It took them a minute to come out, but when they did they were amazing. They were shorter than I would have imagined. They were transparent with specs of silver outlining them. They did look a lot like costume fairy wings.

"May I touch them?" I felt awkward as soon as I asked, but she didn't care.

"Sure".

I walked over to her and touched them. They were soft like smooth silk and warm.

"They are beautiful. Can you fly with them?"

"Thank you, and no I can't. Fairies aren't able to fly. That is a Hollywood made up thing. However, it would be neat if we could.

"Yes it would be and I remember you telling me fairies can't fly before."

Her wings slowly ascended back into her back. After a minute they were completely gone, and her back was smooth once again.

"Back to you, now. You said last night you felt an energy come from within you. Can you explain that again?"

"Alright. During the attack, I felt a rush of strong electric energy course through my body. It wasn't like what I felt when I run or compel people. This was different and stronger. I forced him away from me. I wanted him gone and he was. As soon as I thought it, it happened."

"Interesting."

"Interesting?"

"Yes, I have never known a vampire to experience anything like what you described."

"So, I am a freak of nature. Great!"

"No, I didn't say that. This is just unusual. It is fascinating though. You controlled the demon with your mind. I want to see if you can do anything else. I want to see if you can do what other witches can do. We will keep it small though."

"Um, okay. What do you have in mind?"

She thought for a moment. "Alright, be right back." She walked into the front room. When she came back she had a wicker basket full of feathers. She laid the basket on the floor across the room, then walked back over to me.

"I want you to make the feathers float in the air."

"Are you crazy?" I asked, knowing it wasn't going to work.

"No, this is something easy for a witch to do. All witches have some sort of telekinesis; some are stronger than others. I am wanting to see how strong you are."

"Okay, I'll try."

I looked at the basket, nothing happened.

"You look like you're trying too hard. Don't force it, relax your mind. It will happen."

I tried again. This time I took her advice. I took a slow deep breath and cleared my mind. I saw in my mind the feathers float up one at a time. As I was thinking about it and looking at the basket it happened. One by one the feathers lifted into the air.

"That is incredible. You definitely have more powers than a normal vampire."

I looked at her and smiled. When I did all the feathers dropped to the floor. I lost my concentration and connection to them. Alright, I had to stay focused.

"That sucks, they fell."

"We can work on that. I want to try something else." This time she grabbed a candle from one of the boxes and placed it on the floor.

"You want me to make the candle float?"

"I want you to light the candlewick with a flame."

"I don't think it will work, but I will try."

I cleared my mind again and concentrated on fire. Nothing happened still. I was starting to get annoyed. I couldn't do this. Maybe I had powers, but they weren't very good.

"You can do this, stop trying to discourage yourself."

I tried again. Still, nothing happened. "Focus Jade! You got this!" I screamed at myself.

After trying a few times, I saw a small spark. That gave me hope. I started a chant in my head. "Fire show me a flame, fire show me a flame, fire show me flame." The wick lit up with a small flame.

"I did it, oh my gosh, I did it!"

"Yes you did, that is amazing". Jade, I do believe you have witch blood in you. I wonder why it took so long to surface."

"Please don't tell anyone. I want to figure out what this means. I want to see if we can learn why I have these abilities if hybrids aren't supposed to exist."

"I will not tell anyone, I promise. We can be discreet."

"There is more I need to tell you. First, I have been having dreams, strange ones. They started before I turned into whatever I am. Some of the dreams were about a fairy warrior who was a healer. Others were about a shapeshifter who changed into a falcon."

"A fairy warrior?"

"Yes, she was beautiful. She had hair that was close to black, green eyes, and a mark on her arm. It was similar to the one I have."

"What mark?"

It was my turn to turn around and show her my back. I took my shirt off and heard her gasp. "It showed up after the transformation, it wasn't there before. In my dreams, the fairy had one like mine, but with one star and the shapeshifter had two stars."

"What were their names? What was the fairy's name?"

"The fairy was called Jewel and the shifter was called Jahana. I haven't had many dreams about either. Jewel, the fairy was dancing around a fire with people of her tribe, then she was saying goodbye to what I assumed was her husband and child. Jahana I saw turn into a falcon, then she was murdered by her people. That is all I remember."

I put my shirt back on and turned toward Lavy to see her back up against the wall and slide down the wall. She started to cry, tears quietly running down her face.

"What is wrong? Did I say something wrong? I am sorry if I did, you asked and I wanted to answer honestly."

She looked up at me, her eyes shiny with the tears. "Jewel was my mother."

Chapter Fourteen

I was dreaming about Lavy's mom. How was that possible; why me? Why did we have similar marks? Why didn't I realize that Lavy was Lavender before? I guess because she didn't look like she did when she was a child, except for the eyes. She was human then. She also didn't look like her mom or dad. Maybe a mixture of the two. She was taller than her mother was but lighter than her dad. I couldn't beat myself up over it. There was no way for me to know.

"Your mother?" I asked, still in shock.

"Yes, you were dreaming about my family. My name is Lavender, but I go by Lavy. I have for centuries now. My mom used to call me her little fairy girl. I don't remember her well because I was really young when she died. My father used to talk to me about her all the time;

including about that special mark before I decided I needed to be on my own."

"I had no idea who you were. I'm sorry. I never thought Lavy was a nickname. I never thought you were the small child in my dreams. From dreaming about your mother, I could tell she loved you and your father deeply. She was incredibly strong, brave, and had a huge heart.

"That is what my father said. He remembers everything about her: the way she looked, smelled, her laugh, everything. He has never gotten over her, and I don't think he ever will."

"I am sure, from what I have seen, they were in love. They were soul mates. You could feel their strong connection. It was an intense bond. Lavy, she loved you so much too. When she had to leave you, it broke her heart. She didn't have a choice. She had to leave and be strong for her people in the war. She knew your father would protect and love you no matter what."

"Yes, my father was great. My mom was gone for close to a year before we heard of her passing. I was too young to understand. He simply told me that she wasn't coming back anymore. He said she was in a better place un-

.

til he finally revealed the truth when I was older."

I went over to where she was, sat beside her and held her hand. She laid her head on my shoulder and cried. I know I didn't tell her anything new, but it was the shock that someone new in her life, had dreams of someone she lost so long ago. I was sure, she would have given anything to see her mother one last time. I know I would have. I missed my family so much that it hurt, physically. She cried for a long time and I let her. I felt her release the pain she had been holding on to for so long. She never got to say goodbye or to really cry over the loss of her mother.

When she finished, she went to the bathroom and shut the door behind her. She emerged a few minutes later with a freshly washed face and semi happier mood.

"Sorry for that."

"Don't be, sometimes you have to let it out, to feel better."

She opened the store back up. I swept the floor, even though it didn't need it. She looked over our inventory and made a list of what to order. It was quiet for a while. Not really an awkward quiet; just a quiet where we were in our own thoughts.

"I'll ask around about hybrids. I won't mention you at all. I want to know what's going on", she said as she broke the silence.

"Thanks, I want to know, as well. I feel like I'm a big mystery; even more than I thought before. I don't like, not having answers to questions I have."

"I am the same way, I like to know things. No more secrets, please. I understand you didn't show me the mark before because you wanted to make sure you could trust me. Please know I will never do anything to hurt you, I promise. I feel protective of you."

"I feel the same. You're family to me."

She smiled at that. "Thanks."

I nodded and smiled back. The day went kind of fast after that. We got a few customers; one or two were regulars. The rest were tourists. The whole tourist thing was weird. I liked my city for the most part, but I didn't understand why people wanted to come here, except maybe the whole twin-city thing. You could go to our post office and stand in the middle: have one foot in Arkansas, and the other in Texas and be in two places at once. I have to admit, I liked it too when I first got here, but it got old fast.

I was still stressing over Falcon when I left the shop. Something still felt off about him. I really needed another girl to talk to about him. That is when I thought about having a girl's night with Alexa. It had been awhile since it was just the two of us. Lavy was leaving for the weekend to go spend time with her father. She made the plans after I told her about my dream. She hadn't seen him in a while and wanted to fix that.

I sent Alexa a message to see if she was up to spending the weekend with me.

"Need a girl's weekend, boy trouble, need my bestie... you interested?"

"This coming up weekend?"

"Yeah, that k, was thinking Fri & Sat?"

"Sure, I have nothing to do. Please have snacks and movies."

"Of course! What ya want?"

"I want nacho cheese chips, salsa, varieties of chocolate candy, and caffeine."

"Can do! Chunky or normal?"

"Chunky please, love the peppers; also, extra butter popcorn."

"Added to the list. Movie sug?"

"You choose. Wait, scratch that. I want horror movies, something good. Get Amityville, the original one."

"Ah, you and ghost movies."

"I love them, you know that. What boy trouble?"

"Blah, I'll tell you Fri."

"Fine!"

"You can wait... hehe."

"I guess I have to. Got to do homework. Will talk to you later."

"Bye."

I didn't miss that at all; having to do homework. I was still thinking about taking some college courses online but wasn't sure what. I had a lot of interests, but wasn't sure what I wanted to do, professionally. I have always wanted to work with animals or maybe photography. If reading could be a profession, I would do that. I decided to worry about it later. I was still only sixteen and had time to figure out what I wanted to do for a living.

The week passed by, and nothing special happened. Lavy hadn't been able to talk to anyone yet about my powers. She was planning on asking her father since he had been around longer then she had; there was also the fact that she trusted him more than anyone.

Falcon didn't talk to me unless I talked to him. It was mostly a lot of "Hi" and "How are you?" I felt stupid still, feeling crazy over a boy. I really liked him though; more than other boys I had crushes on in the past. Hopefully, I would get answers from him Sunday.

It was finally Friday. I had all the snacks and movies that were requested plus some. We were going to have the apartment to ourselves, so we could be as messy and loud as we wanted. I could pretend to be a normal teenage girl for a few hours. I had drunk the blood I needed the night before so I would be on my best behavior and wouldn't have to drink any in front of Alexa.

She was used to what I was, but it didn't mean I had to flaunt it. I hadn't told her about the special powers yet. I wasn't planning on it until I figured out what they meant. This week-end was supposed to be just normal fun: scary movies, junk food, gossiping about boys and getting some advice I felt I needed.

I heard Alexa walk to the door before I smelt her vanilla body spray. I could tell she was excited about our weekend. It made me feel good. I opened the door before she could knock.

"Hello!"

"Were you standing at the door waiting for me?"

"No, I heard you walking to the door from the street."

"Right, the vampire hearing."

I winked at her. "Sorry, can't control it."

She laughed. "No worries."

"Come in. I got snacks galore, the movie you wanted and one I wanted, along with a couple of others. Thought we could order takeout later?"

"Sounds good. Now spill, what boy trouble?"

"Drop your stuff off in my room. Then we can talk."

"How about you take my stuff to your room. You're the one with vamp speed. I want to know what the boy drama is. It has been driving me crazy all week. I have a feeling I know who it's about though."

Before she finished the sentence, her stuff was already in my room. I was sitting on the couch waiting for her when she finished. She walked over to me, looking amused, and sat down beside me.

"Alright, it's about Falcon."

"Figured so, spill."

"We have been talking to each other some, ever since I changed. At the New Year's party a couple weeks ago he kissed me. The kiss was amazing! He kissed me really, but I kissed him back. As soon as it was over he left without saying anything. He practically ran away from me. He didn't talk to me for the first week. I got annoyed, so I sent him a text. We made plans for Sunday, but we haven't talked much since."

"Hmm, okay. I think he likes you, but he may be scared you don't like him. It is also possible he is playing hard to get."

"Boys! That aggravates me. I like him. I know I shouldn't because I don't know him that well, but I do. Also is it too soon to want to be with someone? Nick didn't die that long ago."

"Forget Nick! What he did to you was wrong. You deserve to be happy, especially with everything you have been through."

"That makes me feel better. I know Nick did something horrible to me, but I am afraid of how it will look. I don't want to jump from one guy to the other."

"Since when do you care what people think?"

"Good point. Maybe I am worried that I am overthinking the kiss with Falcon, and he really doesn't like me that way."

"I don't think he would have kissed you if he didn't."

"It was at midnight, so maybe he felt obligated."

"I see the way he looks at you, I think there is something there."

"Maybe. I just have to wait I guess. I hate second guessing myself and stressing over this. It was easy with Nick, even if it was a fake relationship. He made it easy."

"Not every relationship will be the same. That is a good thing. I am sure of it."

"You have a great relationship with Trevor. I'm a little jealous."

"We have our ups and downs like all couples. We communicate so that helps."

"True, blah. Okay enough talk about my guy trouble for now. Anything new happening?"

"I am in charge of the prom committee."

"Wow, how did that happen?"

"I am the only one who signed up."

"That's funny. Still congratulations. At least this way you get to go before you're a junior or senior."

"I know, I am excited. I am forcing Trevor to go with me. He isn't happy about it, but he knows it is important to me. I also have pull for you to come and bring a date."

"Um, I am not much of a dancer. You know that."

"Yes I know, but it will be a lot of fun. You can even bring Falcon."

"Ah, I don't know."

"It's not until March. We are having it early this year, but it's still a ways off. Think about it please."

"I'll think about it, but don't get your hopes up. Do you have a set date?"

"I was thinking March 26th. It is a few days before my birthday; figured it could be fun."

"Alright, since it's so close to your birthday, I'll come. I swear you thought of that on purpose, just so I would come."

"You know me so well. I don't want to go to my first prom without you."

"Let's hope I have a date. If not I'll have to be the third wheel", I said sticking my tongue out at her playfully.

She threw a couch pillow at me. "I'm sure you will have a date, crazy. I don't think any boy could resist the girl next door look."

I blushed at that. The only boy I wanted didn't seem to want me. "Jade stop thinking like that", I yelled at myself.

We stopped talking for a little while, so we could watch a movie and munch on sugary goodness. By the time we were finished with the remake of Carrie, we were starving for actual food. I ordered a couple of pizzas and chicken wings. When the food arrived we dug in. I ate the thin crust pepperoni and she ate her pan supreme. I didn't see how she ate that; too many toppings to me.

When we were full, we watched another movie, trying to get our stomachs to stop hurting. Of course, we over-ate, we always did on nights like this. I started to feel restless before the third movie was over.

Alexa could sense it or maybe she was feeling the same way. She paused the movie and looked over at me.

"Want to go out? It's Friday and it's not that late", she asked.

"Sure, I am feeling cramped in here. What do you have in mind?"

"We just watched almost three movies, so that is out. Want to go to the mall?"

"Really?" She could tell that was a no, by the way, I was looking at her.

"Okay... Okay... no mall. How about bowling? We haven't been in a while."

"Sure, let's go. That actually sounds fun."

We put on shoes, brushed our teeth and hair, and then headed to my car. There weren't many vehicles in the parking lot. I was relieved. We walked to the counter and picked up some bowling shoes and were given the ticket for lane 7. The overhead lights were off in the bowling area. In their place were neon lights at the end of the alleys, a few strobe lights by the computers where you kept track of your score, and long black lights on the ceiling.

I was wearing all black, so I didn't light up like Alexa did. She had on light jeans and a white sweater. We picked out our bowling balls. I got blue and she got pink. It took us a few minutes to find the right weight and fit we wanted.

I let her go first. She had always been a better bowler than me. I could have cheated and used my new abilities to win, but I didn't like cheating of any kind. She kept getting strike after strike. I was lucky to get a few pins down, but it was still fun.

Alexa won the first game. That wasn't a surprise. Before we started the second round, I offered to get us some drinks. She looked sweaty and was starting to get red in the checks.

"Water would be great, thanks."

"Sure thing, want anything else?"

"No, just water. I had plenty to eat earlier."

"Alright, I'm hungry again. Some nachos sound good to me."

"You and your appetite. It is amazing how much you can eat."

"Hey, it's healthy! A girl has got to eat."

She laughed at that, as I was walking away. I walked up to the counter, looking at the menu on the wall when someone walked up behind me. I would recognize his scent anywhere."

"Hello", I heard from behind me.

I turned around slowly, trying to keep my face neutral. I was right it was him, but he wasn't alone. A little girl was with him, she looked a lot like him, but she was probably ten or eleven.

"Hi, to both of you", I said smiling.

"How have you been?"

"Good, what about you?"

"Good."

"Who is this?" I asked while nodding my head to the girl.

"Oh, this is Rayvn, my sister."

"Hello, Rayvn. It's nice to meet you. My name is Jade."

She smiled up at me then. "So you're Jade. My brother has been talking about you a lot", she said bright-eyed.

"Rayvn!" he said while blushing.

I smiled at her. "Has he now?"

"Yes."

"Hopefully, only good things", I said, and winked at him.

"Did you just get here?" he asked.

"No, Alexa and I have been here for an hour, maybe. I came up here to get snacks. What about you two?"

"We just got here. He is treating me to a fun night. I passed my math test today."

"Wow! That is great. Math can be hard. Would you two like to join us? We have played one game, but I am sure Alexa wouldn't mind."

"Yes!" Rayvn exclaimed.

"Great, do you mind Falcon?"

"No, if that is what my sister wants, that is fine."

"Want something to eat or drink? My treat."

Rayvn looked up at her brother. He nodded at her, letting her know it was fine.

"Can I have a slushy and nachos, please"?

"Yes, I was wanting the same thing. What flavor do you want?"

"The green kind, please."

"Falcon want anything?"

"I'm fine, thanks."

I turned back toward the man behind the counter. "May I have a green and blue slushy, two water's, two nachos, two fries, and two hot dogs please?"

"Coming right up."

The food was on two trays. Falcon grabbed one, and I grabbed the other. We made our way back to where Alexa was. She looked at me and smiled for a split second.

"I was wondering what was taking you so long. I see why now, and who is this?" she asked while smiling at Rayvn.

Falcon spoke up, "This is my sister, Rayvn."

"Hello there, I'm Alexa. Are you joining us?"

"Yes, they are. Rayvn is celebrating tonight", I said.

"Oh, she is? What are you celebrating?"

"I passed my math test today, so I get to have a fun night", she said excitedly.

"That's great! I have problems with math, so I know it can be hard."

"Yes it is", Rayvn said smiling.

"Let's go get our balls, little sis."

They walked off to go get their bowling balls. I watched them as they did.

"He showed up? Did he know we were coming here?"

"I didn't tell him. I was surprised when I saw him."

"This is good. Maybe you can try to talk to him."

"Maybe."

We stopped talking. They were walking back then. We let Rayvn go first on the next round. She was good at this. Alexa had some competition. Rayvn and I ate while the others took their turns. I slid water and a hot dog over to Falcon. He didn't protest. I could hear his stomach growling before, but didn't push it.

We didn't talk much for the first two games. Both of us lost to Alexa and Rayvn. I didn't care. I wasn't expecting to win. I was having fun and so was everyone else. That is what mattered. Somehow, before the third round got started, we got left alone. Alexa took Rayvn to the arcade section to try to win a prize from the claw machine.

I felt him looking at me. I wanted to look up but fought that feeling.

"Hi", he said.

I looked up at him then. "Hi."

"This is quite a coincidence isn't it?"

"Seems that way, yes."

"How have you been?"

"Okay, I guess. You?"

"Same."

"That's good. Are we okay?"

"Yes, why?"

"I didn't want to get into it here, but you kissed me then left. I didn't hear from you for days. Did I do something wrong? It is fine if you don't like me like that, but you're my friend and I don't want to lose our friendship. I need friends right now, especially from our world."

"I'm sorry. You didn't do anything wrong."

"Then why did you run?"

"I... I got scared."

"Of what?"

"The way you make me feel."

"How do you feel?"

"I..."

Before he could say anything else Alexa and Rayvn were walking back to us. Rayvn had a bright green stuffed frog holding a flower in its hands.

"Look what Alexa won me."

We all smiled at her. She was too cute. We played one more game before we called it a night. It was getting late, so we said our good-byes to each other. I didn't look at Falcon, but I could feel him looking at me.

Alexa and I made it back to my place. We were exhausted by then. Who knew bowling could drain you of energy. We changed into night-clothes and crawled into bed. It didn't take us long to go to sleep, which was nice. The best thing was not having any dreams, or my brain running a mile a minute with thoughts of everything that was going on. I just had a dark deep sleep, exactly what I needed.

Chapter Fifteen

Alexa was awake before I was. I woke up to the smell of breakfast cooking. She loved to cook. I didn't mind because she was good at it. I could smell bacon, ham, biscuits, and scrambled eggs. I practically flew out of bed to the kitchen. I grabbed a couple pieces of bacon while she was at the stove cooking the eggs.

"Good morning".

She jumped when I talked to her. "You have to make some type of noise", she said when she turned to look at me.

"I'll try to remember that", I said smiling.

She went back to cooking. A few minutes later she was done. I got us plates, forks, and milk. The food was great.

"Have any special plans for today?" she asked after taking a drink.

"Not really. I am actually tired today. I was thinking about a lazy day."

"Sounds good to me. We can finish watching the movie from last night."

We finished eating, and I washed dishes since I didn't have to cook. The afternoon went by quickly. Alexa talked me into going to the mall to get matching hoodies. We both got solid black ones with our names on the back. I chose blue lettering of course and she chose pink. After that, we grabbed frozen coffees and walked around the mall. It was something to do that got us out of the apartment. I got a new ear piercing and got Alexa some skull earrings. After about the sixth clothing store, she received a text from Trevor. I knew she was going to leave me before she even said anything, because of the guilty look on her face.

"Have fun", I said.

"How did you know?"

"You have to ask?"

"Are you sure?"

"Yes, I'll go home and read, anything to get me out of this horrible place", I said as I winked at her.

"You're the best! I'll make it up to you, promise."

"No need, you can get your stuff later."

I watched her walk off to the other end of the mall. I assumed Trevor was already there waiting for her. I went back home and read for a few hours in bed before I drifted off to sleep.

There is chaos everywhere. Bloody bodies lying on the ground covered in mud. I could hear screams from men and women that surrounded me. Fairies, witches, shapeshifters, vampires, trolls, and things I didn't recognize were fighting humans. These humans were strong and skilled.

I could see the vampires and shifters biting and tearing apart the humans. Witches throwing them around like they didn't weigh much. Fairies were fighting with swords, spears, and hand to hand combat. I could feel the humans were the bad ones. They started all this. They hated all of us because we had abilities they didn't. They feared us, these weren't normal humans. They were reapers.

I walked around observing the war. I couldn't do anything except watch. I wanted to help, but when I tried nothing happened. The pain in the faces I saw of the ones being killed made me sick.

Closing my eyes didn't tune it out. I contin-ued to hear the rough metal sound of swords clinking, flesh being ripped apart, and bodies dropping on the ground. When I opened my eyes, hundreds more were laying on the ground than there were before.

I felt her before I saw her. It was Jewel, and she was being beaten by a large man with red hair and a scar slashed across his face. I could see the black dagger and snake on his left arm. He smiled evilly at her. Her leg was broken, and blood was coming out of her mouth. She tried to get up but he shoved her back down to the ground.

"Any last words you filthy creature before you leave this wretched earth?" the man asked. His cold inhuman voice sent chills down my spine.

She looked up at him, trying to smile. "My story will not be over simply because this life will end."

He drew a dagger from his boot and stabbed her in the chest. He missed her heart on purpose. "Elder Cain Diomedes wanted me to give you a message before you die. He has won; he always does. Now be gone with you forever." He turned the dagger slightly to the right. I saw the life in her disappear.

I woke up screaming. The nightmare felt real. My chest was hurting, and tears were coming out of my eyes. I felt sore all over. I felt like I had just fought for my life. It took me a while to calm down. It happened so long ago, but it didn't happen to me. It wasn't me, I was safe in my bed. I had only been asleep for an hour before I woke up feeling horrible. My room was starting to make me feel claustrophobic. It looked like the walls were closing in on me.

I needed to get out in the fresh air. It was close to dark, but I didn't care. I grabbed my new hoodie, put my hair in a ponytail, and then walked out the door. As soon as the outside air hit me, I felt instantly better. I started to walk down the road. I didn't care where I went. I just needed to walk. Downtown was crowded, people were eating and shopping before everything closed down. I passed Lavy's shop and kept going. I walked for a couple of hours before I stopped for a break at Spring Lake Park.

I sat on a bench under a tree, close to the small pond, staring at the water. The park was secluded. It was too late for children to play and joggers to run around the trail. The street lights were lighting up a few sections of the park. I chose a dark spot, mostly to hide. I didn't want to be seen. I wanted to be left alone.

The faces of the people in my dream kept popping up in my mind. Jewel's death was the one that took up the most space. Her last thought was of Lavender and Kegan: how she would never see them again, and how she had broken her promise to them. She wouldn't return. That hurt her more than her broken body.

I was angry. I couldn't help it. I didn't understand why I was seeing this. What did it have to do with me?

I wasn't able to think about it long. I heard three people walking up to me. I could sense that they knew what I was. I didn't move. I let them get close to me. When one of them was right behind me, I got up and appeared behind him. He couldn't have been more than seventeen. He was skinny and blonde. The other two were in their thirties and muscular. One was a red-headed man, and the other was a blonde woman. I knew they were reapers before they got close. They were glaring at me. They wanted to kill me.

"What does a girl have to do to get some alone time?" I asked them.

"Oh, why would a pretty girl like you want to be alone?" asked the blonde male.

"To think, to be one with nature, you know the usual girl reasons."

"Don't worry little Jade, you will be one with nature soon", the blonde woman said.

"Well, I don't like the way you said that. Also, it is rude that you know my name, but I don't know yours."

Before anyone spoke, I changed into vampire mode. The disgust on their faces grew more intense. "What, don't like what you see?" I asked.

The redhead man was the first to try to attack me. He threw a punch at my face, but I ducked instinctively. "Now, now, I thought we were going to be friends", I said.

"You're delusional, you filthy vampire", the woman said.

"That isn't very nice. Didn't your mother teach you manners? My mom told me, if you can't say anything nice, don't say anything at all."

The woman got angry at my little comment. She pulled out a gun. It was a small one, but I knew it could hurt me.

"Now that isn't fair. You have a toy to play with, but I don't", I said looking at the woman.

She pointed the gun at my heart, the two men were on either side of me. I knew they were going to kill me if they could. I couldn't get close enough to compel them to leave me alone. I wasn't even sure if it would work on them.

I remembered in my dream, some of the witches were able to move people by thinking it. I prayed hard that I was that strong. These were humans, not feathers. I focused on the gun, telling it to fly against a tree a few yards away. The gun moved instantly. I felt power circling throughout my body. The look on the three reapers faces was priceless. They were shocked by what I had done.

"What are you? Vampires don't have that kind of power", the redhead asked.

"A little of this, a little of that. Sugar, spice, and everything nice. You know what all girls are made of", I joked.

The redhead got closer to me, moving an inch at a time. He was trying to close the gap between us. I turned to him and he froze, but not at his own will. I made him do it.

"Sneaking up on people is not very nice. You could scare someone, and make them think you mean them harm."

"I can't move!" He yelled at the others.

"That is a pity." I turned toward the other two. Their faces had gone white. I wasn't going to hurt them. They were still humans, only misguided evil ones.

"Let him go", the woman told me.

"Be quiet." She went silent. She tried to talk but couldn't. Her mouth wouldn't open for sound to come out. I wasn't sure how, but I was controlling both of them at the same time. It was awesome, but I couldn't last long, though. I was already struggling with keeping my concentration. It took a lot of energy to control their movements. The blonde male was open mouthed and gawking at me.

"Sleep", I told him. He fell to the ground. I did the same to the woman. After she dropped, I focused back on the red-headed man. He couldn't move, still, I had to take the opportunity to compel him. I still wasn't sure if it would work, but I had to try.

I looked into his eyes, and he was forced to look into mine. I could feel my mind connecting to his the way it had done with others. There was a wall blocking me from his mind, though. I had to break it down or poke a hole in it or something. It was difficult, he was fighting me. I could feel myself letting him slip. I tried harder to focus, but I couldn't.

He started to wiggle his finger. I felt panic go through my body. I couldn't fight him, I was weak from the mind control. Second by second he was escaping my control. I was trying to back away slowly. If he got free I was sure he could hurt me or worse.

A moment later, he was walking toward me. He knew he didn't have to run, I couldn't get away fast enough. I didn't have enough strength to use vampire speed. He closed the space between us quickly. I knew that was going to be it. I was going to die. I saw him take a black dagger out of his pocket. It matched his tattoo perfectly. The twisted grin on his face made me sick to my stomach. I wasn't prepared to die. I needed to do more in life. I closed my eyes and waited for the pain that was sure to come. It never did, instead, I heard a roar and then a loud thump. I opened my eyes immediately. In front of me was a beautiful black panther. He was standing on top of the man who had fainted from fear.

The panther turned around and looked at me. His eyes were warm and concerning. I knew it was Falcon. I didn't know how he knew I was here or needed help, but I was thrilled to see him. Before I could get overjoyed, the blond male woke up and shot me. It wasn't a bullet. It was something sharp. I felt a sting for a moment, and then everything went black.

I woke up on my couch, and Lavy was staring down at me. Boston was by her side, but I couldn't see Falcon. "Where is he?" I asked. They looked at each other, then back at me. "He left after he brought you home. He needed to be alone", Boston said.

I got a sick feeling in the pit of my stomach. "What happened?". This time Lavy answered. "All we know is that the reapers were trying to kill you. Falcon had to stop them, to protect you, so he did." The sick feeling worsened. "Are... are they dead?" "Yes", they both said in unison.

I tried to sit up, but nausea swept over me. "I think I'm going to be sick." I was handed a small trashcan. It was the one beside the couch.

It had a gray trash bag inside. I was glad I put one in it. It would be easier to clean if I puked.

"Take slow deep breaths. I will get you something to settle your stomach." Lavy walked off then and went to the kitchen.

I looked up at Boston, "Is he really okay? Does he hate me?"

"He will be okay, once it sinks in. He has never had to kill anyone before. He doesn't hate you, it's quite the opposite actually."

That surprised me. He didn't hate me. "Do you think he would talk to me?"

"It's best to give him space for now. When he is ready he will come to you."

The nausea was swept away by a strong feeling of sadness. I made him kill someone. I didn't do it intentionally, but if I wasn't out wandering around alone, he wouldn't have had to. He wanted to make sure I stayed alive. He did feel something for me. Not just as a friend, but more. I wanted to go to him, to comfort him. Boston knew him better, so I gave him space. I hoped it wouldn't take him long to come talk to me.

"Here you go. It's warm with a little bit of ginger root in it." Lavy handed me a large mug with blood in it. It smelled wonderful. I took a small sip. That small drink made me feel better instantly. "Thank you."

"You're welcome. It should help."

"It is. What are you doing here? Aren't you visiting your dad?"

"I was. I came back this morning after Boston called me to tell me what happened."

"This morning?"

"It's Sunday night. You have been out for hours. Whatever they tranquilized you with was strong."

I looked out the window. It was dark outside. "Do you know what they shot me with?"

"It was a strong sedative. Something that would be used for a bear or larger", Boston said.

"Great! That explains why I feel like I'm floating. Also, I'm starving now."

Boston spoke up, "Need more blood or food?"

"Food would be great, something greasy. Maybe a burger and fries? I'm tired of the food around here though," I said looking sad.

"Can do. I know a great place that is open until late. I'll be back in thirty."

"Thank you that is really sweet of you", Lavy said.

"Yes, thanks! My wallet is on my nightstand, feel free to grab you and Lavy something."

"No worries, I'll take care of it."

"Thanks, that's nice of you."

"I'll take a chicken salad with double the ranch on the side", Lavy piped in.

Lavy walked him to the door. I made sure not to watch. I heard them kiss. I didn't know how to feel about that. I didn't get a chance to think about it before she was back in front of me.

"What do you want to talk about?"

"How did you know?"

"We have been living together for months and you usually have your food delivered, even if it is across town."

"Good point. Is Falcon going to be alright? Boston said to give him time. He needed to let what happened sink in and come to terms with it."

"I believe he will be. He is strong and he cares for you deeply."

"That is what Boston said. I hope so, I really want to help him, but don't know how."

"Space, for now, is best. I know it will be hard, but remember you needed space when you went through the transformation and other things that have happened."

"I know you're right. It just sucks."

"The time will pass quickly. You're alive and safe. That is what matters."

I changed the subject not wanting to discuss me almost dying. "How did your visit go with your father?"

"It went well. It was nice to see him. We had a lot to talk about."

"That's good." I didn't want to pry too much. She would tell me what she wanted me to know.

"Yes, it is. I did mention you to him. I explained about your mark and your abilities. He was intrigued for sure."

"What did he say?"

"There hasn't been a hybrid in thousands of years that anyone knows of. They are believed to be a myth like I said before. Something to frighten our kind. They are told to be unpredictable and dangerous. They can't control their power and often go insane."

"I'm going to go crazy?"

"It is just a myth, not everything is true. My father doesn't believe that will happen to you. He has a feeling that you're stronger than that."

"That's comforting, but he doesn't even know me."

"I told him what you can do and how I can see your aura."

"You can see my aura?"

"Yes, it's strong. Stronger than anyone's I have encountered. It's beautiful too, mostly white with a thick border of blue around it and in the center."

"I'll take your word for it."

"He thought we should try to train you; to find another witch who can help. He gave me a couple of names. We can search for them when you are better."

"That is a good idea. The power seems to be strong, but it drains my energy fast."

"Yes, Falcon said the same. He watched you throw the gun the reapers had, force the larger one to be still, and made the others fall asleep."

"He saw me do that?" I cringed at that thought, of course, he didn't want to talk to me now. I was a freak of nature. I wasn't a normal vampire.

"Jade, I know what you're thinking. He isn't avoiding you because you have gifts that other vampire's don't. He is angry with himself, not because he had to take a life, but because he didn't come to you sooner."

"Okay."

"Believe me please, give it a few days. He will talk to you. Speaking of talking to you. My father wants to meet you soon."

"How soon is soon?"

"In the next year or two."

"That is a relief. I thought you meant like in the next week or two."

"Our time isn't like a human's time. We can go years without seeing or speaking to each other. It feels like days to us."

"Wow."

"You have a lot to learn, but you will. You are a lot stronger than you think you are, mentally and physically."

"I hope you're right."

"I am."

I left the couch then and headed to my bathroom to take a shower. I needed to feel fresh. My chest ached from where I was shot. I turned the hot water on until steam was coming out of the shower. I undressed. I was wearing the same clothes I was wearing yesterday. When I stripped my shirt off and looked in the mirror, I saw a small bruise close to my heart. If I were human, it would have been worse, I knew that without a doubt. I needed to get prepared for reapers and whatever else was out there wanting to harm me. I was thinking of running, but I was sure they would find me no matter what. I wasn't ready to hide yet. I knew I could get strong with my magic and learn to fight. I also knew something was coming but wasn't sure what.

Chapter Sixteen

I was lying in bed, holding the bracelet I was given on my birthday by my birth mom. I didn't take it out much. It was a painful memory that I was abandoned as an infant. I usually hid it away in my bottom dresser drawer. For some reason, though, I felt the need to hold it and look at it. It was more like the little piece of jewelry was demanding I touch it.

"That is pretty", Legs said.

"It isn't really my style, but thank you. It was a gift."

"I know, I remember."

"You do?"

"I overheard when you received it."

"So you know it was from her?"

"The her being the woman who gave birth to you? Yes, I know."

"I don't understand why she would do it, why leave me?"

"I don't know who she was, but I am sure she had her reasons."

"Maybe."

"There is a way to find out."

"There is? How?"

"A spell of course?"

"A spell?"

"For someone smart, you can seem dumb at times."

"Hey, I am still learning all this. What type of spell?"

"A seeing spell. You only need to find a magic book or create your own spell."

"I can create a spell of my own?"

"Yes, but it isn't easy. The wording has to be right."

"Alright, I'll try a spell book. How do I get one?"

"The internet or Lavy may have one."

"I'd rather not ask her."

"The internet then. It is a simple spell, so a beginner book would be fine."

I grabbed my laptop and began to search for magic books. At first, all I found were ones that appeared to be props for a movie or something, or cult related. After hours of researching, I finally found one. It wasn't even on a website for spells or magic. I found it on an antique resale site. I hoped it would work. It would take a couple of days for me to receive it. I had it shipped to Alexa's. I didn't want Lavy finding it. I felt bad hiding this from her, but if it worked I would tell her. Some things I needed to figure out on my own.

The days dragged by. I was waiting anxiously for my book. I told Alexa to be on the lookout for it. I had it shipped overnight, but I wouldn't get it until Tuesday since I ordered it on a Sunday. I kept checking the tracking number, but it rarely changed. When it finally said delivered, I drove to her house to pick it up. Lavy made me take off for the week, because of what happened. I was glad. I needed the break for what I wanted to do. I made it to Alexa's house pretty quickly, I may have sped some, but I was in a hurry,

It looked better than the picture showed it. It was black leather binding with bronze letters on the front that said Book of Shadows in the middle. Feathers were at the bottom in the same bronze color. Touching it felt strange. I could feel the power vibrating from the book, even from the box that it was in. I placed it back in the package it was delivered in. I couldn't wait to get it home.

"Thanks, Alex, tell Alexa I'll talk to her later."

"You okay? You seem in a hurry."

"Yeah, I'm good, just busy. See you later."

"Later."

I was glad he wasn't a nosy person, I didn't want to have to explain why I had a package delivered to his place and not mine. I felt guilty. I didn't like hiding things from people, especially Lavy. I only told Alexa it was a book I wanted and wasn't going to be able to be home to get it, and someone had to sign for it. She probably knew I was lying but she didn't say anything.

I rushed to get home, I somehow was still able to avoid the police. I had to stop speeding, I didn't want to draw attention to myself. When I made it home I locked the door behind me including the deadbolt. We rarely used it, but I wanted to make sure no one could disturb me.

I got the bracelet from my dresser and set it on my bed. I opened up the spell book, the writing was in small cursive. The penmanship was beautiful, not like my chicken scratch. The best thing was, it was all in English. I expected it to be in some old dead language I couldn't pronounce. I looked through the pages; there were spells of healing teas, crystals, and oils. I also saw spells for memory: to make someone forget or remember something, even to talk to the dead. I finally found the one I was looking for. I was starting to get worried I wouldn't.

"To see Distant Memories"
To look into the past you must have an object or person from the past.
Touch the object and focus deeply with your mind on the time you want to see and whom you want to see.
Once you have the image in your mind, chant the words below three times, while burning Sage and Rosemary wrapped in twine.
Place seven white candles around you to create a circle, ignite them to close the circle around you.

Repeat these words three times. Take me through the sands of time. Show me what I want to see."

The spell seemed simple enough. We kept herbs in the kitchen. I was positive we had some in a cabinet somewhere. I walked to the kitchen and found them the first place I looked. The issue was finding twine or rope. I assumed a shoestring would work. I took one from a shoe I hardly wore, I could always replace it. Candles were easy, we had candles all around, Lavy was obsessed with them. I grabbed seven small teacup candles and placed them in a circle on my bedroom floor. I put the bundled up herbs on a glass plate and lit them on fire. I got into the circle with the bracelet then lit the candles. I took a few deep breaths to calm myself. I was afraid it wouldn't work, but also afraid it would.

"You can do this. Focus", Legs said.

"I know, let me concentrate."

She went back into her house and left me alone. "Jade you got this, stop stressing", I told myself out loud. I closed my eyes and focused. I wasn't sure what my birth mother looked like or exactly where I was found. I had to try still, I knew that it was sixteen years ago and at a warehouse in New Boston, Texas.

I focused on what I wanted. I wanted to see my birth mother. I wanted to feel what she was feeling. I wanted to know why she gave me up. I held her bracelet close to my heart and started to chant the words from the spell book. "Take me through the sands of time. Show me what I want to see." Nothing happened. I could feel my heart sinking into despair.

"Try again, put your own spin on it. Be specific". I opened my eyes and looked at Legs, she was at the front of her terrarium looking down at me. I did as she suggested. I had to remind myself I was new at this when I first tried the spell, I didn't feel anything. I tried again, still, nothing happened. I didn't want to give up. I tried again, trying to relax and focus at the same time. I prayed for the power I felt before to embrace me again. I hadn't felt it since waking up a couple a days ago from being drugged. I didn't think my power was gone but didn't have a reason to until now.

I changed the wording a little. "Take me through the sand of time. Show me why I was left behind." *Blurry images started to appear* in my mind. It was mostly dull colors, like a watercolor painting. I kept repeating the words and feeling the power connect with me again. It wasn't as strong as it was before, but I had to keep trying. I was close, I knew I was. A large building started to become clearer. I pushed myself toward the dark-colored metal building. I could hear the rain pouring down outside before I saw it.

I looked around. The streets were deserted. It was late at night, I think. It was dark out. I looked back at the warehouse and saw a door. Walking through the door, I followed the cry of a baby. She sounded scared. As I got closer to the cry, the image became clearer. The feeling of regret practically punched me in the chest. I saw a woman holding a baby in a blue and pink blanket. The woman was rocking the baby trying to get her to stop crying. The woman's back was facing me. I walked around so I could see her face. She was beautiful, and I knew instantly she was my birth mother. She didn't look much like me in the face, but we had the same hair and eye color. She was taller than me by a few inches and her skin was pale. She was wearing black *pants and a black shirt. Her hair was in a long braid going down her back.*

I stepped closer to her, wishing I could touch her. I looked into her eyes and they were filled with so much love for the baby she was holding. I could feel her heart breaking. She didn't want to leave the baby. She didn't have a choice. She knew the child was in danger, or at least she would be when she became of age.

The woman kissed the baby on the cheek, and placed her down in a box with a small pouch beside her. "Goodbye my precious Jade. Please know that I love you and always will." The woman walked away toward a door that led into the street. I followed her out. I didn't want to leave the child, but I didn't have a choice. I came to see this woman. I watched her walk a couple streets over to a pay phone. She dialed 911.

"Hello, is this an emergency?"

"There is a baby in an abandoned ware-house on Main. She is alive and healthy but she needs help."

"May I have your name please?"

She hung up the phone then. When she left the phone booth she ran away with vampire speed after looking around to make sure no one would see.

I came back to reality then. I didn't want to open my eyes. I wanted to go back and see my mother again. She didn't hate me or want to get rid of me. She loved me, I could feel that she did. She was trying to protect me. I wondered if she was still alive. I opened my eyes reluctantly to see that I was laying in my bed. Lavy was looking down at me with concern.

"What were you doing?", was the first thing that came out of her mouth.

I looked up at her. She looked worried but angry. "I was doing a spell."

"Yes, I know that. I saw the spell book, candles, and the burning herbs. I'm not a witch, but I know what casting a spell looks like. I got worried. You were on the floor passed out. You have been out of it for a couple of hours. It's late at night now."

"I was trying to understand why my birth mother left me."

"Did you find out?" she asked, looking surprised.

"Yes. She was trying to protect me from something or someone. She loved me unconditionally. She didn't want to let me go. Lavy, she was beautiful. I need to find her, and make sure she is alright."

"First tell me what you saw. We will go from there."

I explained the vision I had of my birth mother. The vision didn't last long enough for me to know exactly what she was hiding me from. Maybe she knew what I was going to be: a hybrid with vampire and witch blood.

"I saw a tracking spell in the Book of Shadows. It requires two witches for it to work. I want to ask one of the witches you found to help me. I need to find her."

"We will. First get some rest, you look exhausted."

"No, I need to find her as soon as I can."

"I will call Theodora tomorrow. I believe she will be the best one to help us. She is older than me and her magic is strong."

"Please call her now."

"If you go to sleep, I will call her."

"Fine." I didn't want to sleep, even though I felt I needed it. Using so much magic drained me again. I needed to get stronger. I had to be able to protect myself. I felt the intense fear my mother had. I hoped the witch Theodora could help me not only find my mother, but help me control my power.

I laid in bed listening to Lavy as she made the call. The voice on the other end sounded like she was in Africa. Her voice was strong. She sounded wise even on the phone. I heard the whole conversation. It was rude to eavesdrop, but this was about my life so I didn't care.

"Hello?" asked someone on the receiving end of the call.

"My name is Lavender. Is this Theodora?"

"Yes, how can I help you, child?"

"A close friend of mine could use your help. This is a unique situation. This must be done in secret. Lives could be at risk."

"I understand. I assume you will provide more information if we meet in person?"

"That is correct. I would like to meet in a neutral place."

"That is fine. You choose the place."

"It needs to be somewhere that it is not crowded."

"Rhondo Cemetery", I pipped in. Oops, I thought, oh well, damage done. She probably already knew I was listening to them.

"Do you know where Rhondo Cemetery is in Texarkana?"

"I am sure I can find it. It will take me a couple days to get there. Shall we meet Saturday?"

"That will be fine. Please mention this to no one."

"You have my word child, I will not."

"See you soon. Thank you."

"You are welcome."

She hung up the phone then. A minute later she was back in my room. "Happy?" she asked, looking worried.

"Yes, thank you."

"Please sleep now. We have a few days until she will be here. You need to get your energy up."

"I know. I will. I'm sorry."

"For what?"

"I hid the spell book from you and what I was doing. Also, you found me on the floor. I'm sorry I didn't tell you. I was afraid it wouldn't work."

"I don't want to say I am not upset because I am. Please remember I am here for you no matter what. I will do whatever I can to help you."

"I know, thanks."

"You're welcome. Good night."

"Night."

I dreamed of my adoptive parents that night. They were in heaven, I believe, with Grams watching over me. They seemed so happy. I felt they were guiding me, and telling me to keep going forward that I was on the right path. They knew what I needed to do and what I wanted. They wanted me to find my birth mother, to find out about what I was capable of, and what my purpose was. They knew I would love them and miss them no matter who would come into my life. They may have been gone from Earth, but they were always with me. I was to never forget that.

Chapter Seventeen

Saturday had finally arrived. I hated it when I wanted something to come around so bad that it made time drag on longer. I knew it was all in my head; time never slowed or sped up. It was all about perception, but still. I felt I was being taunted because I was close to hopefully finding out more about my birth mother and where I came from.

Theodora called us when she was close. We decided to meet at night. It was a full moon and we could draw from the power of the moon. We were told to bring candles, in case we needed the power of a circle. We didn't tell her what I wanted to do yet, but she assumed it had something to do with magic. Why else would we have called her?

When we arrived a little while after sunset, she was already there. She wasn't what I expected. She was shorter than me, a little on the chubby side, with long dark braids in her hair. Even though she was barely over four foot, she made up for it in confidence. She looked strong and powerful. Her eyes showed that she had power. It was like they could see into your soul and knew what your darkest secrets were.

"Hello, children."

It was strange for her to call us children. I know she was older than us, but she looked younger than Lavy.

"Greetings", Lavy said.

"Hello", I said.

"You must be the young lady I talked to on the phone", she asked looking at Lavy.

"Yes, that was me. Thank you for coming."

"Yes, thank you", I said.

"You must be the one needing help."

"I am. I want to track someone with this." I held up the bracelet so she could see it.

"Bring it closer to me please."

I did as she asked. She held her hand open and I placed it there. I hoped we could find my mom. I wanted to see her in person. I needed to let her know I was alright; scared but alright.

"I am trying to find my birth mother. This is all I have of hers. I don't know where she is or if she is alive."

"I will do my best child. May I see your hand?"

I didn't want to give her my hand. I wasn't really all that worried she would hurt me, okay maybe I was, but she didn't seem evil. I held out my hand. She touched it and closed her eyes. I could tell she was concentrating on something. When she opened her eyes, they went wide. She was giving me the strangest look.

"Is there something wrong?" I asked.

"You are quite different aren't you? Not only a witch but a vampire. You are a hybrid."

I took my hand back, backing away slowly. "Yes, I am."

"Child, you have nothing to fear from me. You are special. Your secret is safe with me. You have great power."

"Please do keep this a secret. No one knows but a few people. I am afraid of what might happen if the wrong people find out."

"Yes, as you should be. The elders would find you particularly interesting."

"I am sure they would, but I'd rather them not know."

"Of course not, as I said, you are special. I feel you should be protected. You have a great destiny ahead of you."

"I don't know about that. I just want to know where I came from and where my mother is."

"Let's get started, shall we?" Lavy chimed in then.

"Yes, lets. I assume you brought a spell book to work with?" she asked me.

"It is one I found on the internet. It worked for me to get a vision of my mother leaving me when I was a baby."

"You did that on your own? With no proper training?"

"Yes, is that bad?"

"No, it is fascinating."

"Why?"

"People your age don't generally have the ability to do a spell so complex, even if it is for most beginners. You do have great power young one."

"I guess I am full of surprises, then, huh?"

"Yes, you are."

"You ready?"

"Yes. Let us start. Lavender, you stay back a little way please."

"I'll be by the car if you need me", Lavy said, as she looked at me.

I nodded my head at her. Theodora and I walked over to the church. I wasn't sure why she wanted to do the spell there but didn't care to ask either. She was already helping me out by doing the tracking spell with me.

"Put the candles down on the ground and form a large circle."

I obeyed pulling out the candles out of a duffel bag I brought with me. She pulled out a small golden box, opened it and poured white stuff around the circle. The smell hit me shortly afterward. It was salt. It didn't smell like table salt though, it smelled weaker. She then walked into the circle and sat down with a dark blue candle and lit it.

"Come into the circle, sit down, and close your eyes."

I did as she asked. When I entered the circle, I could feel the power inside. My body vibrated and felt electric. I could feel the power inside me awakening.

"What do you want me to do?"

"Concentrate on the image of your mother and yourself. Concentrate on your bond with her and the bracelet. Concentrate on the answers you seek."

"What I see, will you be able to as well?" I was afraid of the answer but had to know.

"Yes. What I see will stay with me. I have many secrets young one. I assure you. I will not share this with anyone. I feel a need to protect you, as I stated before, even though I just met you."

"Alright, here goes nothing." I closed my eyes holding the bracelet while visualizing the image of my birth mother in my mind. I focused on the way she looked when I was a baby, the love and sadness she felt, and the way she smelled of roses. I tried to imagine a link going from me to wherever she was: a light blue line connecting us, a mother and a daughter.

"Earth, Air, Water, Fire, Spirit, guide us to what is lost. "
"Earth, Air, Water, Fire, Spirit, lead the way to what we seek."
"Earth, Air, Water, Fire, Spirit, open our hearts and minds to see."

Theodora chanted those words over and over again until images started to flood through my mind. It was like it was before, blurry at first, then it became clear. The first thing I saw wasn't my birth mother; it was Jewel.

She was giving birth to Lavender. Kegan was there holding her hand. Theodora was there with them wrapping the baby up in a woven blanket. She handed Jewel the little girl, and the look on her face was pure joy.

Lavender was then crawling around a grass field with wildflowers on a bright sunny day trying to walk. She kept falling, but each time she did she would laugh. She would then get back up and try again. Jewel was encouraging the little girl to come to her. She had her arms open, waiting for the child. After a few failed attempts, the little girl walked over to her, hugging her and laughing.

Jewel was crying and angry because she had to say goodbye. She was going to war to fight the humans to protect her people. Her only regret was leaving her daughter and her husband. She loved them more than anything.

She was then fighting the man who killed her. She didn't feel fear, even though she knew she was going to die soon. She was weak and tired from lack of food from the past few weeks. She knew the war with the humans would continue to go on without her. Her warriors were brave, and so were the other creatures who were fighting with them. The humans would be defeated. She had to believe that. She had to hope for that.

The red-headed man pushed the dagger into her chest. She still wasn't afraid, even when she could feel herself slipping away. It didn't matter. Her daughter and her love were safe. She would see them again one day, even if it wasn't in this life.

When she died, her soul left her body. It was more beautiful than she was. Her soul was a shimmering sky blue shadow of pure energy. It radiated love, hope, joy, strength, and power. It was pure with no evil in it at all. Her soul then disappeared into the sky.

I saw the same spirit go into a young woman who had copper brown skin and long black hair. The woman several months later gave birth to a beautiful girl with dark black curly hair. "Her name is Jahana", the woman said, before she died. Theodora then took the child and gave her to a woman, who I believe was her aunt. The woman looked like Ja-hana's mother.

Jahana grew up playing in trees, swim-ming in the ocean, and hunting animals. She wasn't popular among her people because she was different. She was more of a free spirit than they were. She was curious about every-thing. She loved to explore the lands she was raised on.

When she turned sixteen, she went into her transformation alone in the forest. She knew it was coming and that it would hurt, but she didn't know it would feel like she was dying. The pain she experienced was horrible. Sweat was pouring from her body, and she felt like her bones were breaking. She felt like she was going to die, but she knew that it was coming unlike me. When she was done, she turned into a Falcon. She was magnificent. Her feathers were clean and perfect, her eyes clear and fo-cused. She soared into the sky, with the sun lighting up her wings.

Next, she was being dragged out of her tent. She was awakened by being dragged by her hair by a man in the village. She didn't know why she was being treated like this. She knew she wasn't liked by her people, but that didn't mean they hated her entirely, surely. When she was brought in front of the Chief, she got a little scared. Not because she knew they feared her, but because she saw darkness in the eyes of the Chief. She was being controlled by false fear and only had death on her mind. Jahana didn't hate her people; she feared for them. A disease was killing them, and she knew now they blamed her, but she didn't know why. When Jahana died, the same blue spirit shadow left her body and disappeared into the night sky.

The next thing I saw was my birth mother. She was so happy and carefree. She was talking with a man she just met. He was tall with dark brown hair and hazel eyes. He was a witch, a powerful one. He looked at my mother with curiosity. He knew she was a vampire beneath his class, but he didn't care. There was something about her that was intriguing, unlike anyone he had met before. He was used to strict rules and had his life planned for him, but this woman wasn't like that. She could do as she pleased. She was open with herself. The man took my mother to a room. When they were alone he kissed her.

The same blue shimmering shadow went into her then. She knew that night with him she became pregnant. She didn't know how it was possible. Species of the Shadow Realm weren't supposed to be able to mix. She left her home that night, she didn't want anyone to find out. She feared for her unborn child. I watched as her belly grew with the unborn child inside. She never stayed in a place too long, because she was scared she would be found.

The baby was born. My mother was alone, but she cut the cord and cleaned the baby up. She made sure she was healthy and fed. The baby girl was perfect. She had all ten fingers and toes, her eyes changed from green to brown depending on if she was happy or sad. My mother knew she would have to give her child up to protect her. The only thing she could think of was to let her grow up in the human world. She would come and check on her when she could. In sixteen years, she would find a way for someone to help her daughter with the transformation, if it happened. She wasn't sure what the child would turn into.

My mother went to a pay phone to call 911. She explained a baby was left in a warehouse

and she needed help. I watched as police offi-
cers found the child, my mother staying hidden, and watching as the baby was taken
away. The baby was taken to the hospital. She
was checked over by a doctor, blood taken,
shots given, changed and fed.

A man and a woman came into the room
the little girl was in. It was my adoptive parents. My mother picked up the baby and
looked at her with pure joy. The couple took
the little girl home. I watched as they set up a
nursery that changed to a toddler room, then
a little kid room. I watched as I grew up from
a baby into a teenager. I saw myself at the
hospital saying goodbye to my mother. I
watched as I went through my transformation
with Lavy. I said goodbye to Grams in the
hospital, then again at the cemetery after she
was placed into the ground.

The last thing I saw was my birth mother
watching me as I said goodbye to Grams. She
was in the cemetery with me that day watching me cry. She wanted to come to me then but
was afraid I would reject her and that I would
hate her. She still loved me and wanted to
make sure I was okay. She had been watching
me my whole life. Years may have passed be-

tween the times she came to see me, but she tried when she thought it was safe. She thought I was beautiful, brave, and smart. She thought my adoptive parents raised me well.

I saw her leave and go to a large city. She was in a large city somewhere in Arkansas. People were constantly moving there. She wouldn't stay there much longer because she was afraid someone would find her. She thought my dad was searching for her. She heard when she first left that a high powered witch was looking for her. He never got her name but he described her in every detail. She made sure she only came out at night and not for long, she didn't know who would be watching. She changed her hair a lot and her style of clothing to make sure she wasn't recognizable. She only fed mostly on animals and human blood when she just had to. I saw her go from town to town, city to city, state to state, but she always came back to get a glance at me.

The visions ended. So many memories flooded through my mind. I remembered the lives of Jewel and Jahana. They were me or I was them, I wasn't sure how to explain it. We were all connected: my soul was theirs. This was my third life. Each life had the same mark, but the stars increased. Jewel had one, Jahana had two, and then I got three. I lived before, but I didn't remember until now. I was a fairy in my first life and a shifter in my second. I was now a vampire-witch hybrid.

A couple of realizations hit me then. I had been married with a child. I had a daughter. My daughter was Lavender. The second thing was: this Elder Cain Diomedes was the one person who had Jewel and Jahana killed. He was going to come after me too, but I wasn't sure why. As far as I could tell Jewel, Jahana, and I hadn't done anything to him. I had to be on guard and figure out if he knew about me, but I had to keep it secret. I couldn't put anyone in danger. The third thing was: I knew about where my birth mother was. I had to make plans to go find her. I wanted to go as soon as I found out, but I had to get things in order and I had to have an actual plan that involved the people closest to me.

I opened my eyes then, after what seemed like hours of trying to comprehend everything I had learned. Theodora was looking directly at me. The way she was looking at me, I knew she saw everything I did. Her eyes and face were a mixture of things: respect, love, sadness, heartbreak, but must of all understanding. She felt what I felt then as well. I felt a deep connection with her then. She had been there in my past lives, Jewel giving birth to Lavy, Jahana being born, and now she was here, helping me as if fate had brought her to me.

I looked over at Lavy then, feeling a different kind of love for her. I felt the way a mother loves her child. I saw her the way Jewel saw her. I couldn't tell her, though. I wasn't ready to, and I don't think she was either. Maybe one day, I would, but not for a while. This life of mine was complicated enough. I turned back and looked at Theodora.

"Your secrets are safe with me child", she whispered to me.

"You know all of it don't you?" I asked, knowing the answer already.

"Yes. I know you have had many lives. You are special young one. Your destiny will be great."

"I'm afraid of what is to come. Do you know who this Cain Diomedes is?"

"He is a powerful witch. He is dangerous. Stay away from him."

"Why did he want me dead in my past lives?"

"I am sorry, child, I don't know. I need to leave now. We used a lot of magic, and I need to regain my strength. Continue to use your power. I know it frightens you. The more you use it, the stronger it will be. I don't think you need any form of training. You seem to be doing well, by following your instincts."

"Thank you for everything."

"You are most welcome. If you need me, think of me and I will come. We are connected. You are now family."

I nodded. I blew out the candles and waited until the melting wax became cold. I, then, gathered them up and put them in my bag. I stayed on the ground and watched Theodora leave. I wasn't ready to be around Lavy. I didn't know how to act around her anymore. I had to remind myself that she doesn't know about me, I wasn't ready for her to know. I needed to act the way I always did, even if it was hard.

I got up and took a few deep breaths to clear my mind. When I felt I could control my emotions, I walked over to Lavy. I did my best not to look at her too much. She looked so much like Jewel and Kegan. She made a great mixture of them both.

"Did you learn what you needed to? Theodora didn't say much before she left."

"I did. I know where my birth mother is. At least, I know where she was. That is a start. I need to make plans to start looking for her. We can go home and rest now. I will start making plans tomorrow."

"Are you okay? You look like you saw a ghost", she joked.

"I'm fine. I'm just really tired now. That spell took a lot out of me. Blood will liven me back up and a long hot shower."

I smiled at her and got into the car. I let her drive. This way I could stare out the window, and sift through the memories I had gained tonight. I never knew so much love and heartache before. I reminded myself Jewel and Jahana were gone. I was Jade now. Whatever they had been before wasn't meant for me, even if I did want it. Destiny had another plan for my new life now as Jade. I simply had to figure out what it was. Tonight I would eat and sleep. Tomorrow I would make a plan to find my birth mother and say goodbye to my human life once and for all.

Chapter Eighteen

I could see a blonde haired male with brown eyes who could be eighteen talking to an elderly woman. The woman was scary. She had crazy sprung out white-gray hair. Her eyes were yellowish around her black pupils. The man looked kind and innocent. He was dressed in a cream-colored robe with a dark brown rope tied in a knot in the front. The woman was dressed in dirty old rags that were torn at the bottom and sleeves. He looked to be wealthy because he was clean and looked healthy. The woman looked weak and her bones were showing through her skin.

"Listen to me, Master Cain. I speak the truth."

"You keep saying that old woman, but I cannot believe thee."

"You must master. I have nothing to gain by giving thee false words."

"If thee are speaking thy truth, when shall this take place?"

"The female who holds the mark of a crescent moon and star of blue will be your downfall. I do not know when this shall take place or who it shall be. This female will have great powers, unlike anyone has ever seen."

"You have seen this in a vision that you speak of?"

"Yes sir, I have many times."

"I will put a stop to this female of which you speak. I will have control of our world and the human world. The humans will fear us and be our slaves. We are the more powerful of beings. They will know this to be true."

"Yes, they will if you get rid of the female I speak of. She could be any creature among us. It is possible she isn't born yet master. Beware I say, beware."

He changed from looking good and pure to evil and twisted. He could have the face of an angel if he wanted and then could change into the face of a beast. I knew he was planning something, but I couldn't figure out what.

Also, it wasn't good. A lot of people would be dying.

I woke up to the sound of a text message. I was relieved. I didn't want to stay in that dream any longer. Being that close to Cain made me feel ill. I grabbed my phone off the nightstand, unplugging it from the charger.

"Good morning, think we can hang out today... I would like to talk to you alone..." The message was from Falcon.

"Sure... I would like to talk to you as well..."

"Good, b/c I am at your front door right now..."

I jumped out of bed and ran to the front door. When I opened it, he was there in dark blue jeans and a black t-shirt. He looked tired; like he hadn't been getting any sleep. It had been a week since I had seen him, but it felt longer to me. I didn't realize how much I missed him until I saw him. He gave me a half smile when he looked at me.

"Did I wake you?"

"Yeah, but it's okay. I needed to wake up anyway. I had a bad dream."

"Oh, I'm sorry, you okay?" he seemed saddened by my nightmare.

"I will be. How are you?"

"I'll be alright." He didn't look like he would be, but maybe more time would help.

"Give me five minutes and I will be ready. Come in and make yourself at home."

"Thanks, I'll wait on the couch."

I heard him close the door and walk to the couch. I ran up the stairs, grabbed some clothes and headed to my bathroom. I went as fast as I could brushing my teeth and hair. My hair took a minute. It was a tangled mess. I assumed it was because I slept roughly the night before. I threw on socks and shoes before going to the living room.

"Hungry?" I asked. My stomach grumbled then.

"No, but you are. You should eat."

"What are the plans for today? Stay in or venture into the big scary world?" I realized my bad joke after I said it. It had only been a week since I was attacked, and he took human lives, even if they were reapers.

He didn't cringe at my horrible joke, which was good. "I want to take you somewhere that is special to me. We get there by train. Warning you ahead of time: it will be an all-day thing."

"Sounds good." I grabbed a blood bag and put it in a mug to drink. I suddenly felt self-conscious around him and didn't want to drink blood. I don't think he noticed which was a relief. I drank as fast as I could, without making a mess. I didn't want blood breath, so I went back to the bathroom and used some mouthwash.

I went back up to my room, grabbed my wallet and a hoodie. Something I could put my phone and wallet in, without carrying a bag.

"I'm ready," I said walking down the stairs.

"Let's go then", he said smiling at me. He almost looked happy.

I sent a text to Lavy telling her I would be out with Falcon. She had said she would be with Boston today and didn't know when she would be back.

We left the apartment to walk down to the train station. It was only a few blocks from the apartment. It was hardly used anymore as a way to travel. I had never been on one before. I was a little excited to get to do this. I hadn't really done a lot I supposed. Besides not riding on a train, I had never flown on a plane. The station wasn't crowded: maybe, ten people or so waiting to be picked up.

"Wait here", he said, as he walked to the ticket booth. I watched as he slipped a piece of paper to the person selling tickets. She handed him two tickets and told him to have a safe trip.

"Why did you hand her a piece of paper?" I asked curiously.

"You have excellent hearing. I didn't want to ruin the surprise for you."

"Good point", I said jokingly.

"The train will be here in a few minutes. We got here right in time."

"Awesome. I am excited. I have never done this before."

"Road on a train or gone off with a guy on some random trip?"

"Both, actually."

"Glad I get to be your first."

That made me blush a little. His mood was lightening up a lot. I was relieved. He didn't seem angry at me, which made me feel a lot better. I was still afraid he blamed me for what happened. I hoped, on this trip, we could talk about everything.

I heard the loud whistle and assumed it was time to board. I was right. Falcon grabbed my hand and walked me to the opening door. He gave the tickets to the conductor who checked them and handed them back. He then led me to the fourth train car. He opened the door and let me go in first.

It was exactly like I saw in movies. There were booths on two sides and a window between the seats. The walls were dark maroon and the seats were black leather. It was still early in the morning, so the sun wasn't blinding through the window. It actually looked like it was overcast; as if it may rain.

"This is my favorite train car. I have a slight issue with numbers. I like even numbers rather than odd. So when I ride the train I get into the fourth car."

I smiled at him before I sat down. "Good to know."

He sat across from me. Looking at me, I felt like he wanted to ask me something, but wasn't sure how. I had questions for him too but didn't want to be the one to start talking. I crossed my legs to get more conformable. I let ten minutes pass by; before not being able to stand the awkward silence any longer.

"I want to talk to you about a couple of things. I would like honest answers."

He gave me another half-smile. "Okay, I'll do my best to answer." He looked relieved that I broke the silence, as well.

"First, about last weekend. Are you okay? Like really okay? Boston said you had to be by yourself, and needed me to leave you alone. I didn't want to. I wanted to come to you but was afraid I would scare you off. I was afraid you hated me for what happened: like maybe you blamed me. I am sorry. I really am. I feel horrible about it. You saved my life, though. Thank you.

He looked stunned by what I had just said; well, sad more than anything. He got up and walked to me, then sat beside me. I was looking at the floor when he did this. He picked up my hand and held it. It took him a minute to say anything.

"Jade, I could never hate you. I don't blame you for what happened. I am relieved that you are safe and alive. I did what I had to do to protect you. They deserved what they got and much more. I did need to be left alone. It was a confusing time: I had to deal with it on my own, in my own way. I am sorry if I worried you."

Tears were starting to appear in my eyes. He didn't hate me. That was a relief! "I am still sorry you were put in that situation. If I could take it back, I would. I would never ask you to do anything like that for me."

"I know. Everything happens for a reason, whether it's good or bad. I am sorry about what you had to go through. It couldn't have been easy. I'm also sorry I wasn't there when you woke up. I felt out of control after you were attacked. I had to leave, but I made sure you weren't alone first."

"You were out of control?"

"I let myself lose control because I was angry. Those reapers were going to kill you. I couldn't let that happen. I went to your apartment, but you weren't there. I called your phone but didn't get an answer, so I tracked you by your scent and found you at the park. I got there when the woman pulled the gun on you. I saw you move it, and then put the two blondes to sleep. After that, I saw the older male come at you with a dagger. Everything was happening so fast. I couldn't help but change and attack him."

"I'm sorry", I whispered. I felt horrible. If I had kept my phone with me, maybe this could have been avoided.

"It is over with. There is nothing we can do to change what has happened. We can simply learn from it. I am better now, I promise."

"What were you doing at my apartment?"

"I wanted to talk to you about the night before and New Year's."

"Okay, what did you want to say?"

"I think you know."

"I don't think I do."

I turned to look at him then. During our, I'm sorry speeches, I was looking at the floor. I couldn't bear to look at him. I was afraid I would cry even harder than I already was. He was looking at me kind of strangely. I wiped the tears away and smiled at him slightly, hoping he would speak up.

"About New Year's: I know I kissed you and ran off. I felt an electric shock when I kissed you. That shock was making me start to shift. I couldn't do that in front of all those people, especially you."

"I felt the shock too. I thought you regretted kissing me, to be honest, and you didn't like me that way."

"Are you crazy, have you looked at yourself? Besides being beautiful; you are kind, strong, brave, and a good person, which is hard to find.

I know I haven't known you that long, but I feel something for you: I assure you, I don't regret kissing you."

He made me blush. "Thank you. I feel something for you as well. I don't know how to explain it exactly either. I know that I like to be around you and when I'm not, I miss you and think about you a lot."

"I know what you mean. I couldn't stand to be away from you any longer. I had to come see you. I knew you were alright, but I had to see it for myself."

"I'm glad you did."

He brushed his finger on my cheek, dragging his finger slowly down to my chin, then leaned in to kiss me. His lips were warm and soft, the electric shock was there once again, but not as strong. I pulled away embarrassed.

"Sorry about that", I said in a low voice.

"For what?"

"I think I'm shocking you."

"I think so too, but I don't mind."

I giggled at that. I couldn't believe I did that. He didn't care, though. He just smiled at me. It felt really good to be around him again. I felt the tension between us fade away like it had never been there. However, I was afraid it was going to come back, but I had to know.

"I have another question."

"Shoot."

"What do you know about me exactly?"

"What do you mean?" he asked looking confused.

"Do you think I am different from other vampires?"

"I don't think I understand what you mean."

I could tell he wasn't lying to me. He wasn't sure what I was talking about. I knew without a doubt I could trust him. I decided to tell him everything, I was hoping he could accept me for what I was. Lavy said he knew, but maybe she assumed he had figured it out already like I had.

"I'm not just a vampire. I am more than that."

"What do you mean?"

I took a deep breath before answering. "I'm also part witch. I'm a hybrid."

He was quiet for a few minutes. I could tell he was thinking about what I had just told him. I knew it was a lot to comprehend. He could tell I wasn't lying either. A good thing about having excellent hearing was that we could hear each other's heartbeats. Mine didn't skip a beat when I told him the truth about me.

"Cool."

"You're not freaked?"

"I knew there was something special about you the first time I saw you. I thought hybrids were extinct: something that had died out thousands of years ago. Knowing the world we live in: anything is possible."

"It is crazy that you are so calm about this. I got freaked out when I found out. I didn't want to be special or different. It was weird enough that I was a vampire. Speaking of, you don't care that I am a vampire, you know the blood drinking part?"

"I don't care. Sometimes I eat freshly killed raw meat."

"Gross", I teased.

"Hey, not cool", he said smiling at me again. I loved his smile. It was warm and welcoming.

"I don't care either. We are what we are. I have learned, well kinda, to accept I am not normal."

"I'm glad you're not normal; that would be boring", he joked.

"Right. Who needs normal?" I asked, smiling.

"How did you find out you are a hybrid?"

"Ready for a long story?"

He looked at his phone; then back at me. "We have at least another hour before we get to our destination, so I'm not going anywhere."

I sighed. "Where to begin?"

"The beginning is a good start."

I told him everything; just not all the gory details. I explained about the dreams I had been having of Jewel and Jahana, the incubus attacking me and how I stopped it, Legs talking to me and being my familiar, and the spells that I have done with the bracelet I was left by my birth mother. I explained how I saw her in a vision when I was trying to figure out why she left me, and also, about where she was right now, or where I think she is. My long story ended with me having past lives as Jewel and Jahana and our shared mark.

"That's it', I said taking a much-needed breath. I felt like I hadn't taken a good breath since I started talking.

"Interesting."

"Interesting?"

"It is definitely something. I don't know how to explain how I feel about it, and all that hasn't happened to me. I do have questions."

"Shoot", I said copying him from earlier.

"Can I see the mark?"

I blushed a little at his request. I stood up, pulled my wallet and phone out of my pockets, and laid them on the seat. I then took off my hoodie and placed it on the seat as well. I turned my back toward him and took off my t-shirt. I was glad I wore a spaghetti strapped shirt underneath it. I pulled my hair to my left shoulder. I heard him stand up behind me. He then touched the crescent moon and the stars with his fingertips. His touch was soft and made my skin tingle.

"Beautiful", I heard him say.

"What?" I asked, wanting to make sure I heard him right.

"The mark is beautiful, and so are you."

I turned around to look at him then. He was looking down at me with such affection that it made me blush even more.

"Thank you. You're not so bad looking your-self."

He sat back down, then, pulling me down with him, until I was sitting on his lap. He kissed me softly on the lips; then my neck. I pulled away teasingly. He pulled me closer and kissed me harder. We kissed until we were both out of breath and my stomach growled. I was extremely embarrassed, knowing I should have eaten more.

He laughed at me, "hungry?"

"A little, I admit. I should have eaten actual food earlier."

He picked me up and sat me down on the seat.

"I'll be right back my lady."

He was gone for a little while, but just when I was starting to get worried, he came back. I got really happy. He brought chocolate, chips, and water.

"You're smart. Chocolate is a girl's best friend", I said, giving him a small wink.

Chapter Nineteen

We rode, ate, and joked the rest of the way to the place Falcon was taking me. It felt great to be around him. I was relieved he knew about me not being normal, as far as normal goes for our world. The best thing was: he didn't act differently around me. He actually seemed more like himself. Maybe it was because we didn't have any huge secrets between us anymore. I was sure he had more questions for me, but he was waiting to ask. I had questions for him as well.

When we arrived at our stop, I was anxious to know where we were. We entered into another train station, not much different than the one in Texarkana. It may have been a little smaller, but not by much. I used the bathroom and washed my face. I looked at myself in the mirror, looking back at me was someone who was happy. I wasn't a sad person, but the past hour I have been a lot happier than I had been in a while.

Falcon was waiting for me outside the door. He greeted me with a warm smile and another bottle of water. "Ready to go?" he asked. I nodded. He took my hand and led me outside. I gasped at the sight. The view was spectacular with various trees of all colors and huge mountains in the background.

"Welcome to the Ouachita Mountains. This is one of the best natural locations in Arkansas", he said.

"They are beautiful."

"I thought you would like them. I like this place. It's easy to be myself here. I don't have to hide what I am, and I can be free in those mountains", he said pointing at them.

"You change here?"

"Yes, when I can. I can run and hunt here."

"Thank you."

"For what?" he asked sounding confused.

"Bringing me here. Showing me something that is special to you."

"I was hoping it could be special for you, too."

I smiled up at him. "Thanks." We walked to the trail that looked to be overgrown. It didn't take long for us to hit the woods. The trees were thick. As soon as we entered them, the view of civilization disappeared. It was just Falcon, me, and nature. I could hear the animals scampering around, smell the clean air, and feel a connection to the earth. My body became alive. My senses became more alert. Maybe, it was because we were out of the city. I tried my best to fight what I could hear, smell, and see in the city. It was a lot to deal with, but here I invited it all in. I felt free. As soon as we left the trail, it was an instant change.

"Feel it, right?"

"Yes, it is like I am one with nature. The outside world is just gone."

"That is why I like this place so much. There aren't a lot of hikers around this time of year. It's too cold for them, but not for us", he said, winking at me.

I laughed. It was definitely nice not getting cold anymore. We continued to walk, not really talking. I was taking the scenery in: the sun was out and above the trees. The different colors of greens, browns, reds, and yellows looked like a crisp painting. The woods seemed to go on for miles, but I didn't care. I wasn't getting tired, and I enjoyed the company of who I was with.

We walked for an hour before the woods ended, and we hit the first set of mountains.

"Hope you're good at climbing", he joked.

"Guess today we shall find out", I replied.

I followed him down a little way until we reached a place that looked easier to climb. He started to climb up the mountain grabbing certain parts.

"You have done this before, it seems."

"Maybe once or twice", he joked.

I grabbed where he grabbed. It wasn't hard. It felt natural to climb up the rocky mountain. I used to be afraid of heights but wasn't now. When I looked down from halfway up the mountain. I saw the trees below us, looking like various clouds of green, orange, and red. It was beautiful. I turned back to the mountain, to see different shades of black, gray, brown, and white. All the colors making random patterns to form the mountain. I let the rest of my senses awaken further, letting the place in. I could hear animals running around and smell the trees, dirt, and water around me. I loved that feeling: of being free and being myself.

When we made it to the top, the view was more spectacular than I could have imagined. The sky was blue with white clouds. The sun was lighting up the trees, the mountain, and the small town below us. I was sure if I only had human sight I wouldn't have been able to see it.

"This is amazing."

"You haven't seen anything yet."

"What?"

"The place I want to take you is even better."

"Let's go."

I couldn't imagine a prettier view than the one I had just seen. Falcon led the way. Of course, there was more climbing down and up mountains. I still never got tired. The more I went, the more I felt alive and free. We reached his secret spot two hours after getting off the train. It was worth the trip. He was right. This was better than the mountaintop. There was a large river in the middle of the mountains with wildflowers and berry bushes surrounding it. At the edge of the river was a waterfall that was slowly releasing water into the large body of water. The water was clear. You could see all the way down to the bottom. Several large fish were swimming around, along with turtles and tadpoles. Dragonflies and honey bees were flying around, avoiding us.

"You were right, this is better."

"I told you", he said playfully.

"Yes you did", I said, smiling at him.

I went to the bank of the river, watching the little world in the water. It was amazing how on this big earth, there are small little worlds everywhere. Everything had a purpose in life, even if they were small or different from everything around them.

"What are you thinking about?"

"My purpose in life?"

"So nothing deep then, huh?"

"I'm scared."

"Why?"

"I think I am supposed to stop this Cain guy, but I don't know why or how."

"I'm sorry. I know this is a lot to deal with. I'll be here with you to figure it out."

"Thanks. The first thing I want to do though is to find my birth mother."

"We will, I promise."

"I'm glad I have you."

"I feel the same. I do have a question."

"Yes?"

"Are you going to tell her?"

"Tell who what?"

"Tell Lavy, that you're her mother reincarnated?"

"No, at least not for a while."

"She should know."

"She will one day. I'm not her mother; not in this life anyway. Plus, I am sixteen, and she is thousands of years old."

"I don't think she will care. You have all of Jewel's memories right?"

"Yes. I feel love for her as a daughter, but also as a friend of someone I have just met."

"Do you feel love for Kegan?"

"Why would you ask that?"

"Curiosity. I have strong feelings for you. I have ever since we met. I want to know where I stand. It wouldn't matter if you cared for him, or remember him in that special way. I will always be here for you, no matter what."

I sighed, "I remember how Jewel felt about him. It is like a distant memory. I don't know him in this life. I know you. I want to be with you."

I walked over to Falcon, closing in the few feet between us. I put my hand on his cheek, willing him to lean down and kiss me. He did just that. The spark between us was just as strong as the first time he kissed me. His soft lips felt warm when they touched mine. The kiss started to heat up and become stronger. I pulled away needing to think and breathe.

"Lets' take this slow, okay?"

He was breathing heavily, "We can do that."

My stomach started to grumble. I was getting tired of being hungry every few hours. I know I liked to eat, but my stomach made noises at the wrong time.

"Hungry, I assume."

"Yes, unfortunately. I'll be alright, though. I don't want to leave."

"We can eat here. Like to fish?"

"I have never been fishing."

He gave me a strange look, thinking I was joking. When he realized I wasn't, he laughed.

"Today would be a good day to learn."

"We don't have fishing poles."

"You're right, we don't, but we have something better."

"What's that?"

"Me."

"You?"

"Yes, I am a natural fisherman and hunter. Watch me."

He took off his shoes, socks, and pants. He had shorts on underneath. When he was un-dressed, shorts remaining on, he jumped into the river. I saw him swim fast to the bottom. He was stalking a group of large fish. I watched him grab one from its mouth. He swam back up to the river bank and threw it on the ground.

"Wow, that's impressive."

"I'll get us a few more. You start a fire."

"I don't have any matches or a lighter."

"Jade you have powers. Use them", he said before swimming back to the bottom of the river."

He was right. I had powers. I was part witch. I could do this. I was sure conjuring fire wasn't going to be hard. I mean I lit a candle. How hard could a larger flame be? Before I tried to make a fire pit, well the flame part, I gathered some rocks to make a circle and found some small sticks and dead leaves from the bushes. I wanted to have something to light up. After I felt it looked safe enough, I thought about fire. Small sparks started to appear. I didn't try too hard to make the fire appear. I simply willed it and it happened. I wanted the sparks to grow into a small flame and that is what happened.

"Looks good".

"Thanks".

I looked over at him then. He was dripping wet from the river and holding four fish. He walked over to a large flat rock and placed the fish there. He then went back to his pants and pulled out a pocket knife. I watched as he skinned the fish and dug the bones out. Stuff like that never bothered me. When the fish were cut up he went to the waterfall, disappeared behind it and brought out two metal skewers.

"Where did those come from?

"I left them here, along with a few other things. There is a small cave behind the waterfall, where I can safely leave stuff."

"You are full of surprises today, aren't you?"

"Just a few."

He put the fish on the skewers, then placed them in the fire. As the fish cooked, they smelled amazing. My stomach grumbled more. I walked over to the berry bushes as the fish continued to cook. The blackberries were safe to eat, but the red ones weren't. I wasn't sure how I knew that, but I did. Perhaps I read it in a book somewhere. I picked some and brought them over to where Falcon was.

"Want some?"

"Sure, I'm glad you didn't get the red ones. Those make you sick."

"Yeah, I know."

"Impressive", he said, copying me.

"Fish done yet?"

"Close, about another minute."

We ate all the fish and berries I picked and drank from the waterfall. It was all amazing and fresh. When I felt full, I laid on the ground and looked up at the sky. I saw the clouds change forms into what looked like animals, boats, and flowers. He laid down beside me and held my hand. We stayed like that in silence for a long while, enjoying each other's company.

He sat up suddenly. He didn't look scared more like a sudden idea popped into his head. He looked down at me and smiled.

"Want to run?"

"What?"

"We are supernatural creatures. We are alone. Do you want to run?"

"Sure. Will it be hard to run on the mountains?"

"No, it's actually a lot more fun."

"Can you run fast in human form?"

"No, but I was planning on changing."

"Here, now, really?"

"Yes, is that alright?"

"Please do, I want to see you."

"Good, but turn around. I have to strip, and I'm modest."

I laughed but did as he asked. I heard him strip off his shorts, then heard bones start to break and turn. It sounded painful, but he didn't let it show. He did tell me before, turning into an animal got easier over time. I heard a small growl. When I turned around, Falcon was gone, and a beautiful black panther was in his place.

The panther walked over to me and pushed his nose into my hand. I petted his head and looked into his eyes. His eyes were golden brown, but it was still Falcon looking back at me.

"You're beautiful", I said. He pulled away then, motioning with his head for me to come along. Before I could think about it too much, he was running up the mountain, back the way we came. I ran after him, easily catching up to him. The rush of energy I felt running was still fascinating. I raced him down the mountain. I was practically flying. We raced through the trees seeing who could go faster. He was almost as fast as me. Before I got too close to the trail and the train station, I turned back around. I headed back to our spot. He followed me easily. Running through the trees, seeing them pass by so fast, but yet so clearly, was incredible. I needed to let myself be free more often. It was an amazing feeling. I started to run back up the mountain, beating him with a little more ease than before. When I was close to the top, my hand got caught on a sharp rock. The rock sliced my hand open to the bone. The pain was intense and sudden, causing me to forget what I was doing. I slipped and started to fall down the rocky mountain. I felt my arms, legs, and head banging against the rocks. When I hit the ground I blacked out.

When I came back to consciousness I was back in the amazing spot Falcon brought me to. My body was a little sore, but I didn't feel any broken bones or bruises on me. I sat up and saw Falcon staring at me. He looked like he was in pain.

"Are you okay", I asked.

"I was worried about you. You were out for a while"

"I'm sorry. I lost my balance."

"I don't understand how. You're a vampire. You're supposed to be able to control that."

"I can be clumsy sometimes, it happens", I joked.

"Please don't joke. I thought you were going to die. You were bloody and bones were sticking out, your clothes were ripped. You really scared me, Jade."

"Hey, I'm fine. I have super healing remember. I should have been paying more attention. I was having too much fun and got distracted, but really I feel fine."

I looked down at myself then and saw why he was worried. My clothes were ripped and gross with blood and dirt all over them.

"I know you are now, but I wasn't sure you were going to be."

"I'm sorry. I really am. I am fine, though."

"I gave you some of my blood to make you heal faster. I knew you would heal; at least I hoped you would. I don't know how a hybrid works. I hope you're not mad I made you drink from me."

"Why would I be mad?"

"When a vampire drinks the blood of a supernatural, a psychic bond can be formed. They can sense each other's emotions. If either of them is scared, in pain, or sometimes other things. That is why most vampires drink human or animal blood. It doesn't happen all the time, though."

That took me by surprise. Did that mean Lavy could feel what I felt? Did she know that something was wrong with me? Did she know that I was her mother in another life? If she did, she didn't say anything.

"I drank from Lavy before, after my Grams died. Do you think she could sense my emotions changing after the meeting with Theodora?"

"I don't know. The more blood you drink, the stronger the bond. How much did you drink from her?"

"I don't know. I don't think that much. She hasn't said anything to me. She hasn't been acting differently around me."

"She probably doesn't know then. It has been months. It is possible that a bond wasn't created. Have you felt anything from her? Have you felt feelings that weren't yours or sensed anything different?"

I thought about it, digging through my memories of the last few months. Trying to find anything that could suggest some type of blood bond had happened. "No, nothing like that."

"Good, then I don't think she knows anything. It may work differently since you're a hybrid. I do still think you should tell her, though. She will find out eventually. Also, it is better if it comes from you and not someone else."

"The only person that knows besides you and me is Theodora, and she promised she wouldn't saying anything. I know I won't say anything until I'm ready. You won't either right?"

"Of course not, you have my word."

"Good, thank you. I will tell her everything, just not right now. I have other things to work out."

"Like?"

"I need to find my birth mother, which is obvious. I also need to figure out what type of witch powers I have and control the vampire thing a lot better, including my pain tolerance. I also need to break away from my human life. I need to let it go. It just isn't going to be easy."

"You don't have to leave your human life behind."

"I feel that I do. I don't want Alexa or anyone else getting hurt. I know something is coming. I can feel it. I am just not sure what it is."

"Whatever it is, we will face it together."

"I know. Thank you."

"You don't have to thank me. I will always be here for you."

"I know, I am grateful for that."

He smiled at me, then leaned over and kissed me on the forehead, before placing his forehead against mine. He closed his eyes, breathing me in. After a moment, I pulled away and looked into his eyes.

"There is one thing I would like to do before I turn away from my old human life completely."

"Okay, and what is that?"

I smiled at him, "Will you go to prom with me?"

Chapter Twenty

Prom is happening tomorrow night. I have been excited about it for the last couple of months. Falcon said yes, of course. I knew, well hoped he would. Also, there wasn't any bond created. I was relieved, I didn't want to be connected to anyone in that way.

Besides looking forward to prom, I have been working on controlling my magic and making preparations to leave Texarkana. This weekend is all about prom, next weekend before I leave, is about Alexa's birthday.

Alexa has been planning prom and making sure it was going to be perfect. This is our first prom together. She doesn't know this is going to be my only prom. I hadn't told her I was going to leave and didn't plan to. She had been excited for months. I didn't want to spoil her plans.

We went dress shopping together. I never found the perfect dress, so I decided to make one of my own. I got the sky blue fabric I wanted, silver lace, fabric glitter to go with it. I used magic to create it. It didn't require a spell. I only had to will what I wanted to happen and it did. Alright, it took a little more effort than that: I had to concentrate on every detail and it took a good four hours of focus to make the needles and thread do what I wanted. It was better than trying to sew by hand for days.

My dress turned out exactly how I imagined it would. It was made of blue silk and I made it look like a princess dress. The dress went down to my ankles and swirled when I spun around. It had off the shoulder sleeves, a V-neck top, and long blue gloves to match. The dress sparkled in the light from the glitter on the skirt and the three silver stars on the neckline. I had silver flats to go with it, I didn't want to do the whole cliché of clear shoes. Falcon got me a silver crescent moon necklace that completed the outfit. I felt like I was in a fairy tale in the dress. I didn't care to dress up usually, but wanted the dance to be special: something to hold on to.

Falcon rented a black and white suit that had a sky blue tie to match my dress. I offered to get him one of his own, but he declined. "I wouldn't wear it again. There isn't a reason to get one." I left it alone. He had a point. After prom I wouldn't be wearing the dress again either, I figured I would donate it. Maybe another short girl would like it as much as I did.

I needed to get some sleep but was anxious. I never cared for school dances, but this one I was excited about. After lying in bed for a couple of hours, I decided to get out of bed and watch some TV. I knew I couldn't concentrate on a book, so I flipped through channels. Nothing was on, but that wasn't a surprise it was two in the morning. After an hour of staring at the TV, I turned it off and went back to bed. I hated doing sleeping spells, mostly because when I woke up I felt druggy, but I needed sleep.

"Jade wake up!" I heard Alexa yelling.

"I just went to sleep", I groaned.

"It is a little after one in the afternoon. How late did you stay up?"

"What? I didn't mean to sleep so long", I said, as I sat straight up in my bed.

"I'm sure you didn't, but you did. We have a lot to do before tonight. Especially you girl, your hair is a mess!"

"Need coffee please."

"No, you don't. You will be hyped up for hours. I'll make you some green tea."

"That stuff is gross."

"Maybe, but it will wake you up without too much caffeine."

"Fine, be mean then, I don't care", I said as I fell back on my bed.

She walked down to the kitchen and started to boil some water. I dragged myself slowly out of bed a couple of minutes later and walked down to the kitchen. She handed me a mug of tea. I liked southern ice tea, but not that green tea stuff. I gulped it down, so I wouldn't have to deal with the taste.

"Next time, maybe add a little honey to it, to sweeten it up please."

"Next time, don't do a sleeping spell. Some passion flower would have done the same thing but not had bad side effects."

"You need to stop reading all those herb and plant books."

"You know you love it. Go get dressed. We need to make it to the salon on time. I don't want to miss our appointments."

"Alright, give me ten minutes."

"You have five", she said sternly.

I grabbed some clothes and changed as fast as humanly possible. I brushed my hair and teeth, as well.

"Ready", I said smiling.

"Great, you had one minute left", she joked.

We made it to the salon on time for our appointments. I paid in advance, so we wouldn't lose our spots. I wanted something simple, so I went with a waterfall braid and the rest of my hair was loosely curled. Alexa, on the other hand, wanted something elegant and fancy. She went with something called a Chain Braid Chignon. It looked like a low curly bun with braids intertwined into it. She also added some jeweled clips into her hair.

We were out in two hours; hair was done and so were our nails. I went with clear polish and Alexa went with a soft pink to match her dress. Her dress came down to her knees. The skirt was pale pink and wavy. The top was white with floral print. She had decided on strappy pink heels to go along with it. I told her she was brave, I would trip continuously all night, even with vampire balance. She laughed and agreed.

We made it to the dance early, to make sure everything still looked the way we left it yesterday. It looked better. We were in the gymnasium. The walls were covered with silver and gold stars everywhere. On each wall was either a crescent or full moon. The ceiling lights were dim to make it dark. Battery operated candles were on the thirty round tables that surrounded the dance floor. Two large disco lights were hanging from the ceiling on opposite sides of the gym. Silver and gold round paper lanterns were covering the ceiling, hanging lower than the disco balls. Strings of flashing Christmas white lights covered the edges of the ceiling. The theme of the prom was a Twinkling Twilight Masquerade Ball.

Face masks were optional, but I played a good sport and wore one. It was silver to match my shoes. Alexa and Trevor decided on white, and Falcon agreed to a black one. He would do anything for me, including wearing a silly mask.

I couldn't wait to see Falcon. I hadn't seen him the past three days. I was too busy helping

Alexa with decorating and organizing. I made her hire several caters to cover food and drinks, and a DJ to cover music, but she insisted she had to be in charge of decorating. She wouldn't trust anyone else to do it, except me. I followed her orders exactly how she wanted. She was a little bossy, but the end result was worth it.

We had about an hour before the dance was supposed to start. I sent Lavy a message to bring our dresses. I also talked her into being a chaperone and having Boston come with her. She acted like it was going to be horrible, but I think she was excited to come as much as I was. She had never been to a human dance before, let alone a high school dance.

Alexa and I sat at one of the tables, admiring our work as we waited for Lavy to show. She appeared a few minutes later in front of us making Alexa jump.

"Hi", she said.

"Remember this is a human dance. You can't be poofing in and out."

"I know that. I was sure no one else was here and Alexa already knows about me", she said while smiling.

"Yeah I do, but you nearly gave me a heart attack", Alexa said. Trying to get her heart to stop racing.

"Sorry", Lavy said.

"I'm okay. No worries, now that I can breathe normally again. Lavy, you look incredible."

"Thank you. I haven't worn this in decades."

"Decades?" Alexa and I said in unison.

Lavy laughed at the two of us. "Yes, I have had this dress since the forties."

Alexa and I looked at each other in surprise. I know that Lavy has lived a long time, but I never think about it. She looked amazing in her vintage dress. It was a simple black cotton spaghetti strap that went past her knees. The skirt of the dress looked like a poodle skirt from the fifties. She had on black flats to match the dress. Alexa couldn't see what I could see. The black fabric made Lavy's orange and purple shimmering skin stand out more and the black mask made her green eyes pop. I still hadn't told her about my past lives, even though Falcon kept telling me I should. Alexa didn't even know. I felt she knew too much already about our world, but that was going to change soon.

We changed and actually managed to not mess up our hair or makeup. Out of the guys, Trevor was the first to arrive. He was in an all-white tux with a pale peach tie. It looked nice on him. Falcon and Boston arrived together a few minutes later. Boston was in black pants and a long sleeve black shirt. He wasn't wearing a tux, but he did wear a black masquerade mask. The untrusting feeling went away towards Boston the past couple of months. He has been really good to Lavy and to me. He knew I was a hybrid now. At first, he was afraid of me, but he came around quickly. I was as much of a mystery to him, as I was to everyone else who knew.

People started to show up in large groups. We all danced to several songs and enjoyed each other's company. Falcon was an amazing dancer, but I still wasn't. He didn't seem to care, though. He held me in his arms and we swayed from side to side when there was a slow song. I copied what others did when there was a fast song playing. I didn't really come to dance. Mostly, I wanted to make memories with Alexa.

There was a king and queen of prom and a prom court. I had no idea who the people who won were, but they seemed to be a good fit. Both were tan blonde seniors who seemed to be well-liked. After they were announced prom king and queen, they shared a special dance. Once their song was over, everyone else rejoined them on the dance floor.

I decided to get some food instead because I was starving and hadn't eaten all day. It was mostly finger food: mini sandwiches, fruit, vegetables, cookies and several small mini cakes to choose from. I didn't eat much. I wanted something more filling.

"After this, I want some real food, y'all want to grab some burgers or tacos?" I asked everyone.

"Yes, sure, sounds great," they all said.

Prom ended around midnight. Alexa hired a clean-up crew, so we didn't have to stay. I would have helped but was really glad I didn't have to. We were the last ones to leave, so we could make sure no one was locked into the school. After everyone was officially gone, we grabbed some food at an all-night diner in town. We stayed there for hours eating and talking. It was nice hanging out together; pretending to be normal. I finally got tired and needed to go home. Trevor took Alexa home.

Lavy was going to stay with Boston, so I offered to take Falcon home. Instead, he wound up coming home with me.

I changed into pajama pants and a t-shirt took my hair down and washed all the makeup off. It felt nice to be myself again.

"You're more beautiful like this, than in a fancy dress."

"You think I'm beautiful?" I joked.

"You know I do."

"Thank you for going with me."

"I would do anything for you."

"I know. I would do anything for you too."

"Good, how about we get some sleep then?"

"I thought you would never ask."

We both fell asleep on my bed listening to each other's heartbeats. It felt nice to lay beside him, with his arm around me. We were still taking things slow. We had both agreed to. I wasn't ready for the next step and he understood that. He got me, and I loved that about him.

The week zoomed by. I had confirmed the plans for Alexa's sixteenth birthday. It was weird that I was older than her, even if only by a few months. I swear she acted more like an adult than I did. For her actual birthday, she would be spending time with her family at a restaurant, but I had the weekend. I couldn't wait. It was going to be epic.

We went to Alexa's favorite Chinese restaurant to celebrate. I was informed I had to come because I was family as well. We got our own room and had them bring us all of our favorites. Alexa and I both ate too much, but it was worth it. I ate plenty of spicy shrimp rolls and peppered shrimp. Alexa made sure to have plenty of noodle soup and crayfish. I wasn't sure how she ate that stuff, but she felt the same way about me and sushi. I picked up the tab because her family was struggling financially; not that I would ever tell Alexa that. I did have to compel her mom to let me pay, but that wasn't hard.

After the restaurant, we went to a small park and had cake. She had a small square cake with the pale pink roses and green vines on it. It was pretty and definitely her. I gave her a silver chained necklace with a pink rose in middle. The rest of her gifts would come later.

"What are we doing this weekend?" she asked when she walked me to my car.

"It is a surprise, but we have to leave tomorrow night to get there on time."

"Come on, I want a hint."

"Nope, not going to happen, I'll see you tomorrow. Enjoy the rest of your birthday."

"Night."

I went home and fell asleep, instantly. The past few nights, I had been having dreams about my birth mother, my past lives, and Cain. I relived my mother giving me up, the deaths of Jewel and Jahana, and Cain talking to the old witch. I hadn't been able to find a lot of information about Cain, except that he was powerful and an Elder, which I already knew. He seemed to be a private person.

I have also been looking for my birth mother for the past couple of months with the help of Lavy and Falcon. We made small trips to find her. With each place we went to, she had already left, by the time we arrived. I'm sure she knew someone was looking for her but wondered if she knew it was me. I tried not to stress over it. I knew one day I would find her.

When I woke up, I felt refreshed. There had been no dreams at all. I already had my weekend bag packed and my lunch box of blood. I didn't have much to do, except to wait until Alexa got out of school. I tried to get her to skip, but she didn't want to ruin her perfect attendance record. "Perfect attendance looks good on college applications", I could hear her saying in my head. I knew she was right and she worked hard for this, so I left it alone.

I felt restless after only being awake for an hour. I offered to help Lavy at the shop, but she declined my offer. She had Boston helping her. I tried to text Falcon, but he was at work, so that left me alone.

"Ugh, I'm bored", I said out loud.

"You can always talk to me. I do talk back now, whether you want to hear it or not."

I jumped up, startled. I still forgot that Legs could talk, because she rarely did.

"You scared me Legs."

She chuckled at that. "I'm sorry, well mostly."

"Glad I could amuse you."

"Me too. What is the matter?"

"Ready to get the weekend started."

"Does Alexa know about this weekend?"

"She only knows we are going to do something fun. After the weekend is over, I'll tell her what she needs to know."

"Are you going to be able to?"

"It doesn't matter. I don't have a choice."

"Jade, I am sorry."

"Thanks, me too", I said almost crying.

I conjured up a few crickets and gave them to Legs. She drained them quickly. Still restless, I studied the spell book I got a few months ago. I have looked it over hundreds of times and remembered every spell. I still looked at it, thinking I had missed something. The book never changed, as it shouldn't. That would be too weird if it did.

The day dragged on until it was finally time to leave. Falcon stopped by when I was on my way out the door.

"Hello there, beautiful. You leaving?"

"Yes. Alexa's birthday weekend."

"Duh, I forgot. Please be safe, babe."

"I will."

"You're telling her this weekend right?"

I sighed. "Yes, I have to."

"I'm sorry."

"Thanks, I know, me too."

"I'm going to miss you."

"I'll miss you, too, I'll call you when we make it. I'll bring you back a souvenir."

"Thanks. Again, please be safe."

"I will. I promise I can handle myself."

"Yes I know", he said winking at me.

I kissed him goodbye after he walked me to my car. I watched him disappear in my rear view mirror. I started to cry. This weekend was supposed to be fun. I had to relax and enjoy it. The hard part wasn't coming until the end. I had almost two full days to have fun. I wasn't going to ruin this weekend for Alexa. I refused to do that.

Chapter Twenty One

After picking Alexa up from school, I took her to her house to pick up her stuff. After that, we were on the road headed toward our first destination. We had to drive to Dallas, Texas to fly on a plane. It would take more than a day by car. This way we could make it there in a few hours and get to enjoy the trip.

We made it to Dallas with about two hours to wait for the plane to leave. I was starving, as usual. We noticed there were a lot more restaurants in Dallas than there were in Texarkana, but Dallas was also three times its size.

"What do you want to eat?" I asked.

"Anything is fine with me."

"Well this is your birthday weekend, so you choose."

"Alright, let's do some Mexican food. None of that Tex-Mex stuff you like. I want the real stuff."

"Deal", I said, trying not to laugh.

We saw several, but finally decided on a small family-owned restaurant. The place was incredible. The walls were bright orange and yellow, with multi-color tile ceilings. The waiters wore sombreros and ponchos. All the workers were family and friendly. It was a Friday, so the place was busy, but we got seated quickly. Alexa ordered some rice and tacos, which looked delicious. I ordered sour cream chicken enchiladas, chips, and queso dip. For dessert, we had home-made ice cream and churros.

We ate until we were over-stuffed, and it was close to time to go to the airport. When we arrived, I walked to the counter and picked up our first class tickets. That was the first time either one of us had ever rode on a plane. I wanted it to be amazing!

Alexa was looking at all the flights that would be taking off soon when I went back to her. I hope she got to go to all those places that were listed and more someday.

"Here you go", I said as I handed her the ticket. Her eyes widened in disbelief.

"Are you serious?" she asked with surprise.

"Yes, that is where we are going. I thought it would be the best place for your sweet six-teenth."

"You are the absolute best. Salem, Massa-chusetts is perfect. You know I have wanted to go there for years. Thank you, Jade. You're such a great friend!"

"You're welcome. What are best friends for, if not to spoil their best friend? I hope we get to board soon. Then, we can sleep on the flight. I want to be awake when we get to the hotel, so we can plan our day."

"Sounds good. There is so much I would like to see."

"We have all day tomorrow and Sunday."

"Thank you again. This will be the best trip ever."

"No problem. I have to spoil my little sister sometimes", I said winking at her. We may not be blood, but she had always been like a sister to me.

"Good point", she joked.

We boarded the plane ten minutes after she found out where we were going. We both liked the idea of Salem, but she was more fascinated by it. The plane ride lasted a few hours. I tried to sleep, but I couldn't relax. The lift-off had me freaked out some, and then knowing I was high in the sky made it worse. I tried not to think about it too much. I had to remember I was doing this for Alexa, not for myself. She slept the whole time. I was a little jealous, to be honest.

When we landed, I was relieved and ready to get off the plane. I had rented a car a couple weeks in advance, so it was waiting for us in a car lot next door. The black SUV was exactly how the picture showed it. I didn't want anything too fancy but wanted to be comfortable.

After we picked up the rental, we went to the hotel. It was a large twelve story building. We were on the eighth floor in a huge suite. It had two bedrooms, two baths, a living area, and a small kitchen that was stocked with food. We also had several menus from the hotel and surrounding restaurants. I wasn't hungry yet but was really tired.

"Welcome home for the next two days. I need a small nap. You can get food, watch TV, or take a shower. I'll set an alarm for four that should give me about three hours of sleep."

"I think I am too excited to eat, take a shower, or really do anything."

"I can do a calming spell on you if you like."

"Thanks, but no thanks. I'll find some tea to calm me."

"Suit yourself."

I went to my room with my overnight bag. I put on some comfy pajamas, crawled into the king size bed and went to sleep within a few minutes. I was exhausted more than I realized.

I woke up with my alarm going off. I swear I had just gone to sleep, but hours had passed. When I became fully conscious, I heard the TV in the living room playing some old television show. She laughed at something one of the characters said. I was going to miss her laugh.

I got out of bed and walked out of my room. She was eating donuts and coffee.

"Got more coffee?"

"Of course, they have a cappuccino machine. It is all set up for you to make one."

"You're the best."

"I know, don't forget it."

"I won't, don't worry."

"When you wake up fully, we can talk."

"Talk about what?"

"The weekend, duh."

"Right, of course."

I made me a cappuccino. After that, I found some banana nut bread in the cabinet. I devoured the whole small loaf of bread and drank two cappuccinos, after that I finally felt more human and not so groggy.

Alexa went to take a shower and get ready for the long day ahead. I did the same, using the oatmeal honey shampoo, conditioner and the honey-scented body wash, provided by the hotel. The hot water felt great. I let the heat wash away the stress I had built up.

By the time I was done, it was a little past six in the morning. Alexa was waiting for me anxiously in the living room. She had her laptop out and was making plans for places she wanted to go check out for the day. She had already made a list of museums, cemetery's, gift shops, a small witch village, and old houses.

"Oh that isn't a lot is it", I joked.

"We can break this up into two days."

"I think that will be a good idea."

"Sorry, I am just excited. I didn't expect to come to this place until after college."

"It's fine, promise. I want you to enjoy this weekend."

Then, a knock on the door came. I was hoping it was another surprise for Alexa. I opened the door and it was. Alex and Carol were standing in front of me with luggage. I was hoping they were going to be able to make it. I didn't tell Alexa because I didn't want her to get her hopes up. I wanted her family to spend this time with her, as well. I gestured for them to come in.

"Hey Alexa, we have company."

"Mom, Alex, what are you doing here?!" she exclaimed as she hugged them both.

"Jade had two tickets held for us at the airport in Dallas. We weren't able to go when y'all did because of my work schedule, but I got the rest of the weekend off. I don't know how Jade did it, but somehow she managed to talk my boss into it," Carol stated.

"Jade just told me I better be here", Alex piped in.

"I am so happy that y'all are here. Thank you, Jade, this means so much."

"They're family, we couldn't have your birthday weekend without them."

"How was the flight?" Alexa asked.

"It was strange riding first class, but very cool. There were some cute flight attendants", Alex said jokingly."

"Ignore him. The flight was nice. We slept most of the way here, so we got a power nap."

"How did you two get here from the airport", Alexa asked.

"We grabbed a Taxi. Jade said she has a rental car already, and we could share."

"Yep, that is why I got an SUV instead of a car; plenty of room for all of us."

"Got any food? I'm starving?" Alex asked.

"Sure we have plenty or would you rather go out for something?" I asked.

"Let's stay here and eat. That will give us time to rest for a bit before we get our day started", Carol said.

"Make yourself at home. Carol, you and Alexa can share her room. Alex, sorry dude. You get the couch to sleep on. But you can use either shower if you need to.

"A lot of food and drink choices are in the kitchen. I'll show you where everything is", Alexa told her mom and brother."

I let them get settled in and get something to eat. I was glad Alexa was happy that her family was here. She was close to her mom, which was nice. When they were done eating and had showered, we decided to leave and go explore the long list of what Alexa wanted to do while we were in Salem.

The first place on our trip was a wax museum. It was so creepy how the wax figurines looked so real. They wore clothing and had their faces painted on. It was like you were looking at people, but could tell they looked off at the same time. Some of the scenes were of witches being hanged from the 1600s, witches locked up in prison cells, or showing men and women trapped in pillories. It all looked sad and barbaric. I know the exhibits weren't real, but I was part witch. It kind of made me angry. I did my best to ignore the feeling. That was a part of history and how people could be ignorant, who wanted an excuse to hate something or someone.

After walking around for about an hour, we decided to go to another place on Alexa's list. We went to a couple of cemeteries where some of the witch trial council were buried. The graveyards were small and the grave-stones very old. I could feel the hate coming from the graves of the council members. It was eerie. The graves didn't affect anyone else, it seemed, but me.

I was happy when we left. As soon as I walked out of the small gates, I felt better immediately. By that time, everyone was ready for a small break and to get some food. We went and found a little restaurant that served different types of seafood. It was amazing! We all over-ate, but we didn't care. We decided to leave the rental car parked; this way, we could walk around and explore everything.

We went to several gift shops, museums, and small old villages. The first day was great. We followed a red line in the brick road to several places we went. It was like a map for all the Salem witch stuff. There were several people dressed up in 1600's costumes: some were presumed witches, others were council members or normal citizens. I never felt magic from any of them. I was relieved. This place was unique and good for visiting, but I wouldn't want to live here.

When the day was over, we had a few bags from places we went. I made sure Alexa got a spell book (no it wasn't real), jewelry, candles, and a Salem history book about the witch trials. I made sure Carol and Alex got something they wanted too. Carol got a jewelry box and Alex got a jar with a fake eye in it.

I took plenty of pictures of our visit here, but I deliberately left myself out. I wanted to make sure they all had a lot of memories from this place. When we made it back to the hotel, we were all tired. I ordered a few pizzas, so we could relax and eat. We watched a movie and talked about our long, but fun day.

I went to bed shortly after the movie. I needed sleep and blood. I made sure to lock my door. I didn't want anyone coming in. After a blood bag, I got into bed and went to sleep. I was hoping for a dreamless sleep, but I didn't get that. I had another dream about Alexa: it was more of a nightmare.

I was walking down a white hallway, and the long fluorescent bulbs were flickering continuously. It was so quiet I could hear the eerie ringing noise in my ear. When I got to the end of the hallway, there were two gray double doors with a sign above them that said, Morgue.

I walked through the double doors and felt a chill throughout my bones. The smell of death and decay burned my nose. I felt sick to my stomach. There were autopsy tables everywhere, which had bodies on them covered up in white sheets.

Each body had a tag on its toe. Each tag was blank, except for one. I slowly walked over to the unknown body with an actual name tag. The name on the label was written in red and said, Alexa Thompson. I walked up to the top of the table and pulled the white sheet down slowly. Laying there was Alexa, with puncture wounds on her neck. Her body was drained of blood, her face pale, her lips blue, and her eyes were wide like she was terrified.

The next thing I knew, I was at her funeral. Everyone was all in black. Her mom and brother were laying black roses on her coffin. I tried to get closer to say goodbye, but she appeared in front of me. Blood was running down her neck. She lifted her arm and pointed at me, and mouthed, "You killed me."

I woke up wanting to scream, but nothing came out. My throat was dry and tears were running down my face. I knew I would never hurt her, but that was the third time I had that dream since my transformation. I ignored it at first, then my witch powers started to form. The attack from the reapers happened, and I had that sick feeling of hate in the graveyard. I knew I had to let her go, even more now than I did before. It was going to be hard, but it had to happen. I had one more day with her. I would miss her so much, but her safety was more important. I couldn't be selfish with her.

The second day was the same as it had been yesterday. We went to another museum, which was mostly displays from the witch trials, led by a tour guide. She was very informative, explaining how it was mostly women who were stated to be witches. Most of them were hanged, and how the trials were held in several small towns. I tuned a lot of it out. I was too distracted by the nightmare I had.

When the tour was over, we grabbed lunch. I didn't eat much, but the others enjoyed their food. Alexa noticed something was wrong, and questioned me about it.

"You okay? You didn't eat much and you have been quiet today."

"Yeah, I'm fine', I lied and she knew it.

"Why are you not telling me the truth?"

"I'll talk to you about it later", I signed.

"You better."

"I will let's just enjoy today. I need some coffee; that will help probably."

We found a small cafe, and I got a large cappuccino with extra caramel drizzle. Alexa got a hot chocolate, Alex got black coffee, which looked gross, and Carol got an apple cider. We were walking around drinking our warm drinks when I noticed a reaper. I could sense the reaper before I could see her. She appeared to be on the hunt for something that was in the opposite direction of where I was.

I wanted to get away from her, so I talked Alexa into a ferry ride around Salem before we had to go back to the airport. We all loved it. I always loved the feeling of being in or on water. The boat trip took a little over an hour. When it was over, we headed back to the hotel to grab our stuff. I checked us out and drove us to the airport. We didn't have to wait long to board before we were lifted into the air to fly back to Dallas.

Alexa rode with me back to Texarkana and Carol let Alex drive their vehicle. We made it back to their place in a couple of hours. Alexa and I didn't talk much. I didn't know what to say. I was sure she knew something was up with me but wasn't sure what. When I parked in their driveway, I got out of my car. I walked in the house with her to her room. She closed the door behind her and turned around and glared at me.

"What is going on with you? You have been acting strange ever since this morning. Are you mad or something?"

"No I am not mad, I don't have a reason to be."

"Than what is it?"

"I had a nightmare that you died and I killed you. I think it was more of a vision. I would never hurt you intentionally, though, I promise."

"I know you wouldn't, it was a nightmare, it wasn't real Jade."

"It felt real. It doesn't matter. I am leaving anyway."

"What do you mean leaving?"

I walked over to her bed and sat on it. I looked up at her and told her what I had been dreading for a while.

"I am leaving Texarkana for good in a couple of days. I have a few things to do before I leave."

"I don't want you to leave. You're my best friend. I need you in my life", she said with tears running down her face.

I started to cry. "You won't remember me."

"How will I not remember you? You are one of the most important people in my life."

"I had a friend set up a spell for me. After midnight tonight, you and everyone else will not remember me. It will be like I never existed. Your memories will be intact, but I will not be in them. "

She looked at me, with more tears starting to populate in her eyes. "How could you do this to me? How could you take away my memories? I feel like you're ripping my heart out."

"I'm doing this for you. I love you, you're like a sister to me. I want you to be safe! You're not safe with me here! I am so scared something will happen to you. I couldn't live with myself if that happened."

"You're taking away a part of me. How can you play with my mind like that?"

"In a few hours, you won't care. You will be happy about the weekend you spent with your family in Salem for your birthday weekend and ready to go to school tomorrow."

"Jade, please don't do this. I will not tell anyone your secret, I promise. I know you would never hurt me. Please, you're family. Don't leave me."

"It's too late, even if I wanted to stop it, I couldn't. Magic doesn't work like that. Once a spell has been set in motion, you can't stop it."

I walked over to her and looked into her eyes. I felt the connection form from my mind to hers. I could tell her heart was breaking, and her mind was flooded with memories of how we met and all the things we have done together. I ignored it, so I could compel her.

"Alexa, I want you to listen to me very carefully. Can you do that?"

"Yes."

"I want you to give me your friendship ring and bracelet. You want me to have them." She slid the ring off her finger and bracelet off her arm, then gave them to me.

"Here take my ring and bracelet. I want you to have them."

"I am going to leave in a minute. I don't want you to remember that I told you I was leaving. You will only remember me saying I had to leave so I could go home. You are going to go to sleep in a few minutes because you are exhausted from the trip. When you wake up in the morning, you won't remember me or anything about the shadow realm. Now walk me to the door to say goodbye. Do you understand everything I have said?"

"Yes, I understand."

I left her mind. She shook her head a little and smiled at me.

I washed away my tears quickly, so she wouldn't see.

"What were you saying?"

I smiled at her. "I'm tired and need to go home. It has been a long weekend, but I had a lot of fun."

"That is probably a good idea. I could use some sleep too. Let me walk you out."

She walked me to the door and I left, practically running to my car. I held back the rest of my tears until I was in my car and driving down the road. It hurt so much leaving her. It hurt worse knowing that in a few short hours she wouldn't even know who I was.

I made it back to the loft. When I walked in everything was nearly packed up. Lavy was on the floor eating take out with Boston and Falcon. Falcon got up and walked over to me, I slid into his arms and cried.

"I am so sorry babe."

"It hurts so badly."

"I know it doesn't mean much now, but you're doing this because you are a good friend."

"Maybe, but it sucks."

Lavy walked over to me then and gave me a hug and some tea. "This will help relax you."

"Thanks." I drank it. Letting the tea warm my body. I started to feel calmness drift throughout my body. "Did y'all get all the stuff from her place?"

"Yes, we got all the pictures, gifts, and anything that could remind her of you", Lavy said.

"Good. No one else has anything I need to worry about", I said.

"Oh, the deed and banking information came in yesterday while you were away", Lavy said, as she walked over to her bag.

She pulled out some envelopes and handed them to me. I pulled them out and looked at them. They were exactly what I wanted. I was leaving Grams house, including the furniture, to a women and children's shelter. I had already removed all the photos that were left last week. The second set of documents was an inheritance I left for Alexa and her family, but it was from a deceased family member on Alexa's dad side who wanted them to have it. The letter was vague but got to the point. The money was legally theirs, and no one could take it from them. I set them up with two hundred and seventy-five thousand dollars. I wanted to make sure Alexa could go to whatever college she wanted, and her mom wouldn't have to worry about it. I knew she would do great things with her life; the money just insured it.

I put the papers back in the envelopes and put them in a bag I had in my room. I planned to take them to a lawyer who was from our world tomorrow. He would see that everything was done correctly.

My room was boxed up, and the mattress was bare. It looked so empty in here, but I knew it would before I came back. Seeing and knowing are two different things, though. Legs was in a plastic tote ready to travel. I opened up the lid and saw that she was staring up at me.

"I'm sorry Jade. Are you okay?"

"No, but I will be."

"Yes, you will. She will have a good life."

"I know, but I won't be in it."

I put my hand in Legs' tote. She walked up on my hand, then my arm, and sat on my shoulder.

"You're strong, Jade. Remember you have all of us here, and soon you will have your mother."

Knowing I was leaving to go do a better search for my birth mother was the only thing that kept me going. I know I had Lavy, Falcon, and Boston, but they weren't Alexa. Alexa was more than my best friend. She was my sister. I was going to miss her, even if she wouldn't miss me.

Chapter Twenty Two

It's been a week since I left Texarkana. We donated all the stuff in the apartment. Lavy closed
down Children of the Sun and Moon and stored
all the extra merchandise in a storage building
Boston had. I saw the papers be handed to
Carol. When she read the documents, she
started to cry. I watched Alexa at school. She
was happy and the same Alexa she had always
been. I said goodbye one final time to Grams'
house and visited Grams' grave. I felt like I was
saying goodbye forever. I donated all my books
to the used bookstore downtown and only took
clothes I needed, the basic essentials, and of
course Legs.

Falcon came with us. He quit his job so he
could come with me, but he was told he could
come back anytime he wanted. I made sure his
family would be taken care of while he was

gone. He didn't want me to, but he had to agree to it if he wanted to come with me. I was not going to let his family go without because of me. He finally agreed because he didn't want to be away from me.

Boston stayed behind. He wasn't much for trips, and I think him and Lavy were just good friends. They tried to be more, but it didn't work out. I left my car with Boston. I loved my bug, but it wasn't a good road trip car. I bought a used Durango. Falcon went with me to look over it the day I got it. We packed up and started to drive. We went from town to town looking for my mother. With each place we went, I could sense her. I knew she was there at some point, but it was like we just missed her.

I finally ran into someone that she trusted and had been helping her for years. He was a nice, old, dark-skinned man with long white hair, who had known my birth mother before she gave birth to me. I found him wandering around a nursing home. Something led me to him. It was like a force I couldn't see was pushing me toward him. He seemed to know I was coming, even before I knew I needed to find him.

I didn't trust him at first, and I tried to compel him. To be truthful, it didn't work. There was something blocking the compulsion.

"If you are trying to compel me, it won't work."

"But... how did you know?"

"I may be human, but I have a few tricks up my sleeve."

"Understood."

"You don't have to trust me, but if you're looking for Luna, I will give you the address of where she will be heading to next."

"Why would you give up the information so easily?"

"I may be old, but I am not blind. You don't resemble her except for the hair color, but I know you are her daughter. You are so much like her, honest and strong. Also, I have been expecting you for quite some time, now."

"How?" I asked stunned.

"She told me about you a little bit. I met her before she had you, Jade. She was a sad thing; depressed that she had to give you up, but mostly afraid someone was after her and you."

"Where will she be going?"

"She is going to be at the warehouse where it all started."

"Where?"

"If you think about it, you will know. I must go now. Safe travels. Don't worry, I can't say a word about you to anyone. Not that anyone would believe me. Everyone thinks I am a crazy old man."

"Thank you."

"Take care. Tell your mom, Sam says hi."

I stayed on the bench that we were sitting on during our strange conversation. I watched as he walked up a long ramp to the opened door that led to the nursing home. I saw on the back of his arm a faded black dagger and snake tattoo. Alarmed, I stood up fast and walked up to him, demanding to know what he was.

"You're a reaper?"

He turned to look at me then with sad eyes. "Yes, I was. I haven't been hunting in over forty years. Jade just because you're told you are something or brought up to be a certain way, doesn't mean you have to be. I may have been raised as a reaper, but I didn't agree with the lifestyle or hurting anyone just because they were different. I'm not the only one who feels this way. Your mother trusts me. You can, as well."

"I don't know what to say."

"You don't have to say anything, follow your instincts. Not everything in this world is as it seems. You should know that better than anyone. Now, I need to rest. It's been a long day and I'm an old man. Goodbye Jade, I hope to see you again someday. I have a feeling our paths will cross again."

"Bye."

I went back to the motel we were staying at. Falcon was asleep, and Lavy was eating a salad on the opposite bed. I had time to think in the car. It was worth a shot to check it out. Even though I wasn't able to compel him, I was able to listen to his heartbeat and his breathing. He wasn't lying to me. He was being honest. I wanted to ask him more questions, but I could tell his mind wasn't all there. He seemed distant for most of our conversation. I also figured out what he meant about where it all began.

"I know where she is going to be now."

"What?"

"I met an elderly human man who knew her before she gave birth to me. He called her Luna. She will be at the warehouse where she left me as a baby."

"When do you want to leave?"

"Now, you can eat in the car."

"Sure, I'll pack up."

I woke Falcon and had him load our stuff in the car. We were on the road ten minutes later. It was only a couple of hours drive from the warehouse. I did my best to abide by the speed limits on the highway, but it wasn't easy. I wanted to get to Luna, to my birth mother, as fast as I could. I needed to see her in person. I needed to make sure she was real.

When we finally made it to our new destination, I was jumping out of my skin. I was where she was going to be. Now, I just had to wait. I tried to relax and calm my breathing, I kept telling myself to calm down. Saying and doing are two different things for sure. We waited in the car for two hours, before I saw a woman go into the run down warehouse.

"Y'all wait here. If I'm not out in twenty minutes, come in and find me. I need to do this alone first."

"I don't like that, but okay," Falcon said unhappily.

"I agree with him", Lavy said.

"I'll be safe, remember I'm part witch. I can take care of myself. I pretty much have my powers under control."

They both sighed, but finally agreed, sort of.

I got out of the car and walked into the building. It smelled like wet dirt and mold. Windows were broken out, and it looked more rundown than it had in my vision. I tried to walk around as quietly as I could. I didn't want to frighten her, or for her to run away from me.

I was halfway in the building when I felt someone behind me. I stopped and turned around slowly. It was her in the flesh, but her hair was dark red now. She had dyed it recently, but she was still my birth mother. She looked shocked to see me, but she recognized me instantly.

"It's you", I whispered.

"How did you find me?" she asked.

"The elderly, man Sam, told me where you would be."

"He shouldn't have."

I stepped back. The words she had just said felt like a dagger in my heart. She didn't want me to find her? She didn't want to see me?

"I'm sorry, I needed to find you. I have questions and I want answers. If you answer them, I will leave and will not bother you again."

"Jade, you're not a bother to me. I have dreamed of seeing you up close and talking to you so many times. It isn't safe right now."

"I know it's not, but that is why I found you."

My friends came in just then. Luna then ran with vampire speed up to the third floor. I followed her. I was able to grab her arm before she escaped out of a broken window.

"Don't leave. They are my friends. They are safe. They have been helping me look for you. I trust both with my life."

She turned to look at me and nodded. "You're strong."

"I know, I think it has something to do with me being a hybrid."

"You know then."

"I do. Please answer my questions."

"I will do what I can."

We walked back down to the first floor. I introduced Lavy and Falcon to Luna. She still seemed on edge, not that I blamed her. Her daughter she gave up just found her and brought her shapeshifter boyfriend and fairy friend with her.

I didn't want to lose any time I had with her, so I went straight to the important questions.

"Who is my father?"

"A powerful witch. I had only known him a few days when you were conceived."

"Does he know about me?"

"No, you are not supposed to exist. I am still not sure how it is possible that you do."

"Why did you run away and give me up?"

"Hybrids are usually killed. I knew the moment I found out I was pregnant there was something special about you. I had to protect you."

"Is that why you let me be raised by humans?"

"Yes."

"I saw visions of you watching over me, why did you?"

"I wanted to make sure you were taken care of. I didn't want to give you up. I loved you more than you will ever know and still do."

"Did you know I was going to go through the change?"

"Yes, that is why I had your grandmother leave the house. I knew someone from our world would be there for you."

"You knew my grandmother?"

"Yes. I have been in contact with her for years, since before your parents died. I was the patient she was coming to see. I compelled her to think that I looked different than what I do. I knew she didn't need to be there during your transformation. She would have had too many questions, or have tried to take you to the hospital. She told me about Lavy, so I checked on her at her shop from a distance. I knew she was a fairy, and she would help you. It's in a fairy's natures to help."

"What else have you done?" I asked, trying to comprehend all of this. I knew there was more. She impacted my life more than she was letting on. I knew she wouldn't lie to me if I asked the right questions.

"When your adopted mother was in the hospital and dying, I went to see her. I took away her pain. I couldn't heal her. Her injuries were too severe, but I took away the pain that I could. I wanted you to be able to say goodbye to her."

"You were there?"

"Yes. I didn't know about your grandmother until after the funeral. I watched you the next day as you said goodbye. I wanted to comfort you, but didn't want to put you in danger."

"Were you in Salem recently?"

"Yes, I was watching you, until a reaper spotted me. I had to leave after I took care of her."

"I need a minute to process all of this." I turned away from her and closed my eyes, trying to let all of the new information sink in.

She had been watching me for years. She was always in my life one way or another. She was trying to help me in her own way. She knew Grams and she talked to my mom. Everything she told me took a couple of hours to get out of her and for me to accept it. I knew I wanted to know more but wasn't sure what I wanted to know.

Before I could think of something else to ask, the door to the warehouse opened. And large men came in. I knew they were guardians from what Lavy had told me, and from seeing Kegan in my dreams.

ॐ

A week had passed since I had been brought to Nyidalur. My friends were brought here too. I saw them once, but that was two days ago. They were all in separate rooms throughout the castle. We were only allowed to talk to each other for a few minutes. I was sure it was to appease me. I kept demanding to know what happened to them. They looked fed and healthy, which made me feel a little better.

Legs was brought to me a day after I had arrived. She was brought crickets and other bugs to eat each day when I was brought my meals. I didn't drink any blood the first three days, but I had to give in. I could feel my energy slipping away from me. Food was fine, but it wasn't enough to sustain me to keep me at my full potential. I smelled the blood a lot and took a small taste to make sure it wasn't drugged. It seemed fine. Nothing happened to me, except my energy was getting restored.

I was given new clothes when I arrived and was placed in my room. They were exactly my size, and so were the shoes I was given. I was brought fresh towels, and the bedding was changed daily by a maid.

When I stopped fighting the guardians and spoke to them calmly, I was allowed to go outside a couple of times a day to get fresh air. I wasn't able to go too far, and there were at least four guards with me all the time.

The eighth day, well what I believed to be the eighth day, I was brought a light purple dressing gown and ivory colored dressy flats. It had long sleeves, lace on the front, and came down to my ankles. A young woman who brought me the dress came and told me she had to do my hair for dinner.

"Why do you have to do my hair?"

"This is a special dinner, my lady."

"What do you mean special?"

"My lady, the dinner is in honor of you."

"In honor of me?"

"Yes, my lady."

I hadn't gotten used to the "my lady" stuff yet. Everyone who talked to me called me that. They wouldn't stop, even if I asked. When the woman left, I was dressed and my hair was in wavy curls flowing down my back. If I didn't feel like a prisoner, I would have felt pretty.

A guard came shortly after she left, and told me I was free to wander the castle for a little while. As soon as he walked away, I left my room. The castle was huge, I tried to find any of my friends' scents, but I couldn't. It was like my vampire smell had been weakened. I couldn't even hear that well. I wasn't sure what was going on.

I wandered down several hallways with no luck finding anyone. I only saw a lot of paintings, statues, doors, and candles everywhere. Getting annoyed, I made my way back to my room. Before I went in, I heard Falcon call me. I turned around and saw him, dressed in a fitted black and white tux. Lavy and Luna were with him, dressed in dresses similar to mine. I ran to them, kissing Falcon, and hugging Lavy then Luna.

"What is going on?"

They shook their heads. "We aren't sure", Falcon said.

"We know we were told to get dressed up for a dinner", Lavy said.

"The woman who brought me this told me the dinner is in honor of me", I said gesturing to the dress I was wearing.

"I was told the same thing, then told I could explore the castle", Luna said.

"How did y'all find each other?" I asked.

"We were in the same hall on the first floor. We didn't know until we were able to leave our rooms", Lavy said.

"I am sorry about this. I never wanted to put any of you in danger. I wanted y'all to be able to escape, and live your lives. I wanted each of you to be safe."

Falcon kissed me, then. "We are where we want to be. We all love you. Don't forget that."

"He is right", Lavy said.

Luna walked closer to me, placed her hand on my check, and then hugged me tightly.

"Jade, you are my daughter. I love you more than words can say. I won't ever leave you again. You have my word."

"I love you too", I said back.

"Dinner will be ready soon", said a butler of some sort. He was with a guardian, one of the ones that brought me here.

"Before dinner, your host would like to speak with you", the guardian said to me.

"I want my friends to come with me", I said.

"As you wish, my lady."

We followed the guardian down the wide staircase. He walked down another hallway to the right when he left the staircase. We walked past a banquet hall with a large table that had several places for people to sit and eat.

When we finally stopped at the large wooden door, the guardian knocked twice.

"Come in", someone said from the other side of the door.

He opened the door and gestured for us to come in. When I walked in, I saw several people sitting on thrones, actual thrones. One person, I recognized instantly was Cain Diomedes. He was the one in the middle, sitting on the biggest throne. He looked older than he had in my vision. He looked directly at me and smiled innocently. He gestured for me to come closer. I tried to avoid eye contact with him. I looked around at the other people who were sitting on the other thrones. I could tell there was a fairy, a shapeshifter, a troll, a vampire, and other creatures I didn't recognize. I could sense they were really old.

When I turned back towards my friends, they were looking at the elders. I was going to turn back toward our host, but a painting caught my eye. I was looking at myself, but it wasn't me. The painting had to be hundreds of years old. The woman in the painting was older than me, but not by much. She had dark brown eyes and her hair was close to black. It could have been my twin.

"Who is that?" I asked pointing at the picture on the wall. "Why does she look like me?" I demanded.

"My dearest Jade, my precious granddaughter that was your grandmother, my deceased wife. Oh, how I miss her so. The resemblance

between you and her is remarkable is it not?"
asked Cain Diomedes.

Continue the journey with Jade in the next
book
The Shadow Realm
Impossible Choices
Releasing in 2019.

About The Author

J.L. Keathley is a self-published author who
focuses on Young Adult genres. She lives in
Arkansas with her husband and two daughters.
She loves animals and has a variety of pets. She
has always loved to read and decided to write
what she wants to read about. She likes to
travel with her family and find adventures.

Follow the author on social media for updates.

Twitter: https://twitter.com/jlk_ya_author

Facebook: https://www.facebook.com/J.L.Keathley/

Instagram: https://www.instagram.com/j.l.keathley/

www.ingramcontent.com/pod-product-compliance
Lightning Source LLC
Chambersburg PA
CBHW020818180626
46814CB00001B/6